*"Gallagher, if we're going to make this partnership work, we're going to need some ground rules,"*

Mikki said.

"Such as?" Shawn drawled, curling her hair round his finger.

She brushed his hand aside. "First of all, no touching."

"How about if you're falling down?" he asked innocently. "Would it be all right if I grabbed you and broke your fall?"

She gritted her teeth. "Yes."

"Okay. Grabbing's allowed, then."

"Only under certain circumstances, and I get to say when."

"To say what?"

Couldn't he get anything straight? "When," she fairly shouted at him.

Too late, she realized her mistake. Before she could utter a single word of protest, he had her in his arms.

Dear Reader,

With all due fanfare, this month Silhouette *Special Edition* is pleased to bring you *Dawn of Valor*, Lindsay McKenna's latest and long-awaited *LOVE AND GLORY* novel. We trust that the unique flavor of this landmark volume—the dramatic saga of cocky fly-boy Chase Trayhern and feisty army nurse Rachel McKenzie surviving love and enemy fire in the Korean War—will prove well worth your wait.

Joining Lindsay McKenna in this exceptional, action-packed month are five more sensational authors: Barbara Faith, with an evocative, emotional adoption story, *Echoes of Summer*; Natalie Bishop, with the delightful, damned-if-you-do, damned-if-you-don't (fall in love, that is) *Downright Dangerous*; Marie Ferrarella, with a fast-talking blonde and a sly, sexy cynic on a goofily glittering treasure hunt in *A Girl's Best Friend*; Lisa Jackson, with a steamy, provocative case of "mistaken" identity in *Mystery Man*; and Kayla Daniels, with a twisty, tantalizing tale of duplicity and desire in *Hot Prospect*.

All six novels are bona fide page-turners, featuring a compelling cast of characters in a marvelous array of adventures of the heart. We hope you'll agree that each and every one of them is a stimulating, sensitive edition worthy of the label *special*.

From all the authors and editors of Silhouette *Special Edition*,

Best wishes.

# MARIE FERRARELLA
## A Girl's Best Friend

*Silhouette Special Edition*

Published by Silhouette Books New York

**America's Publisher of Contemporary Romance**

To Leslie Kazanjian,
for allowing
a five-year-old dream
to come true

SILHOUETTE BOOKS
300 East 42nd St., New York, N.Y. 10017

A GIRL'S BEST FRIEND

ISBN: 0-373-09652-6

First Silhouette Books printing February 1991

Printed in the U.S.A.

**Books by Marie Ferrarella**

Silhouette Romance

*The Gift* #588
*Five-Alarm Affair* #613
*Heart to Heart* #632
*Mother for Hire* #686
*Borrowed Baby* #730
*Her Special Angel* #744

Silhouette Special Edition

*It Happened One Night* #597
*A Girl's Best Friend* #652

**Books by Marie Ferrarella writing as Marie Nicole**

Silhouette Desire

*Tried and True* #112
*Buyer Beware* #142
*Through Laughter and Tears* #161
*Grand Theft: Heart* #182
*A Woman of Integrity* #197
*Country Blue* #224
*Last Year's Hunk* #274
*Foxy Lady* #315
*Chocolate Dreams* #346
*No Laughing Matter* #382

Silhouette Romance

*Man Undercover* #373
*Please Stand By* #394
*Mine by Write* #411
*Getting Physical* #440

## MARIE FERRARELLA

was born in Europe, raised in New York City and now lives in Southern California. She describes herself as the tired mother of two overenergetic children and the contented wife of one wonderful man. She is thrilled to be following her dream of writing full-time.

Underlined locations are fictitious.

## Prologue

*Dresden, Germany*
*March 6, 1941*

Klaus Wintermeyer, tailor par excellence for the very rich, sat hunched over in his dank basement, sewing by candlelight. A sudden, faint noise had his tired eyes darting from side to side. Nothing. Just the normal sounds of the old house, accentuated by the evening silence. Perhaps it was mice moving about in the shadowy recesses.

The hairs on the back of Klaus's neck bristled. Perspiration ran down his forehead and into his eyes. He blinked to clear his vision. He had to hurry. The boat would be leaving in only a matter of hours.

His delicate hands trembled as he painstakingly sewed the lining of his overcoat back into place. Not a stitch could be missing. A nervous smile seized his lips in a spasmodic movement, flickering away just as swiftly as it had appeared. The shoemaker's children went barefoot, did they not? Why should not the tailor have a poorly made overcoat?

For a very good reason, he thought soberly. He couldn't afford to draw attention to himself. Not to his sudden, secret flight, nor, most especially, to his overcoat.

He wondered if Madam Von Ryan had missed her jewelry yet. He had painstakingly removed only the most precious diamonds from all the pieces. It seemed inconceivable to Klaus to own such treasures and not take them out at all hours, to hold them up to the light, to make love to them with one's eyes as one would to a beautiful woman of breeding.

He was overreacting. These were just stones, nothing more. Their only true value was in their ability to secure his freedom and to provide for his future. The only thing of value he had ever known was Elissa. She had been his treasure. She and Reinhardt. But Elissa was gone. And so was Reinhardt. Elissa had died of typhus, and Reinhardt might as well have. His son had become a stranger. That arrogant, smug young man in uniform who belonged to Hitler's youth corps was not his son.

He had lost his son to a charismatic devil.

He had no one left in this country. Nothing to live for. But people went on living, he thought, completing the last stitch. The will to live seemed to thrive despite one's wishes to the contrary.

He had gone on dispiritedly. And then Madam Von Ryan's safe had hung open so invitingly, filled to overflowing with "trinkets" as she called them.

Left alone in a room of Herr Von Ryan's estate he had been put to work completing the alterations on Madam's dress. There was to be an elegant party tonight. A ball honoring Hitler. And unfortunately, Madam had put on a few more pounds. Klaus had been summoned this morning and kept at the estate all day. She was to wear the blue dress his nimble fingers had been working on. Blue, to match the sapphires. The diamonds would not be worn tonight.

He would not have done it, even in his impoverished state, but Herr Von Ryan had come in and boasted how Hitler would use the youth corps to eliminate the "inferior" races. There was no mercy in his voice. He was a monster, Klaus had thought. A sadistic, compassionless monster.

The plan had crystallized then.

And tomorrow, he would be gone. The diamonds would be his insurance. The army that Herr Von Ryan embraced with such open enthusiasm owed it to him for taking Reinhardt.

For the first time in over a year, Klaus Wintermeyer smiled.

*Borachon, Texas*
*July 29, 1941*

The hot sun beat down on Klaus's bowed head as he rode away from the town. Was he being followed? He wasn't sure. At times, he was certain he was. He could sense it, smell it. At other times, he felt he was imagining it all. No matter. If they were behind him, he was up to the challenge. It gave him the incentive to go on, to match wits with his enemies just one more time.

His sudden departure would have already been noted and more than likely connected to the theft of the diamonds. Most certainly there would be people after him. Von Ryan would see to it. Such people had representatives—no, tentacles—in America. It would be a simple matter for Von Ryan to have him pursued.

Klaus's fear had forced him to wander from place to place. He had meant to go directly to Alfred on the West Coast, but he couldn't risk leading his enemies to his brother. So he had undertaken an expedition through the southeastern part of the country. He had been clever. Very clever. But he had been outsmarted by fate. It would help him rob his pursuers of their revenge, if they were indeed there, as long as Klaus could keep them at bay just a little longer. The doctor in Houston had been kind, but precise. He had diagnosed cancer. There was no hope. Perhaps six months, perhaps less.

But his enemies weren't going to get the diamonds. They had taken his son, but he had taken their diamonds. It could hardly even the score, but it helped.

Klaus thought of his younger brother and smiled. Alfred, the sunny one. Alfred, the lucky one. He had gotten out before the trap had been sprung in Germany, gotten out and made something of himself in a city with the improbable name of Saint Francis. Or was it San Francisco? American names confused him. He had made a great effort to learn the language, but its vagaries still eluded him at times. Not like Alfred. Alfred was clever. Alfred could put the diamonds to good use.

The theft had not been in vain.

*Mission Ridge, Texas*
*August 1, 1941*


Klaus sat in his tiny, airless room at the Hospitality Hotel, writing what amounted to his last will and testament. It was in the form of a letter to his brother. With the letter he put a key to the strongbox that he had left in the hotel's safe this morning. It had been a new experience for him. His last new experience, he thought ruefully, wondering when the pain that had become his constant companion in the last month would totally engulf him. The strongbox contained three things: a map to the location of the diamonds, a note that only Alfred would understand detailing the whereabouts of the diamonds once Alfred arrived in Borachon and the diary he had kept since his clandestine departure from Dresden aboard the freighter. Klaus had left two of the smaller diamonds with the note so that his brother would not think he had succumbed to delirium in the last days of his life.

He addressed the envelope carefully. Now all that was left to do was to mail it.

And to die.

## Chapter One

*Somewhere in Texas*
*May 4, 1991*

When she looked back on it later, Mikki realized that she owed it all to Mrs. Wallace, the whimsical inefficiency of the U.S. mails and a virus.

But as she sat on the Greyhound bus, staring out the window and trying in vain not to sneeze and cough, Mikki Donovan didn't feel as if she owed anything to anyone. If anything, perhaps the world owed her a little kindness for everything she had endured the past twenty-three years.

She was on her way to a little town called Mission Ridge in Texas because she was leaving nothing behind her. She hoped there was a treasure before her.

Mikki resisted the temptation to sneak another look at the letter in her purse. The man sitting next to her didn't really look interested in anything but getting off the bus, but she was taking no chances.

She closed her eyes for a minute, wishing she had packed some aspirin with her. Her head had been aching badly for the past few hours, as was the rest of her. But even if she had the aspirin, where would she get the water? At least she was on the last leg of her journey. The next stop was Mission Ridge. She'd get everything she needed there.

With luck.

Luck had always been in short supply as far as she was concerned. It had deserted her almost as thoroughly as her parents had over eighteen years ago. They had been, she recalled vaguely from conversations she had overheard, on their way to fame and fortune in the movies. A child held them back, sapped their energy, diverted their resources. So, she was cut, scrubbed, tossed away like so much extra ballast from a hot air balloon. Aunt Jane had been the long-suffering recipient. After Aunt Jane came Great-aunt Alice. Then someone named Patience, who didn't have any. And after Patience came a string of foster homes. Eventually, Mikki stopped worrying that her parents wouldn't be able to find her when they returned. She knew they weren't coming back. She knew she was on her own.

From the instant she came to that realization, Mikki began to build a protective shell around herself, layer by layer. She promised herself that she would never knowingly put herself in danger of being hurt again. She also knew that no one was going to do anything for her. Her fate was in her own hands. And when fate had beckoned, Mikki had been quick to follow its call.

Fate had appeared in the guise of a fifty-year-old letter that was delivered to her doorstep. A mysterious letter promising riches. She could only hope that this wasn't one of life's practical jokes.

Until a few days ago, she had been working at Wallace's Bookstore, near Fisherman's Wharf in San Francisco. She had been there over six months and had just begun to feel secure. But Mrs. Wallace had decided to increase the store's profits by cutting down on the overhead. Mikki came under the heading of overhead. The last hired, she was the first to go. She had left with a two week's severance paycheck in her pocket and profuse apologies ringing in her ears.

Thoroughly miserable, Mikki had walked to her second-floor, furnished garden apartment that afternoon. She usually refused herself the luxury of being depressed, but yesterday had been an exception. She had been fired. There was a bleak, dank fog enshrouding the city, and she felt a cold coming on. Her supply of optimism was temporarily exhausted.

The best thing to do, she had told herself, was climb into bed, get some rest and think about this current crisis tomorrow, when she felt better.

Tomorrow. A small smile curved her lips. She'd think about it tomorrow, just like Scarlett O'Hara. Well, why not? Scarlett had always landed on her feet, right? And so would she.

Mechanically, Mikki had checked her mailbox, then stared at the coarse, weathered, thick envelope stuffed into the narrow space. She gently jiggled it from side to side, taking care not to tear the rotting paper. The envelope wasn't for her. Though it bore her apartment number, the letter was addressed to an Alfred Wintermeyer. Sighing, Mikki scanned the names on the long row of mailboxes.

There was no Alfred Wintermeyer listed.

There was nothing to do except mark the letter "recipient unknown" and mail it back. She shivered, pulled her oversize sweater tightly around her and walked up the stairs to her apartment. Closing the door behind her, she tossed the letter onto the table and proceeded to rummage through the kitchen drawer for a magic marker.

The magic marker ran dry as she began to write "return to sender." It figured. It was one of those days when *nothing* went right.

And then she saw it, her defunct marker hovering near the postmark. The cancellation date on it was August 2, 1941.

"Nineteen forty-one?" She had heard of slow postal deliveries, but this was ridiculous. There was a small note taped firmly to the back of the envelope. It was from the post office, apologizing for the delay. The letter, it seemed, had been discovered stuck in a crack beneath some sorting machinery.

As Mikki turned the envelope over to take a closer look at the cancellation date, it slipped from her hand. She tried to catch it, tearing only a corner of the fragile envelope. The letter inside was half-exposed as it lay on the faded green shag carpet, tempting her to pick it up and read its contents.

"Oh, what the heck!" Alfred Wintermeyer was probably dead. He certainly didn't live here anymore, and any forwarding address he might have left would probably be useless by now. Maybe there was something in the letter that would give her a clue about what to do with it.

Having satisfied her conscience, Mikki tore open the rest of the envelope. A key fell out. She stooped to pick it up as she read the letter.

"'My dear Alfred.'" Mikki felt her way to the sofa and sat down. "'By the time this you receive, I no doubt will already dead be.'" Boy, did he ever have that right. Mikki strained to read the rest of the tiny, neat handwriting. "'But please not to grieve. Elissa waiting for me will be. A key enclosed I have for you, belonging to an iron box in the safe of a hotel sitting. Hotel Hospitality in Mission Ridge, Texas. A key to more riches than to tell you I can. Take please, my beloved brother, take key and my love everlasting. Klaus.'" There was a small postscript. "'My English is better, yes? Too bad much longer to use it I cannot.'"

Mikki folded the letter and felt overcome by a wave of sadness for a man she would never know. "Too bad," she echoed Klaus's sentiments, then looked down at the key. "Riches." She turned the word over and over again in her mind. The more she thought about it, the more it intrigued her.

She sneezed and unconsciously reached for the box of tissues on the coffee table. It was empty. Sighing, she trudged to the bathroom, the key still in her hand. She tore off a length of bathroom tissue in time to capture another sneeze.

An impulse began to take hold.

Why not?

What did she have to lose? she thought, looking at the key again. Absolutely nothing. She no longer had a job, and there was no one to consult or consider. There were absolutely no ties to hold her here.

With the flicker of hope beckoning to her, Mikki made up her mind. She was going to Mission Ridge, Texas.

Provided, of course, that Mission Ridge still existed and that it was accessible by Greyhound. She didn't have much money to invest in this uncertain adventure.

But first, there was something she had to take care of. Something to put her conscience to rest. Stuffing the tissue into her pocket, she went down the stairs and out the door, following the winding concrete path to the rental office.

The manager of the apartment complex was getting ready to close up the office early, but his face brightened when he saw his visitor was Mikki.

"What can I do for you?"

He gestured to a chair, but Mikki declined, shaking her head. "Can you tell me if Alfred Wintermeyer left a forwarding address?"

"Friend of yours?" He turned toward the small file box on his desk, which held the forwarding addresses of former residents.

"In a manner of speaking." Her fingers tightened around the key in her hand. "We share a common interest."

The tall, thin man flipped through his cards. "No, no Alfred Wintermeyer here." He scratched his head. "Are you sure he lived here?"

Mikki nodded, then pushed back the hair that had fallen into her eyes. "A long time ago."

"Well, the place was totally rebuilt in '65. There was a fire—"

But Mikki was already out the door. "Thank you," she called over her shoulder. She hurried back to her apartment.

Alfred Wintermeyer was gone without a trace, she thought, smoothing out the torn envelope with the palm of her hand. She looked down at the return address. Perhaps Klaus Wintermeyer was still alive, still living in Mission Ridge, Texas, wondering why his brother had abandoned him without a word. Or maybe his relatives were wondering what had become of him. Perhaps someone might be grateful to her for telling them what had happened to Klaus's letter. Grateful enough to give her a reward. After all, stranger things had happened.

"And why not?" she mused out loud, turning the crumbling paper over. At this precise moment, she needed something to hope for, however improbable. "Why not just this once?"

She walked over to the phone, picked up the receiver and called information, asking for the Mission Ridge area code. It took the operator five minutes to find it.

The friendly operator in Mission Ridge took less time than that to tell Mikki that there was no number listed for a Klaus Wintermeyer. Or anyone named Wintermeyer for that matter.

"Could he be unlisted?" she managed to ask before she sneezed.

"Bless you. Honey, *nobody's* unlisted in Mission Ridge." It was Mikki's first clue that Mission Ridge was probably the size of a postage stamp.

Her brain felt a little fuzzy, but excitement buzzed through the rest of her. She refused to give up hope. "Give me the Bureau of Records."

"Now them I can reach," the woman said cheerfully.

A minute later, she heard the phone on the other end ring. The man who answered was polite enough, but the information he finally gave Mikki was both dispiriting and puzzling. There was a death certificate for Klaus Wintermeyer dated September 2, 1941.

Mikki thanked the man, then hung up. Klaus had died a month after he'd mailed the letter, she thought. What if the strongbox was still in the hotel safe, unclaimed? She had read about such things happening. Her mind began to race in several different directions. She pressed her hands to her temples, telling herself to calm down and think things out logically. It was likely the hotel was gone, burned, torn down or blown away. She was probably getting excited for nothing.

Still, she refused to let this newest spark of hope die. She dialed the information operator in Mission Ridge again.

"Hi, honey."

The woman obviously recognized her nasal voice, Mikki thought. "Is there a Hospitality Hotel located in Mission Ridge?"

"There sure is. One sec." Before Mikki knew it, the woman was connecting her with the hotel.

"Hospitality Hotel. Harold here."

Mikki's mind went blank for a minute.

"Hello?" the man named Harold shouted into the phone.

His tone jolted her back to the present. "This is Mikki—Mikki Wintermeyer. Do you have a safe in your hotel?"

There was a pause before he answered. "Yeah. It's not used much, though. Matter of fact, I can't remember the last time I had a reason to open it." The puzzled tone became hopeful. "Are you planning on making a trip here?"

Mikki's pulse was beginning to race. No one used the safe. Maybe the strongbox *was* still in there. "Yes." She could hardly keep the mounting excitement out of her voice. "Thank you. Thank you very much." Mikki hung up, grinning. She stared at the letter for a long time.

It was a challenge from fate and one Mikki felt she was ready to take up.

The next morning, armed with three fresh packets of tissues, Mikki locked up her apartment and set off with her suitcase to seek her fortune.

Maybe.

The bus pitched and swayed, making her feel utterly miserable. The simple cold she thought she had was turning into a full-fledged, rip-roaring case of the flu. Not for the first time, a cough began to claw at her throat.

The man sitting next to her shifted in his seat, trying to move as far away from her as he could. The bus was packed, and there was nowhere else for him to sit but next to Mikki. "You really should see a doctor," he snapped at her, not trying to hide his annoyance.

Mikki paused to blow her nose. "It's nothing. It'll pass away."

So will I, she thought, retreating into silence. Her headache had now spread. Her whole body ached. It was just her imagination, she told herself. That, and the fatigue that resulted from rattling around in the bus for so long. How could she not expect her body to ache?

Besides, she never got sick.

She shivered and wished that the driver would turn down the air conditioner. Never satisfied, her mind mocked. Half an hour ago, you were perspiring and wishing that he'd turn it up.

What she fervently wished for, she knew, was for the trip to be over.

Finally, it was.

Mission Ridge didn't look too impressive as she peered out the window of the bus. Forlorn people moved in slow motion through long, desolate streets. It looked even less impressive when she stepped out of the bus. Stopping the first person who crossed her path, Mikki asked directions to the hotel. The man pointed to an uninviting building in the distance. Thanking him, she took a deep breath, tried not to cough and began to walk toward the Hospitality Hotel.

Shawn Gallagher was standing across the street from the bus depot when he saw the tall, slender blonde get off the bus. He noticed several men turn to look her way. She had class written all over her. What was she doing in a town like this?

He knew what he was doing here. Looking for something he had lost along the way. His faith in humanity. A self-deprecating smile curved his lips. He should have known better.

Shawn pushed his hands into his pockets, still watching the blonde's progress. He had convinced his editor at the *Houston Chronicle* that a series of articles depicting life in small-town America could be a winner. Eccentric characters, perfect subjects for human-interest stories, abounded in many small towns. And he was the man to do the piece. He had been born and raised in a small town and had desperately wanted to escape when he was young. Now, thinking back, he realized that the people living in these towns were survivors, expert at coping with everything from boredom to locust. He needed to get back in touch with that kind of spirit.

The series was a far cry from the pieces he usually wrote as an investigative reporter, but his editor had sensed Shawn's need to do the articles and had authorized him to go ahead.

Yet what Shawn thought he could find by returning to the world he had grown up in wasn't there. There was no spark to be found, no determination to overcome obstacles. Instead of hope, he found despair. Forlorn, worn-out people walking through the shadows of their lives. These were dying towns that didn't seem to have the good sense to accept the fact and fade away. They were places that had sprung up around oil fields and had hung on after the oil boom ended. The wells ran dry. So did the people.

Still, Shawn supposed even that had a human-interest story in it.

But it wouldn't be a story that would give him back his soul.

In the seven years he had been at the *Chronicle*, he had dealt with the baser human emotions, with the seamier side of life. He had become a man who lived on wits, adrenaline and coffee. He hadn't always been that way. Or maybe he had and the other life, the memory, had all been an illusion. At times, he doubted if there *was* a good side to humanity. But he still experienced a vague longing to be proven wrong. That was the reason he was here. Searching. It was his third town in as many weeks.

He felt restless.

He watched the blonde with the million-dollar figure make her way to the Hospitality Hotel. It was the same place he was staying. The only place to stay if you didn't want bedbugs as companions.

He wondered what sort of companion she would make, then upbraided himself for letting his mind and his hormones wander.

He turned his back on Mikki and walked in the direction of the town center. He had a few more places to check out before he left.

Mikki felt woozy. Summer heat, she told herself, as she let her suitcase drop with a thud to the floor of her hotel room. She needed to pull her thoughts together before she attempted to secure the strongbox. A good meal would fix her up fine. She wondered if she could find one. The small town didn't look as if it had a wide variety of restaurants.

"Best meal in town is at Big Kate's," the desk clerk whose nametag identified him as Harold said. He went on to inform her that they had no eating facilities on the premises. "Eat at Kate's myself whenever I can." He leaned forward over the desk. "To tell the truth, the wife's cooking leaves a little to be desired." His eyes skimmed over Mikki with a look akin to a child gazing into a candy store-window.

"Thank you," Mikki mumbled. She passed the back of her hand across her forehead. Her skin felt damp as she wiped the perspiration away.

"Hey, you okay?" The look on the man's face was a blend of curiosity and concern. "You look a little pale."

"I'm fine," Mikki answered quickly. "It was just a long trip, and I'm a little tired."

"I could send out for something," the clerk offered. "And maybe bring it to your room for you?" He ended the statement hopefully, and Mikki knew what was running through his mind.

"No, thank you." When she came back from dinner, she planned to ask for the strongbox and take it to her room. Alone. She was too smart to let someone like Harold in her room. At the very least, she knew she'd have one heck of a time getting him to leave.

The ache in her head was beginning to take on a persistent, deadly beat.

The sun seemed unusually bright, she thought, as she made her way down the street in the direction the clerk had indicated. She wasn't really hungry, but it had been quite some time since she had eaten and her stomach was pinching, hurting, demanding something to fill it. Maybe a little soup would help.

The thought brought on a fresh wave of perspiration. Mikki shivered involuntarily. Chicken soup, she amended firmly. Best medicine in the world. Except maybe, she thought, for the chicken.

She was getting giddy.

Big Kate's was just what she had expected of this dusty little, windblown town. It was small and smelled stale. It was no more than a greasy spoon, a truck stop with a few homey touches. She took the first unoccupied table she saw.

Shawn watched her slide in. For the second time that day, he was struck by how odd it was that someone who looked as if she belonged in the big city had voluntarily come to a tiny place such as this. He was certain she didn't belong. There was a sophistication about her that made her stick out like a sore thumb. He grinned. On the more practical side, he had seen her ask someone for directions.

He watched her unobtrusively over his coffee cup. Might make an interesting addendum to his story, he decided. Was she visiting friends? Family? Then why was she staying at the hotel? His natural curiosity was peaked.

It didn't hurt any that she was the best-looking woman he had seen in a long, long time, either.

He waited until she had begun to eat before he left his booth. "Excuse me."

The deep, pleasing baritone voice cut through the fog that was wrapping vicelike fingers around her brain. Mikki looked up and saw a handsome, dark-haired man with vivid green eyes grinning down at her. Carelessly hooked onto two fingers, a gray-blue windbreaker was slung over his right shoulder. The image reminded her an of old Frank Sinatra record album cover she had once seen in Aunt Jane's house a long time ago.

What was Frank Sinatra doing here?

Mikki stared and blinked several times, trying to focus her eyes as well as her mind. She was beginning to drift too much.

"Yes?"

"Would you mind if I join you?" Shawn began to sit down at her table.

"Yes, I would."

Shawn stopped. "What?" He wasn't used to being turned away, certainly not by women. In his line of work, he depended on his engaging manner almost as heavily as he did on his sharp instincts. He had a way about him that made people open up, talk to him. Why had his usual charisma suddenly failed?

"I said . . ." Mikki took a deep breath. It hurt her lungs. "Yes, I would mind you joining me."

He was slightly taken aback, but unfazed. There were always his credentials to fall back on, and resistance intrigued him. "Maybe I should explain that—"

"Maybe you shouldn't," Mikki cut in. He was trying to pick her up, and she was definitely in no condition for word games. She felt too tired and light-headed to hold her own against anyone, especially a handsome, confident stranger. What she needed, desperately, she decided, was to lie down—before she fell down. Her body felt strangely disjointed.

She fumbled with her purse, drawing out what she thought was the price of the half-eaten bowl of soup. The face on the five-dollar bill multiplied before merging into a two-headed creature.

Bed. She needed bed. Now.

"I'm afraid I'm leaving," she told Shawn. She rested her hand on the back of the plastic chair for support as she pulled herself up. Her legs suddenly felt rubbery, as if they were unable to support her. Perspiration began to slide down her back. Clammy, everything was becoming clammy. The soup hadn't helped. In fact, it had made her feel worse. The churning sensation it created in her stomach rose up to her pounding head.

"Well, then," Shawn tried again, "at least let me walk you to your hotel." He noted the sheen of perspiration. "You don't look very well."

Things were getting foggy. And his voice echoed in her head. Mikki closed her eyes and opened them again. It didn't help. She was about to ask him how he knew she was staying at the hotel when everything began to shrink away from her until it disappeared into blackness.

Mikki was out before she hit the ground.

## Chapter Two

Mikki opened her eyes slowly. She blinked several times, attempting to bring her surroundings into focus. Slowly she distinguished mint-green curtains billowing softly at the open window. She didn't own mint-green curtains. Where was she? She felt so stiff. That table under the window, that wasn't familiar, either. What was going on here? She turned her head slowly.

"Oh my God, who are you?" She struggled up to support herself on her elbows and glared at Shawn. "What are you doing in my—what are you doing here?"

He placed his hands on her shoulders and gently tried to make her lie down. "Getting an incredible backache for one thing."

The gentle approach obviously did not work with this woman. She continued to struggle against his grip. Well, at least her strength was returning, Shawn thought wryly.

"Don't exert yourself so much. By the way," he said nodding at her torso, "your sheet's slipping."

Mikki's eyes darted down. She was wearing her night-gown. It only added to her confusion. She stared at the garment, then quickly pulled the sheet up to her chin and held it there with both hands. "How did I get here?"

"I carried you."

There was something entirely too intimate, too familiar about the way he sat down on the edge of the bed. Mikki pulled as far away from him as she could.

"You carried me?" she echoed incredulously.

Slowly the pieces started falling together. The lost letter, the bus ride, feeling sick, the soup, the man in the restaurant...

Him.

Mikki's eyes narrowed as she took a closer look at Shawn. He seemed friendly enough, but what was he doing in her room? This was one hell of a compromising situation. Her instincts told her to be wary. He didn't know her. Why was he being so nice? Just what was he up to?

She needed to get up and get dressed. She'd feel more capable of handling whatever this man had to "offer" if she could be on an equal footing with him. That meant standing up, for openers.

"It isn't often a woman faints when I ask to join her." His smile touched the corners of his eyes.

She realized that the incredible pounding in her head was gone. "That's not quite how it happened," she corrected tersely. "I was sick."

He shook his head. "You were five degrees past sick, on your way to dead. I carried you over here and had the desk clerk call the doctor."

She glanced down at her nightgown. "Was the doctor the one who—?"

"No." He made no effort whatsoever to suppress his amusement at her dilemma.

He was a bastard all right, Mikki thought. She looked at him accusingly. "You—?"

"No." There was a trace of wistfulness in his answer. "In the interest of not being subjected to more temptation than I could safely withstand, I sent for the desk clerk's wife. She undressed you. You were soaking wet with perspiration and shaking violently. I did get to cover you several times, though." His grin broadened. She felt like punching him without knowing exactly why. "You sleep pretty fitfully, you know."

"No, I didn't know." Mikki pushed her hair out of her eyes. She couldn't remember the last time someone had gone out of his way for her. *Why* had this stranger put himself out?

Maybe he was just being decent. But those eyes of his— they weren't the eyes of a Good Samaritan. They were the streetwise eyes of a man who had been around. A lot. Those types generally didn't do good deeds without a reason. She didn't like being cynical, but life had taught her it was always better to be safe than sorry. "And you stayed here with me?"

He shrugged in a studied fashion. "I couldn't very well abandon you after you fainted at my feet."

"I fainted," she corrected. "Your feet happened to be in the way." She pressed her lips together, afraid to ask the next question. Or rather, afraid of the next answer. "What else did you do?"

"Nothing." Although, God knew it had been a Herculean feat to keep from reaching out and touching her. There had been something nearly overpoweringly sensual about her when he had first noticed her getting off the bus, but when she slept, she made him think of a delectably tempting innocent who beckoned and held a man at bay at the same time. "Your virtue is still intact. I like my ladies to be conscious when we make love. I find it's a lot more rewarding that way."

The man was an egotist as well as a voyeur. "Maybe," she bit off. "For you."

He looked at her for a long moment. With her hair tousled, her expression accusingly petulant, she was the most beautiful sight he had ever seen. And he had been far from sheltered. "When you're better," he said softly, tracing the outline of her mouth with his finger, "perhaps you'd like to find out."

She pushed his hand aside. "I'm better," she informed him. And miraculously, she was. "And I have no intention of finding out." Mikki dragged her hand through her hair. "How long did I sleep?"

He moved back and studied her, the Sleeping Beauty waking up and taking a swing at the Prince, he mused. "A day and a half."

"A day..." Her voice trailed off, stunned.

"And a half," he completed.

She had thought it had only been a matter of hours. "And you stayed here all that time?" It hardly seemed possible. He didn't look like the selfless type. He looked more like a man who enjoyed living on the very edge of excitement.

"Yes."

The man was neither a Boy Scout troop leader nor a saint. "Why?"

What made her so distrustful? Was it just the situation she found herself in? Maybe, but he doubted it. He knew people. It was his business to be able to see beneath the surface, and there seemed to be something more at work here. She was really beginning to intrigue him. For more than one reason.

"You didn't seem to have anyone." The nonchalant tone camouflaged his thoughts. "And, you looked like a helpless kitten, lying there." He grinned, and the lines of hard, fast living on his gaunt, angular face softened. For a moment, he looked appealingly boyish. "I'm a sucker for helpless kittens."

She doubted it. She doubted if he was a sucker for anything. Despite his banter, he looked to be a man who would quickly gain control of any situation he found himself in. She'd bet her last nickel on it.

"Who are you and how do you know I don't have anyone?"

She was a tough one, all right. "Shawn Gallagher." He took her hand in his. But he didn't shake it. He raised it and pressed his lips to it, his eyes penetrating hers.

Mikki shivered. The fever hadn't totally gone, she thought.

"And I looked through your purse."

"You—you—"

"Looked through your purse," he repeated. Her flashing eyes only managed to entice him more. "Only in your best interests, Mikki. I was trying to find someone to notify." He could see by the hard set of her mouth that she wasn't taken in at all. Somewhere within him, admiration stirred along with his curiosity. "Who's Klaus Wintermeyer?"

She knew it! The man was a thief. Or worse. "None of your business." She yanked her covers up again in a defensive gesture.

"Cold?" he asked.

"Annoyed," she retorted.

"I would be, too," he nodded his head in sympathy, "if I came all the way from San Francisco on a Greyhound to see this Klaus person and found that he was gone."

"Gone?" Just how much did he know about it?

Shawn leaned back. "I made some inquiries this morning. There's no Klaus Wintermeyer living in Mission Ridge." He paused, waiting for her to absorb this last bit of information. Then he added his headline. "Although, the strongbox he left in the hotel safe is probably still there." He watched her irises darken. God, she looked sexy. He steadied himself by taking a deep breath.

Mikki struggled not to be crushed by disappointment. He had gotten to the strongbox before her. "Did you use the key?" she asked dully. Of course he'd used the key. Why wouldn't he? All this way and for what? To be beaten out be a two-bit opportunist. She should have used the bus fare to buy herself something useful instead of a pocketful of dreams.

Shawn took her hand. Mikki snatched it away. Undeterred, he took it again. Gently, he rubbed his thumb along the inside of her wrist. Beneath her anger and frustration, Mikki felt herself reacting. "Mikki, what do you take me for?" The question was half playful, half probing.

"Someone I can trust only as far as I can throw." A con artist probably. He didn't seem to fit in this town. He didn't have that worn-out, small-town look. No small town could hold someone like him. He seemed too vital, too alive. Shawn Gallagher made her think of a man who had learned the hard way, who had risen up using his wits and maybe his fists. It wasn't the type of education one got in a one-horse town such as Mission Ridge.

He took the key out of his pocket and pressed it into her hand. "The key is still here," he said. "And the strongbox is still unopened. I just asked the desk clerk a few questions. Seems he doesn't know the combination to the safe. Says it's around somewhere in the back room."

His answer surprised her, but she kept her expression blank. "Well, you're honest," she muttered. "I think." She wound her fingers around the key. Maybe there was still reason to hope.

"Like a Boy Scout." He winked. He took both her hands in his. Mikki didn't uncurl her fingers. "How do you feel?"

"All right."

This time, she slowly slipped her hands from his, the hostility temporarily on hold. She didn't know how it was possible, but she felt totally well. Just before she had passed out in the restaurant, all she had wanted to do was curl up and die. Now she felt as if she had never been sick.

"What did the doctor say was wrong with me?"

"Just a virus. Treacherous little devil that plays havoc with your system for about a day or so and then leaves without so much as a calling card."

Thank heaven for small favors. "I'd like to get dressed now." Shawn made no move to go. "If you'll leave the room," she added pointedly.

"Why don't we get you something to eat first?" he suggested. "Then we'll talk about getting up and getting dressed."

"'We?'" she echoed.

"Why, Mikki, you don't mean to tell me that after fate has flung us together this way, you would entertain the idea of tearing us asunder so quickly?" He ran his forefinger along her cheek.

She pulled her head away. "Yes," Mikki answered with some effort.

"I see you're a hard lady."

Mikki's eyes narrowed, and she squared her shoulders. "I'm a lady used to making my own way in the world."

Yes, he believed she was. There was something so strong there, in the way she held her head, in the way she spoke. He had had a sense of it the moment she had gotten off the bus. "Don't spoil my fun, Mikki. You're the first person I've ever nursed back to health. Let me bask in my good deed for a while." He smiled at her. "I never did finish my introduction."

"You mean there's more?"

He nodded. "I'm a reporter for the *Houston Chronicle*."

Wonderful. He was going to plaster the story all over the newspaper. Wait a minute, all she had with her was an old letter. He didn't know that it was delivered fifty years too late. For all he knew, it was just a piece of family memorabilia. And it didn't tell him very much. Just enough, unfortunately, to arouse his obvious interest.

She had to get rid of him. "Mr. Gallagher—"

"I've mopped your sweat-soaked forehead," he told her. "Call me Shawn."

"Shawn," she conceded. "I don't know why you did what you did—"

"Milk of human kindness."

Despite herself, she felt a smile forming on her lips. "I'd like to thank you and your milk, but I'm perfectly capable of handling my own affairs right now."

He shook his head. "That's what they all say."

"All?" she asked, confused. "Who's all?"

"The doctor said there might be a false sense of well-being at first. He told me to watch you." A smile threatened to conquer the corners of his mouth, but he managed to keep a straight face, uttering the words as if they were gospel.

She waved her hand and the sheet fell. She grabbed it, pulling it back into position. "I relieve you of your responsibility," she said dryly, avoiding his eyes. She didn't want to see the laughter there. "And how did you get a doctor to come up here, anyway?"

"I threatened the desk clerk with bodily harm if he didn't get a doctor for my wife."

She could see how that might frighten the desk clerk into—Hold it. "Your wife?" she cried.

He nodded. "It made it easier to handle things."

"But I signed in as Mikki Wintermeyer." Her suspicions returned, full-blown. Reporter or not, the man was first and foremost a con artist.

Shawn shrugged. "I told him you were your own woman and kept your name after we were married."

She held up her left hand. "No ring."

Shawn grinned. "That's what he said. I told him you didn't like jewelry."

She studied him. "Got an answer for everything, don't you, Gallagher?"

"I try."

He was quick, she thought. And someone who would require watching. "Well, thank you very much, Mr. Gal—" Shawn raised a dark eyebrow "—Shawn," Mikki amended. "But there is really no need to put yourself out any further. I—"

There was something very unnerving about his smile. She tried to ignore it. "Oh, I think there is," he said softly. "Besides, I don't like to see things through only halfway." He crossed his arms across his chest. "How do you propose to get into that strongbox?"

And she had almost fallen for his act! She should always go with her first impression. People were always after something. Her voice was deadly still when she answered. "The usual way. With the key."

Her distrust rankled, although he told himself he had no business feeling disturbed by it. She was just an interesting stranger, nothing more. He knew even then that he was lying to himself. What he didn't know was why. "You don't look like a Klaus Wintermeyer."

This was ridiculous. Why was she in her nightgown carrying on a discussion with a perfect stranger about how she was going to gain possession of a strongbox? It was none of his damn business.

Still, she thought it best to answer him. It was obvious he wasn't about to leave unless she satisfied his curiosity. Of all the men's feet she could have fainted at, why did she have to pick his?

"I'm not. I'm his niece."

"Alfred's daughter?"

She could tell by the inflection in his voice that he didn't believe her. Damn him and his smug smile.

"Yes. He was my father." The word sounded so strange on her tongue. "My father passed on, and I was going through his things."

"I see." His eyes mocked her, but he said nothing to contradict her. "And, I suppose it's safe to assume, since he left his strongbox behind in the hotel safe, that Klaus has passed on, too.''

It was a game to him. Mikki struggled to keep her temper. Don't waste your energy on this man. You'll need it to see this thing through.

"Yes."

Shawn shook his head. "You don't lie very convincingly, Mikki."

"I'm not lying." She met his stare unwaveringly.

He moved closer to her, his eyes freezing her into position. "It's my job to see through people, Mikki. You'll never fool the desk clerk. Why don't you let me handle the details for you?"

"That's like handing the fox the keys to the henhouse and showing him where the frying pans are stored."

Shawn laughed, tickled with the analogy. "Look, Mikki." His voice was soft, silky. Mikki stiffened. "Why don't we send out for lunch and put our heads together? I think I might be able to come up with a way we can get our hands on that strongbox with a minimum of trouble."

How did it go from "I" to "we" so quickly? she wondered, amazed. Talk about fast workers. "I don't need your help. I can get my uncle's strongbox without you."

Shawn grinned and picked up the phone. He rang up the desk clerk. "My wife's just recovered," he said. "And shows signs of an appetite."

So did he, Mikki thought grudgingly. Like a vulture. How on earth was she going to get rid of him?

She was starving. She hadn't realized it until the food from Big Kate's had arrived and she had taken her first bite. One taste led to another and another until the food on the makeshift tray Shawn had provided for her was gone. She eyed his sandwich covetously.

"Wish you'd look at me the way you're looking at my ham sandwich." Shawn surrendered the second half to her.

"You wouldn't taste good with mustard." She took a bite and closed her eyes. Heaven.

"You'll never know 'til you try."

Mikki chose to ignore his comment.

"What's Mikki short for?" he asked. "Michelle?"

She shook her head, waiting until she finished chewing. The rye bread needed help sliding down. She took a long drink of her soda. "Michael." She swallowed. "My parents wanted a boy," she said flatly. That was about the only thing she did know about them, that even her gender had displeased them.

He discerned something in the tone of her voice, but thought it best not to probe. Shawn looked at the outline beneath the sheet. She had a body that invited loving. "They sure didn't get one."

She saw the way he looked at her. It struck a responsive chord, one she didn't want strummed, at least not by him. Time to get the future into order. She wiped her mouth with the stiff napkin from Big Kate's.

"I'd like to get dressed now, please." She looked at him expectantly.

"And you'd like me to leave?" he guessed.

"That's the general idea."

"Mikki." Shawn shook his head as he rose. "I am beginning to think that you don't know how to have fun."

"I'll work on it," she promised dryly.

"I'll wait for you outside." He pulled the door closed behind him.

"I never doubted it, Gallagher." Mikki sighed, frustrated.

There was no getting rid of him, she realized, hurrying into her clothes. Oh well, she did owe him something, she supposed. He could have just left her there, lying on the restaurant floor. He certainly didn't have to stay with her.

The thought of his hands covering her, adjusting the sheet around her body, brought a tingling sensation that zipped through her, like lightning down a rod during an electrical storm. She pushed the thought aside. She didn't need lightning. She needed luck. The good kind. And plenty of it.

Maybe he could be helpful. He seemed to know his way around. Must be his journalist's instincts.

When Mikki opened the door, she found Shawn leaning against the wall, waiting. He straightened immediately, and his eyes slid over her with the ease of a man used to appraising women. Yes, she was one hell of a looker. He wondered how long it would take to melt the icy barriers with which she surrounded herself. He had always loved a good challenge.

"It's nice to know you can recover so fully so fast."

"One of my attributes." The look in his eyes made her tense.

Shawn took her hand and threaded it through the crook of his arm. "I'm looking forward to cataloging the others."

Don't hold your breath, she thought as she offered him a false, sunny smile. Once that box is opened, we part company.

The desk clerk looked both surprised and pleased to see Mikki come downstairs. Shawn preceded her by half a step and leaned his elbow casually against the desk. "We'd like to see your safe now."

Harold looked at him incredulously. "You want to put something in?"

"No," Mikki cut in, "take something out. My uncle left a strongbox here."

The man shook his head. "Nobody's left anything here since I took over ten years ago. Like I told your husband—" he raised his eyebrows toward Shawn "—I don't even know where the combination is."

Mikki was too close to give up now. The excitement that rose within her made her overlook the fact that the clerk had referred to Shawn as her husband. "My uncle left the strongbox here in 1941."

A raspy chuckle came out of Harold's throat. He obviously didn't believe her.

Shawn leaned forward. "We'd like you to find that combination. Please." The word had never been said with quite such force.

Harold closed his mouth as he took a step back. He raised both hands before him, palms out. "Okay, okay. It's going to take a while, though." He looked at Shawn, hoping that his excuse would make him give up on the idea.

"We'll wait," Shawn told him.

The clerk left, muttering under his breath.

"Do you always sound as if you're threatening people?" She wasn't sure if she liked his style or not. The thing she did know was that it did seem to get results.

"Only when things get slow."

She decided it was better not to explore that comment.

It took the desk clerk a half hour to unearth the combination from a stack of papers shoved into one of the multitude of cubbyholes in the back room. When he returned to the front desk, Harold's lean face bore a crafty expression. It was obvious that he had done some thinking while he was searching. "I found it."

"Wonderful," Mikki exclaimed. She had all but given up hope. She began to walk around the front desk, intent on going into the back room.

"Not so fast." The desk clerk put up a hand to stop her. When Shawn raised his eyebrow, Harold dropped his hand. He clearly didn't need to be told that the man with the quiet voice was not one to be crossed. He seemed to flip quickly through his options. "I'll need some proof of your identity." He addressed his words to Mikki.

Mikki dipped into her shoulder bag. "I have a letter from Uncle Klaus." She didn't look at Shawn as she said the name. "He mailed it to my father, but for one reason or another, my father never acted on it. He was quite ill, you see."

"This thing's been here a long time," the clerk said, his voice tinged with suspicion.

Mikki shrugged innocently. A perfect performance, Shawn thought. Maybe the lady *had* been around.

"He must have forgotten about it. I only found the letter while I was going through his things." She paused for effect. "He died last month."

Shawn wasn't sure whether to offer her a handkerchief or merely applaud.

"Sorry to hear that," the clerk said mechanically. He scratched the back of his neck as he mulled over Mikki's story. "Can I see the letter?"

Mikki unfolded it and passed it to him quickly. She never took her fingers off it. Just as quickly, she returned it to the envelope. She wasn't about to let him read it.

Shawn took out his press card and flashed it for the clerk's benefit. "My paper is doing a human-interest story on this." He smiled genially at the man. "You might even get your name in the *Houston Chronicle*."

The clerk eyed the press card, then watched Shawn take it back. "I guess it's all right." It must have dawned on him that there was something important in that box, because he walked away muttering curses. Returning, Harold scratched his head again. "'Course, like I said, it's been here a long, long time. There's a charge, you know," he informed Mikki. His tongue darted out, licking his dry lips.

Mikki's eyes narrowed. "How much?"

"A hundred dollars."

"A hundred dollars?" she cried.

Thin shoulders raised and then lowered. "Seems like a small price to pay for something of such sentimental value."

"But I—"

Before she could finish, Shawn reached past her. He placed a fifty-dollar bill on the counter. "I'd say it's worth fifty." His tone was mild. His eyes weren't. They challenged Harold to protest.

The man swallowed, then his hand darted out and took the money. "This way." He gestured for them to follow him into the back room.

She was in Shawn's debt, and she hated being in anyone's debt. The breath she blew out ruffled her bangs. "Thanks."

"Never heard it sound like a curse before," Shawn murmured, taking her arm.

The back room was windowless. Paper-filled cubbyholes covered three walls. Dust seemed to be everywhere. Dust, a rickety table and the safe. They watched as the clerk opened the safe.

The strongbox was the only thing in it.

He placed the small metal box on the table for them. Mikki eagerly put her key into the lock. It took. But before she turned the key, she looked at the clerk. "I'd like some privacy please."

Harold muttered something unintelligible under his breath as he left the room.

Carefully, Mikki turned the key. The lock stayed where it was. Frustrated, she looked at Shawn.

He put his hand over hers. She withdrew hers, and he left his on the key. "Fifty years provides a lot of grit."

She watched his forearm strain as he turned the key. The lock snapped open. Shawn gestured toward the box. "The honor's all yours."

Mikki held her breath as she opened the lid.

The box contained a diary, two carefully folded pieces of paper and two small diamonds that winked and shone in the dim artificial light like souls that had finally been freed. Mikki picked the diamonds up in awe.

Shawn took one from her hand and placed it at her earlobe. "Diamonds suit you."

Before she could offer a retort, Shawn dropped the stone back into her upturned palm. He picked up the diary and flipped through it. Much of it was in German.

"Looks like we have the makings of a mystery here, Mikki." This was getting better all the time, Shawn thought.

There was that "we" again, Mikki noted in mounting exasperation.

## Chapter Three

Anticipation warred with fear as Mikki looked at the contents of the strongbox laid out on the dusty table. She was afraid to hope, really hope.

Yet it began to blossom, to spread within her. The events of the last several days swirled through her mind. Reality and fantasy melded kaleidoscopically, culminating with this morning: waking up semi-nude with a roguishly handsome stranger standing over her.

But this strongbox, the diary, the diamonds, they were all real. Fantasy had become reality. She felt exhilarated, but melancholy at the same time. Her good fortune was at the expense of someone else's misfortune. It didn't seem fair.

Sadness showed in her eyes. Shawn watched, fascinated, as the different emotions flitted quickly over her face. *I'm going to get to know you, Mikki Donovan, before this thing is over, whether you like it or not.*

Taking a deep breath, Mikki put the diary and the papers into her purse. She dropped the diamonds into her skirt pocket.

"Want me to hold anything?" He nodded at her purse. His voice was even, totally controlled. It didn't give away a clue of what he was feeling about her.

He anticipated her reply before she gave it. "No."

Why had she divided the items? "Why didn't you put the diamonds into your purse, too?"

"I don't like putting all my eggs in one basket." Just in case this apparent knight-in-shining-armor turned out to have feet of clay and decided to separate her from her purse, at least she'd have the diamonds, she thought. If they *were* diamonds. Who knew? They might be pieces of glass. This Klaus Wintermeyer person might have been duped. Or, he might have been trying to perpetrate a hoax for some reason.

"Don't worry, Mikki." He grinned knowingly. "I'm not going to steal them off your person."

She narrowed her eyes. Yes, she could see him doing just that. Not by force, but by seduction. She couldn't afford to let him get close to her. "I know judo."

Did she really think he was a thief? Or was she afraid of something else? "How nice for you."

She didn't look as if she was someone who had just found two diamonds. He had seen people more excited when they had discovered a coin in the street. What was behind that guarded expression? He was impressed with the way she was handling this. This whole fantastic tale was something out of a movie, yet she appeared to be in control. She intrigued him more than the twinkling gems.

"Ready?" Shawn asked. Mikki nodded. Shawn opened the door. Harold quickly stepped back, making it clear he had had his ear against the door.

Still he maintained a blank expression. "Everything in order?" he asked innocently.

"Perfect." Shawn smiled. It was not a warm smile. The clerk backed away.

Shawn placed his hand against the small of Mikki's back. She didn't miss the implication of the simple gesture. He was guiding her, she thought, attempting to take control of the situation. "And just where do you think you're going?"

"Back to your room with you." Pound for pound, she was one of the most suspicious people he had ever met. "I want to take a closer look at that diary."

So did she. Alone. "Don't you have a newspaper article to write or something?" She pulled away. Because he was coaxing her toward the elevator, she deliberately headed for the front door.

She was being difficult. Normally, that would irritate him. Instead, her feistiness was starting to endear her to him. His own reaction surprised him. He told himself that it was because he sensed there was a story here and he was always patient if he could extract a story from a situation. But somehow this was different. He was being patient with *her*. He'd wait her out, wait for her to trust him.

He took in the defiant way she held herself, her shoulders squared, her head held high. It didn't look as if trust would be forthcoming.

"Right now, it's the 'or something' that interests me. Watch out!"

But his warning came too late. Just outside the hotel, Mikki collided with a weaving, inebriated old man in a rumpled gray suit. For a moment, their bodies tangled. Only Shawn's hold on her arm kept her from falling.

The man, a wizen-faced creature who appeared to be the town drunk, exhaled a pungent cloud of stale alcohol and doffed his shabby hat. "Excuse me, dear lady. It was entirely my fault. I hope I haven't done your person any harm."

"No, I'm fine." Mikki resisted the urge to brush herself off.

His smile bore traces of a leer. "Yes, you certainly are." He tipped his hat again. "Good day to you."

"What a sad little man," Mikki commented to Shawn as she watched the drunk weave down the street.

"If he is, I think his brain is probably too pickled for him to know it." Shawn nodded toward the hotel's interior, waiting.

Mikki decided, for now, to go along with Shawn. There seemed to be nothing to be gained by being stubborn. And, she reminded herself, he had helped her get past the desk clerk. There was no need to worry. She was smart enough not to let him get past her.

Darting around to the back alley, Malcolm Everett dug into his pocket to see what he had managed to lift from his unsuspecting mark. He had been aiming for the man, but the woman had gotten in the way. It was something small. Maybe it was a coin, although it hadn't felt like one.

Malcolm's coal-gray eyes shone as he looked down into his palm. A diamond, picking up the midafternoon sun, gleamed in his hand. Putting it carefully into the left pocket of his pants, the one without the hole, he kept his hand protectively over his newfound treasure and hurried over to the pawnshop.

Twenty minutes later, Malcolm walked briskly toward the Do Drop Inn tavern. He wore the simple, innocent expression he had worn for the outside world for over forty years.

Malcolm let out a sigh, followed by a cackle.

"You old son, you got lucky." He shoved his hand into his pocket, curling his fingers around the diamond the way a lover curls his hands around his beloved's face. At the pawnshop, Jack had offered him a tidy sum for the tiny stone. But Malcolm had declined. He wanted to hold on to it for a while. When it came time to part with it, who knew, maybe he could parley it into a con. The pawnshop would be a last resort.

Feeling as if he had suddenly been given the power to rule the world, Malcolm strutted inside the bar.

"Whiskey, Brian," Malcolm said, sliding onto a seat next to two men near the door. The men were strangers. Malcolm was familiar with almost everyone in Mission Ridge.

Brian Traherne, a heavyset man in his late thirties who looked closer to fifty, eyed Malcolm suspiciously. He wiped his hands on his wide apron. "Got any money?"

Malcolm's smile was so wide, it showed off a space, well off center where someone had knocked out a tooth twenty years ago. "Got something better."

Brian cocked his eyebrow skeptically, but pulled a bottle filled with amber-colored liquid from the smoky-glassed bar. If Malcolm couldn't pay, he could always make it up in trade later. The place needed sweeping up. "Whiskey it is."

The liquid had hardly settled in his shot glass before Malcolm downed it and pushed it back toward Brian. "Again, Barkeep."

Brian looked down at the bar. "I don't see any money there."

Malcolm wanted to draw the moment out, set the stage for his revelation. "You will, Brian, you will."

"I must be crazy." Brian shook his head. He poured another shot. "Feeling your oats, are you?" he chuckled, looking at the smiling, grizzled face.

"Feeling like a million," Malcolm said. "Yes sir, a million. Oh, that feels wonderful." He let out a long, contented sigh as the second shot met its twin.

Brian began moving away. "Don't you want to know where I'm going to get my money from?" Malcolm's tongue was loosening. It never took a long time.

"The less I know, the less I can tell the sheriff," Brian answered, his voice mildly disinterested.

"No, no, it's nothing like that." Malcolm cackled. "It's treasure. Buried buccaneer treasure." It sounded so much better than saying he "found" the diamond. The lie came easily to him. Lies always did.

The two strangers next to Malcolm looked over in his direction, their interest aroused.


"Why should I trust you?" Mikki asked Shawn as she tucked the map into her purse. She looked straight into his intense green eyes. "I think you're an opportunist who wants to horn in on what he thinks is a good thing."

"Rather bluntly stated," Shawn said, leaning back against the wall, "but not totally without reason, I suppose."

"Suppose anything you like." She snapped the lid on her purse. "From here on in, I go solo."

Shawn sank down on the bed. The springs creaked loudly. Mikki moved away. She didn't want to be within reach of this man. There was something . . . just *something* about him that made her wary, skittish. He had a way of looking at her that confused her. She didn't want to be confused. She wished she had gotten rid of him at the door, but somehow he had talked his way into her room. She was going to have to stay on her guard until she could make him leave.

"If it hadn't been for me, you might have had trouble getting that strongbox. The desk clerk looked as if he wanted to barter for more than just money."

She raised her chin defiantly. "I can handle that type. I've done it before."

Shawn rose and walked over to where Mikki stood. He took her chin in his hand, studying her face. Beneath her bravado he detected a vein of pure vulnerability. He wanted to know what made her tick even though he sensed that the knowledge might be dangerous. For both of them.

"How often?"

She pulled her head away. She liked the feel of his hand. She even found that she liked the fact that at times he acted as if he had watched too many Humphrey Bogart movies.

She liked—and that was dangerous. Every time she let her feelings go, she got hurt. She had never really lost the desire to belong to someone. She was going to have to ignore the warm feeling in the pit of her stomach. It shouldn't be too difficult.

"Enough," she answered evasively.

He wanted to know more, but this wasn't the time. Shawn dropped his hand to his side. Let her keep her secrets. For now.

"I think you'd better reconsider winging this on your own."

She folded her arms across her chest, her feet planted firmly apart. The stance challenged him to convince her. He doubted that she knew how sexy she looked. Something hot and demanding stirred within him, but his expression remained mild.

"I've never heard of this Borachon, but it looks like it's on the border. Texas border towns can be dangerous places. This isn't Acapulco you're planning on visiting. I know. I grew up around Laredo."

"That doesn't say much for Laredo." Mikki shoved her hands into her pockets defiantly. "I can take care of myself. I can—Oh God."

Shawn was on his feet, alert. "What's the matter?"

"The diamonds," she gasped, turning her pockets inside out.

"What about them?"

"There is no 'them.' There's only one." How? When—? And then she knew. "That old man! He must have—"

"What were you saying about being able to take care of yourself?"

Mikki contemplated wiping the smug grin off his face with something lethal.

"And so this guy sezs to me, he sezs, he's after this buried treasure. The chest's full of diamonds and rubies. Stolen from his family more than a century ago." Malcolm was in his glory, embellishing the story for the two strangers, who'd introduced themselves as Rick and Neil.

Malcolm winked. "Y'see, I kinda 'stumbled' in on his conversation with that woman of his. He gave me a little 'bribe' to hold my tongue. 'Here's a little something to keep you quiet about it,' he said." Malcolm raised his shaking finger to his lips, missing them the first time. "Shh, I sezs. Mum's the word." He smiled, content with himself. "But you're my friends, so there's no harm in talking, right? Right," he answered before either man could comment.

"Did you overhear anything about where the treasure's buried?" Rick prodded.

"Rick, the guy's a rummy. This is just something he's making up," Neil insisted, yanking on Rick's arm to get his attention.

"Making it up?" Malcolm echoed indignantly, putting his hands on the bar, palms down, as he tried to draw himself up. "I'll show you making it up." He shoved his hand into his pocket and drew out the diamond. Lovingly, he set it down on the bar. "There." Triumph framed the word. "*That's* making it up."

Rick's hand darted out to cover the tiny twinkling light. He slid the diamond over. "He gave you this?" Rick asked. Neil took it out of Rick's hand and examined it. Brian looked over as he went on drying glasses. The one in his hand almost slipped out.

"Sure did," Malcolm attested.

"Why?"

Rick's tone was almost malevolent. Even in his inebriated state, Malcolm could detect it. He fumbled for a moment. His story was getting confused. "My throat's dry. Hard for me to think when it aches like that."

"Another!" Rick signaled to Brian impatiently. He waited until Brian worked his way back to the center of the bar. "Why?" Rick demanded again.

"I told you, it was to keep me quiet. And, and—he's got a map," Malcolm said quickly to divert attention from himself and back to the story.

"Where is it?" Rick asked.

"Where?" Malcolm raised his shaggy eyebrows, considering the question. "Why, the guy's got it."

"And just where is this 'guy'?" Neil wanted to know.

Malcolm shrugged his frail shoulders helplessly. "At the hotel, mebbe. Or—" Malcolm stopped as he squinted, looking out the tavern window. "That's him." He pointed excitedly.

Rick and Neil turned to look out the window. The world through the smoky plate glass looked dark, but not too dark to make out the people going by.

"Which one?" The friendly facade was gone.

"The guy with the girl. That real good-looking one with the long, blond hair." Malcolm had enough of the story. All he wanted now was to return his attention to his drink.

"Are you sure?" Rick demanded.

"I never forget the face of a man who's given me a diamond," Malcolm said solemnly. "Brian, hit me," he called, holding his glass aloft.

The empty glass slipped through his fingers and bounced on the counter, falling on its side, unbroken. Malcolm closed his eyes and muttered a prayer.

"Thank God it was empty," he said to the men at his side.

But they had already left.

Shawn took Mikki's hand as they walked toward Big Kate's. Very carefully, she removed it from his grasp.

Shawn sighed. "So when are you going to learn to trust me?"

*Trust me.*

The words echoed in her head. He was asking her to trust him. Simple words, difficult execution. But then, what choice did she have? If she was going to go into parts unknown, she was going to need someone with her. He was right about one thing. A woman alone in a border town was an invitation to trouble. If she had to take someone, it may as well be him. As long as she remembered never to let her guard down, she'd be all right.

"Does the expression 'when hell freezes over' give you a clue?"

He wanted to laugh, but he didn't. She could hold her own, and he liked that. He liked a lot of things about her. "How are we going to work together if you take that attitude?"

"Just fine, I expect. As long as I know what I'm dealing with, there'll be no surprises."

He eyed her. "Don't bet on it."

A hot shiver licked at the core of her being. Mikki began to think she was making a mistake. A big mistake. "We'll see."

"Yes, we will." There was the promise of something she didn't quite understand in his eyes. She was going to have to learn to avoid his gaze whenever possible. They were beautiful eyes, mesmerizing liquid green eyes that probably could charm a woman right out of her clothes—and her money.

*I'm on to you, Shawn Gallagher,* she thought. *This is all just temporary because I need you. Nothing more, nothing personal.*

Mikki put down her fork. Her stomach was far too agitated for her to eat. She had ordered a hamburger and French fries under duress. Shawn had pointed out that she was going to need her strength. Probably against him, she thought ruefully, wondering if she was out of her mind, letting him throw his lot in with her. The directions in the map Klaus Wintermeyer had drawn were explicit enough—as far as they went. The note he had included read like a riddle, something about a man suffering from the same malady as their beloved relative, as well as sharing the same name, holding the diamonds to his chest and waiting for Alfred's arrival. It made no sense to Mikki.

As for the diary, it was written in a mixture of German and English. She had a feeling that the key to the whole thing was in the diary. It had to be. Given enough time, she would figure it out herself. She didn't need Shawn.

But common sense told her she did. At least, temporarily.

She watched Shawn consume his steak. "How can you eat like that?"

He glanced up at her. "Easy, I'm hungry. Don't forget, you ate most of my last meal." Shawn stopped eating. He eyed the hamburger with one bite taken out of it and the dangling French fry that hung, half-mast on her fork. "Is the food bad?"

Mikki shrugged. "There's a knot in my stomach the size of Pittsburgh. I can't get this down." She pushed the plate away. "I can't even taste it." Turning her attention to the cola, she swirled the small melting ice cubes with her straw.

Shawn took a good look at her. Again it occurred to him that she was totally out of place in this town. Where did she belong? And to whom? "Who are you, Mikki?"

She looked at him sharply. His voice was like velvet, soft and coaxing. She was tempted to tell him the truth, but knew she'd be lost if she did. He had told her he was a reporter, and coaxing secrets out of people was a talent he had developed in the course of doing his job. Well, not her secrets.

After a moment, she retreated to a half-truth. "I'm not Alfred Wintermeyer's daughter."

He did his best not to laugh. "I had a hunch."

She caught the struggle. "Actually—" she looked him straight in the eye "—he's a distant relative."

All right, if she wanted to play games. "How distant?"

"Second or third uncle, I forget the exact position. I have an extensive family." She tossed her hair over her shoulder. He noticed that her hands were shaking as she said the word *family*. He speculated that saying it made her uncomfortable. He wondered why. "This is a lark for me. An adventure. I got very bored sitting at home, playing the pampered, spoiled daughter."

He nodded, thinking that the exact opposite was probably the case. Why did she feel compelled to invent this story? Had he hooked up with a pathological liar? Instinct told him no.

"Must have been rough."

He retired his knife and fork, leaving next to nothing on his plate, and reached for the cup of coffee at his elbow. He took a sip and frowned. It was weak, but at least it was warm.

"Not much luxury in my family. Just a lot of pulling together." He thought he detected a flicker of envy in her eyes. But then it was gone. He put the coffee aside. Enough was enough. "All right. Our first order of business is to go to the library."

"Excuse me?"

He grinned engagingly. Mikki tried to ignore the way it made her feel. "You don't happen to be fluent in German?"

She shrugged casually. "No, it's one of the languages I neglected to study." Actually, there had been a couple of courses in high school, but there was no reason to tell him that.

"Then we need a German dictionary. This town doesn't have a very well-stocked bookstore. I've been in it."

"But we can't sit in the library translating the whole diary."

He waved for the waitress. "No, we can't."

Mikki eyed him sharply. Just what was it he had in mind? "Are you going to steal it?"

"Let's just call it open-end borrowing, shall we?" And then, because she kept on glaring at him accusingly, he added. "I'll mail it back when I'm through." Once again he waved for the waitress.

"Impatient?" Mikki asked.

He looked at her. The light from the dusty window played on her long, straight hair, making it look even lighter. Pale gold, he thought, wondering what it would feel like slowly sifting through his fingers, brushing against his face.

"About several things." He saw her shift uncomfortably, though she tried not to show it. "The sooner we get going, the sooner we'll get to our goal."

"*If* we get to it," she muttered. It all *looked* promising, but there had been enough disappointments in her life for her never to believe in anything a hundred percent.

"We'll find it," he promised her. "I feel it in my bones."

His answers were too pat for her. "Like arthritis."

"You are one hard lady, Mikki. Didn't you ever believe in Santa Claus?"

She thought of all the Christmases when there had been nothing for her. A wave of uncustomary bitterness rose and then ebbed.

"No," she answered quietly.

Registering the pain in her voice, he cautioned himself not to get involved.

But it was too late. He already was.

The waitress finally meandered toward them, holding a murky glass coffee pitcher. She began to pour into Shawn's half-empty cup without a word.

"No, no, just the check. No more coffee." By calling it coffee, he felt he was paying whoever had made the brew a supreme compliment. Dishwater would have probably been stronger.

The waitress looked accusingly at the coffee she had wasted. Then, murmuring something under her breath, she marched off again with the pot.

"Charming employees this place has." Shawn watched the woman set the coffee down behind the counter.

"It goes with the food," Mikki muttered. Yes, she would be very glad to leave here, she decided. As soon as possible.

"Compared with some of the places I've been," Shawn told her as the waitress returned with her pad and pencil, "this place serves fine cuisine."

Mikki held up her hand, stopping him in midsentence. "Spare me that story."

The waitress appeared only to have heard the last part of Shawn's comment. She beamed and immediately became genial. She wrote the check with a flourish.

"You all come back now, y'hear?" Her words were directed solely at Shawn. She handed him the check as he rose to his feet.

Mikki took Shawn's arm, purposely coming between him and the waitress. She flashed the young, overendowed woman an artificial smile.

"She doesn't mean 'us-all,'" Mikki said as they walked toward the cashier. She gave the girl a backward glance. "She means *you*-all."

"Why Mikki, I do believe you're jealous." Shawn grinned, amused.

"I just don't want you getting distracted. We're in a hurry, remember? Now pay the bill, and let's get to the library."

"Yes ma'am." He gave her a smart, two-fingered salute.

The man, Mikki thought, looking away from his amused face, was impossible. What in heaven's name was she getting herself into?

## Chapter Four

Shawn took hold of Mikki's arm to stop her before she had a chance to charge down the block. She obviously thought she knew where she was going, but seeing the direction she was taking, he knew better.

Mikki swung her head around. She didn't need to say a word. The look in her eyes demanded to know the reason he had stopped her and, more to the point, why he had grabbed her arm rather than just telling her to stop.

There were people who needed to make physical contact when they talked. But too many of the men she had met seemed to fall into that category. They used the simplest of body language to demonstrate their control over her. She had come to hate it. And she wouldn't be controlled. What concerned her was that she didn't react negatively to his touch. Not inwardly. She was beginning to realize that she needed to be very careful around this man. He spelled trouble with a capital *T*.

The whole thing made her nervous, and she didn't like being nervous.

"Now what?"

Shawn grinned. He was growing to like the fire that flamed in her eyes whenever she spoke to him. They darkened until they reached the shade the sky turned just before dusk. "Do you have the slightest idea where you're dashing off to?"

The man could easily earn himself a swift kick for that patronizing tone. And she'd gladly deliver it.

"To the library." Since he didn't let go of her arm, she deliberately pulled it free, her eyes never leaving his.

Shawn folded his own arms across his chest patiently. "Which is?"

She blew out a breath. What kind of game was he playing now? "I don't know. I thought you said that you knew—"

"I do."

His tone was still patronizing. No, on second thought, it was just low and deep and warm. Which was he? A kind, considerate, handsome man, or a deceitful, opportunistic snake in the grass? She decided it was safer to go with the latter. Another time, another place, she'd have given him more of a chance. Clearly, being with him would be an adventure. But she was already on an adventure and couldn't handle any more. Not safely, anyway.

"So?"

His smile grew more expansive and more engaging. She found herself responding to him. She had to ignore the signals he was transmitting to her if she wanted to keep her wits about her and find the diamonds. But she couldn't seem to effectively shut down her receiver.

"So why are you the one who's leading the way?"

Mikki hated him for smugly pointing that out, hated him even more because he was right. She searched for a graceful way out. "I'm just setting the pace."

"Oh."

His eyes laughed at her.

*We'll see who has the last laugh in the end, Shawn Gallagher. If I didn't need you right now, for two cents I'd—*

Mikki felt the diamond in her pocket and remembered the encounter with the drunk. Shawn hadn't been any help there. Why was she so certain he'd be of use in any other situation? It was time he started sharing the load in this temporary partnership of theirs.

"Instead of playing Daniel Boone—" she lowered her voice as someone approached them on the sidewalk and then walked by "—why don't you try to find that old man who stole my diamond?"

He had already given that some thought. "Where do you propose I start?"

"I don't know." She threw up her hands in exasperation. "You're the investigative reporter. Investigate."

When she smoldered like that, he found it very difficult to sustain his train of thought. That was a first, he mused. He had always enjoyed the company of women, women who were far more sophisticated, more experienced than he'd bet Ms. Mikki Wintermeyer or whatever her real name was, claimed to be.

Yet there was definitely something about her that was weaving its way under his skin. She was part firebrand, part lost waif. And all woman. He was going to find a great deal of pleasure in showing her just how much of a woman when the time was right.

Until that time came, though, common sense was going to have to prevail.

Shawn nonchalantly draped his arm around her shoulders and began to guide her in the direction opposite to the one she had taken. Reluctantly, still somewhat uncertain, she let him lead her.

"I think the less attention we draw to this, the better Ms.—what's your real last name, Mikki?"

"I already told you." She looked at him defiantly. "Wintermeyer."

"Yes, so you did." Maybe it *was* her name, but he doubted it. "Have it your way."

She moved her head and turned her face toward his. Though he was at least six inches taller, there seemed to be no space between them at all for a moment. He could feel the soft, gentle flutter of her breath on his face, and it triggered a sudden, urgent need within him. The intensity surprised him.

"That's right, Gallagher. My way."

He laughed softly and hugged her to him for a fleeting instant. He felt her stiffen. "Mikki, you're delightful. Anyone ever tell you you're gorgeous when you're being a brat?"

Enough was enough. She shrugged off his arm. The feel of it on her shoulders generated sensations within her that were far too intimate to suit her.

"Gallagher—" she began warningly.

Undaunted this time, he took her hand and pulled her along. "C'mon, the car's this way."

This new piece of information caught her by surprise. "You have one?"

She had naturally assumed, since they had walked to the restaurant, that he didn't have a car. Of course, the restaurant was only down the next block.

"Actually, this is a rental. Mine ran into transmission trouble just as I drove into this lovely hamlet. The mechanic is trying to revive it even as we speak. The rental car is his. Why he keeps it, I don't know."

She didn't quite understand what he was talking about—until she saw it. Shawn brought her over to the street opposite the hotel. A dusty Mercury Cougar, vintage 1975, give or take a decade, stood in silent repose, sagging against the sidewalk. Its tires were nearly bald and struggled to retain the air he had put in them at the local gas station. The town's *only* gas station. The tires matched the rest of the vehicle. The vinyl roof looked as if it had once undergone a merciless attack by a band of vultures. There was scarcely a place where the vinyl wasn't peeling off in curly waves. Its pale blue paint chipped and cracked, the surface of the car resembled the weathered skin of a hundred-year-old man who had spent his entire life out in the sun.

The car suited the town perfectly.

Mikki stared at it. "Are you sure it's a car?"

"Well." Shawn shrugged philosophically. "It does have a steering wheel and four tires. I guess that qualifies it to be called a car." He opened the door for her. "The town's illustrious and only mechanic informed me that this was the best he had to offer."

"It figures."

Mikki sighed as she tried to slide in. The seat, with its cracked upholstery, tugged at her skirt, making progress difficult. Several tufts of stuffing and the spring coil peered out through the rips in the unconvincing leatherlike material.

The car, she noted with some uneasiness, didn't even have bucket seats. There was nothing to separate her from Shawn. And right now, Mikki felt as if she needed some buffer, however minor, between them.

As she closed her door, the glove compartment fell open, a cracked, jagged edge hitting her knee. She squelched a cry and tried to push it back in place. She failed.

This wasn't going very well. Mikki frowned as she tried to make herself comfortable. She tugged at her skirt and looked for the seat belt. There wasn't any. "This car is as broken down as the town. I'd hate to live here."

Shawn got in on the driver's side and closed the door gingerly. He had the distinct impression that if he slammed it, the door would fall off. "I've seen worse."

"I'm sure you have."

Her icy tone made him turn and look at her, his key still inches away from the ignition. "You certainly have a chip on your shoulder, Mikki."

She tossed her head, her hair spilling down her back like so much liquid gold. "It's my shoulder."

Tempting. The lady was very, very tempting. He doubted she knew how much.

Shawn touched the object under discussion lightly. "Care to share it?"

Maybe the man understood bluntness. "Do you ever stop coming on?"

He shrugged. His hand remained where it was. "Sometimes."

She wondered if she'd have to hit him over the head to make him back away. She also wondered if, once he had, she'd experience a pang of regret. "How do I qualify for that?"

He smiled very, very slowly. "You won't."

In response, every nerve ending stood to attention and telegraphed "Mayday" to her central nervous system. It was far too sexy a smile, and he was far too much of a man for her to handle for long. She had never thought she'd actually feel this way, but she had to admit she needed help. Maybe he'd listen to reason.

"Gallagher, if we're going to make this temporary partnership work, we're going to need some ground rules."

He curled her hair around his finger. Soft, silky, just as he had expected. He wondered if the rest of her would feel this soft to the touch. He was only partially paying attention to what she was saying. The library and the strongbox were temporarily on hold.

"Such as?"

Very coolly, she brushed his hand aside. "First of all, no touching."

"How about if you're falling down?" he asked innocently. "Would it be all right if I grabbed you and broke your fall?"

Mikki clenched her teeth. Others might find him charming. She found him an abominable, egotistical maniac. But why did she have to keep telling herself that? It was a simple fact that shouldn't need reinforcement. "Yes."

"Okay." He nodded, apparently unperturbed by the fact that she had literally hissed the word at him. "Grabbing's allowed then."

She turned in her seat. Unconsciously, she moved toward him, as if her nearness would drive her words home. She meant to keep her voice authoritative, but it wasn't going her way. "Only under certain circumstances." She held her hand up before he could interject. "And I get to say when."

Shawn inclined his head. "To say what?"

Couldn't he get anything straight? Was he acting this densely just to drive her crazy?

"When," she fairly shouted at him.

And then she realized her mistake by the look that entered his eyes.

"Okay."

Before she could utter a single word of protest, he had her in his arms.

It was a trick. She might have known. She should have seen it coming. The man was reprehensible. Mikki opened her mouth to tell him just what she thought of him and his feeble humor when his mouth lowered onto hers.

He had a need, an overwhelming need to get this out of his system before it became an obsession and clouded his better judgment. Being honest with himself, he had to admit that he had been wondering what it would be like to kiss her ever since he had watched her get off the bus. He was sure that once he had kissed her, he would stop wondering.

He hadn't expected to be overcome.

She was furious. Absolutely, positively furious. She had meant to give him a piece of her mind. She had meant to push him away with all the strength that she had in her body. Right out the door if possible.

She didn't push. She didn't castigate. She had all she could do to keep herself from careening wildly off into space. Hands that meant to pummel suddenly grasped his shirt and held on for dear life as some hidden part of herself flashed and exploded to meet the challenge of this man's lips.

It was supposed to be a kiss, a simple, satisfying kiss, but it aroused more than satisfied. Raised questions, not answers. Passions he had been totally unaware of came to the surface at dizzying speed. Simultaneously, she was destroying him and creating him anew, like a phoenix that timelessly rose out of its own ashes. For a moment, he forgot who and what he was, forgot his world-weariness, his jaded view of life. All he could taste was sweetness and passion and need. Hers? His?

Theirs.

He couldn't have been more unprepared for what he experienced than if he had gone skydiving and left his parachute on the plane.

He made her remember. Remember how much she needed, how much she wanted. And could not have. Had never had. It made her moan.

And yearn.

She trembled against him, and Shawn wondered why, when she was the one who had all the power. He had been reduced to nothing but a pulsating hunger.

It took a great deal not to let himself go and taste all of her.

Finally, after what seemed an eternity, Shawn released her. It took a moment for him to get his bearings. He was shaking inside. Getting something out of his system? He had succeeded only in getting her more fully entrenched *into* his system. He would have laughed at himself—if it wasn't scaring the hell out of him.

He was going to have to think about this. Very slowly, very thoroughly.

Her eyes were wide, dark with the passion he knew she was feeling. Passion that echoed his own. He had never seen anyone more desirable. His pulse jumped. He told himself to calm down.

Shawn looked at her hands. "You're tearing my shirt."

Abruptly, she let go, as if the current that had been running through both of them had suddenly been shut off. "You're lucky I didn't punch you."

"Judo and now boxing. Is there no end to your talents?" If he kept his tone light, she'd never suspect that she had just short-circuited all his systems.

Jokes. He was making jokes. Mikki glared at him. "Are you quite finished?"

"For the moment."

The bastard. He had sucked out the very air from her lungs, kissed her as if she were the only woman in the world, made her feel things she had only fantasized about before, and now he was acting as if nothing had happened. "Try forever."

"If that's the way you want it." They both knew that they had started something here that would have to be played out later as surely as the sun rose each morning. But he let her have the lie to save her pride. For now.

"That's just the way I want it."

Even as she said it, a faint inner voice cried out "no." She had absolutely no use for inner voices that were plotting her downfall.

Shawn picked up the key he had dropped on the seat next to her and turned on the ignition. Seeing that his hand wasn't steady, he cursed himself for his lack of control.

"Mikki," he said softly, the feel of her lips still fresh on his, "I'll never do anything you don't want me to do."

"Fine," she snapped tersely. "As long as you don't declare yourself a mind reader, everything will be just great."

He turned down the next long, dusty block. A line of stores came into view. "And if I were a mind reader—" he couldn't help smiling "—what would I read?"

Mikki stared straight ahead. "Your obituary notice."

He laughed. "The library's in this direction."

The car rattled and moaned and filled the silence that rose up between them.

Mikki folded her arms across her chest and said nothing. She didn't trust her voice to keep from cracking. She felt the tears even though she didn't shed them. Damn him. How dare he toy with her? How dare he open up wounds that she thought were healed?

Who was she kidding? The scars that were there were never going to heal. But he didn't have to know that. She dragged her hand through her hair. Well, he had done his worst. From now on, she was just going to have to see to it that nothing like that ever happened again.

And he was right. She did need a man with her when they went to the border town. She just wished he was stoop-shouldered and had a few teeth missing. And didn't have a mouth that made her ache. Or a face that would haunt her dreams for the rest of her life.

*Disturbing*, that was the word for it. The kiss had been disturbing, arousing, demanding and hopelessly tempting. He couldn't remember the last time he had felt like this. It had satisfied nothing. Instead, it had afforded him a fleeting glimpse of a paradise that was far beyond his reach.

Or was it?

He was going to have to keep his distance until he had a few things sorted out. His relationship with women had always been short and sweet, exciting and without depth, ending quickly and with no regrets. Restless by nature, he had always moved on before things got too involved. He had a feeling that this lady was different from the others, and that presented a problem. One that he wasn't sure he could walk away from when the time came.

Stealing a glance at Mikki's profile, he wondered if he could keep his distance.

A sorry-looking one-story wooden building that had weathered over a hundred winters in one capacity or another came into view. Shawn stopped the car in front of it. The vehicle seemed to sigh as he turned off the ignition. Shawn turned toward Mikki. "We're here."

"What gave it away?" she asked, hiding her hurt feelings behind sarcasm. "The word *Library* on the sign?"

She glared at him defiantly. She hadn't liked what had happened between them because she had liked it too much. Too much for her own good. Mikki had absolutely no doubts now that Shawn Gallagher's real avocation was that of a charming opportunist. And she was the opportunity with a capital *O*, nothing more. As long as she remembered that and didn't succumb to his charisma, she would have the advantage. The trick was to remember that. Constantly.

He saw the hurt beneath the anger. He wanted to say things to her that he knew he shouldn't. He wanted to tell her no other woman had ever made him feel the way she did, but he knew she wouldn't believe him. Hell, *he* wouldn't have believed himself if he hadn't experienced the kiss and felt what he had felt.

He didn't want to complicate his life. No matter how vulnerable she appeared, any woman willing to pull up stakes and do what she was doing wasn't meant to be tamed. But he had always liked that in a woman. It made for a relationship that was wild, exciting. And short. This time, though, it was different. There was something more here, something that could hurt. It was time to remember that he was a reporter and that there might be a hell of an interesting story here.

Shawn let his breath out slowly. "If I keep the librarian in there distracted, can you slip out with the dictionary?"

"No."

There was that stubborn tilt of her chin again. He felt like nibbling on it, on her. His lack of control over his own thoughts made him angry. At her. At himself. "Why not?"

"I don't believe in stealing."

"Look," he began patiently, although patience was a commodity in increasingly short supply around here, "without a permanent address in this town, the woman is not about to let us waltz out with a book using the conven-

tional methods. Don't you want to get started as soon as
possible?''

She hated it when he made sense. It gave her nothing to
fight with. "Yes, but—"

"By the time we get everything together and drive to another town where we can *buy* a German dictionary, we'll
have lost about half a day. Do you want to do that?"

She pretended to try to fix the glove compartment door.
But it was beyond hope. As was he. "It's waited fifty years,
what's one more day?" She couldn't believe she was actually saying that when only a little while ago she had been
dying to get started. But Gallagher had a way of making her
want to contradict him even when she knew he was right.

"Remember the drunk who picked your pocket?"

She frowned. He *would* bring that up again. "What
about him? He doesn't know anything."

"No, probably not, but I'd like to keep it that way.
Maybe he knows the desk clerk, Harold, who might mention that someone came asking for a fifty-year-old strongbox. Then our drunk'll show him the diamond."

"He's not 'our' drunk," she said a bit too loudly, her
nerves still stretched to the limit. It was going to take a
while before everything was back to normal again. If ever.
"There's no 'our' anything. And what if he does show him
the diamond?"

"I don't have all the answers, Mikki, but I like to cover
all my bases. As fast as possible."

That much, she believed. Shawn was the type of man
who *always* covered his tail. She'd hate to *really* have to
depend on him. She knew she'd be disappointed. If you
don't expect a great deal, you can't be disappointed. She'd
learned that much about people.

"Now," he said, "I'll be doing the hard part. All you
have to do is locate the book and slip it into your purse."
Her shoulder bag lay on the floor of the car, next to her
feet. "Considering the size of that thing—" Shawn nodded

at it "—it shouldn't be too hard for you to carry out half the library without being suspected."

There was no talking him out of it, and he did have a point. Besides, he had mentioned mailing the book back. If he didn't, she would. "All right, let's do it." Mikki sighed.

"That's my girl."

"Not by a long shot, Gallagher, not by a long shot."

She refused to let him help her out of the car, even though the seat had sagged around her bottom, cupping it like a well-worn beanbag cushion.

Because she glared at him, he removed his hands from her arm. He watched her struggle, his hands raised, his mouth curved. He made no attempt to avert his eyes.

Mikki yanked down her skirt, which had crept up her leg as she tried to disentangle herself from the seat's grasp. She muttered an oath under her breath. "Let's get this over with, Gallagher."

"Mikki, you're always taking the fun out of everything. Well—" he glanced at her mouth "—almost everything."

Mikki decided, for sanity's sake, to pretend she hadn't heard that.

Together, they walked toward the library. Without looking at him, she marched through the door he held open for her. The library smelled old. Old and damp and musty. It was a large, barnlike room with scarred wooden floors that had long since lost their luster and creaked beneath her feet.

Mikki wrinkled her nose. It must have rained recently, she thought.

There wasn't a sound except for the creaking floors. The building appeared to be empty. So much the better. There'd be no witnesses to her first—and last—criminal act. Diffuse light radiated from worn fixtures that hung overhead, and the sunlight that crept in through the windows lost its sparkle as it entered. The place was definitely not warm, or inviting.

Neither, Mikki thought, catching sight of the angular woman in the rear behind the desk, was the librarian. She looked, from this vantage point, like a caricature of her profession.

The impression was not dispelled as they drew closer to the older woman. Alicia Traherne, said the name on her desk.

But by the expression on her face when she looked up, Alicia, Mikki perceived, had never seen anything like Shawn Gallagher. Not even remotely. The books on the desk were forgotten as she rose and made her way toward him.

Mikki saw the barely veiled interest in the tall woman's eyes and felt something stir within her. If she hadn't known herself as well as she did, Mikki would have sworn the feeling was something akin to jealousy. But she knew that was utterly ridiculous. Shawn was nothing to her. She hardly knew him. Why should it matter to her that another woman was looking at him as if he were lunch and she hadn't eaten in a year?

But it did.

"She looks as if she'd like to have you for lunch, Gallagher." The comment was out before Mikki could think better of it.

Shawn gave her a reassuring look that only served to tell her just how much he had been around. "I can handle it."

Mikki began to move toward what she took to be a card catalog. The library was so out-of-date, she noted; the computer age still hadn't reached it.

"Sure you don't want me to tie a lifeline around your waist?"

He grinned. "We'll talk about tying each other up later."

The librarian's thin, crescent-shaped eyebrows rose alarmingly high on her forehead, and she cast a reproving look at Mikki. Mikki turned crimson and swore to herself that she'd pay Shawn back for this embarrassment if it took her the rest of her life—or his.

"Is there anything I can do for you?" the librarian asked Shawn. Her attitude efficiently dismissed Mikki.

Good, they deserve each other, Mikki thought, feeling more annoyed than she knew was reasonable. That only made her angrier.

Shawn smoothly took hold of the older woman's elbow and began to usher her back to her desk. "Why yes, Ms. Traherne, there is. My name is Shawn Gallagher, and I'm with the *Houston Chronicle*. My newspaper is doing a series on small towns...."

His coaxing, velvety voice vibrated back to Mikki as she thumbed through the card catalog. She pushed each card aside with undue force.

An operator, she told herself. The man was nothing more than an operator. He could turn charm on and off like a spigot. That kiss in the car meant less than nothing to him. And to her, she reminded herself. It was a temporary aberration. Temporary, like their partnership.

She realized that the card before her had the name and number of the book she was looking for. Still thinking of what was going on a few feet and one aisle over, she began to write.

The point of her pencil broke. Impatiently, she dug through her purse for something else to write with, inventing creative expletives for Shawn, which she silently heaped on his head as she searched.

## Chapter Five

The library turned out to be unoccupied, except for two very old men Mikki stumbled across sleeping in the reading section. Mikki guessed that there were more people in that tiny, dingy bar she had passed than there were here.

It seemed rather surprising that a town like this would have a library this large. Large and dusty. Unused. Its size bespoke earlier, more prosperous days. But it took money to maintain all this. From the looks of it, though, nothing around here had been touched in a long time. Books didn't get worn-out by just sitting on a shelf. She sneezed. They got dusty.

As Mikki marched up and down the aisle, searching for the dictionary, she could hear the honeyed tones of Shawn and the librarian. A giggle. The librarian had actually giggled. Unless it was one of the old men gurgling in his sleep. Giggling. She couldn't believe that Shawn character. But more importantly, could she trust him? As fantastic as it seemed, she realized she wanted to.

From her vantage point, Mikki could see Shawn's gestures. And even from here, she could see the librarian's wide-eyed expression. The woman was totally intrigued with Shawn. Mikki thought she could have backed up a truck to the front door and emptied the entire building for all the librarian would have noticed.

Her curiosity getting the better of her, Mikki moved two aisles closer. She just had to hear what Shawn was saying. As she edged over within listening distance, Mikki heard him use her name, or rather the name she had given him. His tone had a touch of sarcasm in it.

"Ms. Wintermeyer is my research assistant."

So he was still having trouble accepting Wintermeyer as her name, Mikki thought. Well, that was his problem. She wasn't about to tell him her real name or anything else about herself. The less he really knew about her, the better it would be for her when this venture was all over.

The incredibility of the situation she found herself in struck her then. She was fifteen hundred miles from home, in a tiny backward town, standing in an old, dark library, about to steal a German dictionary. She had a diamond in her pocket, a treasure map in her purse and a charming—a charming what she wasn't certain—for a partner. Mikki stopped for a second, trying to clear her head, overwhelmed by a sense of unreality. Excitement mingling with fear and tinged with anticipation exploded through her. Her fingers and toes felt cold.

"And what is it that Ms. Wintermeyer is researching at the moment?"

The question was asked strictly for the sake of making conversation. Mikki could tell that the woman had absolutely no interest in the answer or in her. Mikki had the distinct impression that Shawn could answer "daffodils" and the librarian would have been satisfied. What she really wanted was standing in front of her in a dark-green pullover and jeans.

Mikki worked her way through the children's section. It was far from extensive. She tried to recall if she had seen many children in Mission Ridge. This wasn't a town that made you think in terms of new families and urban growth. It made you think of dying. Slowly. She shivered and wondered if it had been any different when Klaus had lived here.

As she drew closer to where Shawn and the gaunt librarian were standing and talking, Mikki could almost hear the warm sigh that accompanied Alicia Traherne's question. Man-hungry, there was no other description Mikki could think of and no other man she would have liked to see on the receiving end of it than Shawn Gallagher, she decided, stifling a pleased chuckle. What might have been a tinge of jealousy had completely given way to amusement.

"My assistant is checking to see how many books you have here."

Mikki shook her head. Brilliant, Gallagher. With that mind, in another life, you could have been a master spy.

She moved down the next aisle, into the reference section. It wasn't much of a section. Most of the library, she had noticed, was comprised of fiction, a great deal of which had to do with the West. She skimmed the area quickly, wondering how long it would take Alicia to consume Shawn.

There. She had found it.

The book was worn and old, its yellow and black cover partially torn. But she doubted many of Mission Ridge's citizens had reason to use it. It was obviously a contribution to the library from someone's family. Maybe, she mused, her hand hovering over it, it **ha**d even belonged to Klaus himself. He had been proud of the English he had mastered, but it was plain that he needed the help of a German/English dictionary. This dog-eared copy could well have been his.

Mikki rested her hand lightly on the book, still leaving it in its place on the shelf. For a moment, she hesitated. Even in the worst of times, she had never taken anything that didn't belong to her. But, much as she hated to admit it, Shawn had a point. The book would help them get started faster, and she was curious about what was written in the diary.

The diary intrigued her not just because she hoped to find the clue to the whereabouts of the diamonds but because she wanted to know more about Klaus Wintermeyer. This man had touched her life. He hadn't meant to, but he had. She felt a desire to know more about him. How he felt, what he thought. In a way, she mused, his adventure had become hers.

She thought of the diary in her purse and unconsciously pulled it closer to her. She loved books. To her they represented a link with the past. They were no longer just a source of entertainment and escape, as they had been for her when she was younger. The diary had been written by a man now long dead, but at one time he had been a man with feelings, with emotions. And he had been alone. The way she was. She wanted to know about him, to understand what he had gone through. To find out if, at last, he had found peace. For some reason, she felt a kinship to the man whose letter had been delivered to her doorstep.

Taking a deep breath, she pulled the dictionary off the shelf and shoved it into her purse.

The books that had been on either side of the dictionary sagged against each other. She propped them up and then adjusted the surrounding books to minimize the size of the gap the dictionary had left, hoping the theft wouldn't be detected too soon.

Alicia's voice droned on. She gave no indication that she had any intention of releasing Shawn anytime in the near future.

Shawn knew how to look interested even when he felt as if his eyes were going to slide shut. Very carefully, he glanced at the rows of bookshelves on his left where he had seen Mikki disappear. What was taking her so long? It wasn't that huge a library.

He wondered if she had skipped out on him. No, he hadn't heard the front door close, and he had been listening for it.

Turning his eyes back to Alicia, he tried to keep his impatience from showing. The information she was giving him about the town was boring to put it kindly, and it only corroborated what he had already learned from the bartender, who, he was informed, was her cousin, as were several other people in the town.

Besides, the woman was coming on to him. He was beginning to feel rather uncomfortable about the intense look in her eyes.

Long spidery fingers moved restlessly in slow, nervous circles on his forearm as she talked. Alicia Traherne reminded him of a spider weaving a web. He couldn't feel any sorrow for her. She didn't come across as a lonely woman in need of attention. She came across as a predatory female.

He wished Mikki would hurry up.

"I have a lot more memorabilia available at my house," Alicia announced after taking a decisive deep breath. "Perhaps you'd like to come over for tea and I could show it to you?"

Even if he had been blind, he could have seen her true intentions. Shawn looked over his shoulder toward the stacks and willed Mikki to appear. "Ah, I'm afraid my assistant might need—"

"I'm sure she can manage for herself." This time, the tone was just a shade more insistent. And hopeful.

Mikki thought of slipping out and leaving him to this torture. She glanced over toward the front door. It wouldn't take much to sneak out. She had both the diary and the dictionary. She could manage on her own. She always had before, and it would serve him right for taking advantage of her in the car if she left him now. Mikki moved silently toward the door.

She couldn't do it. At this point, though she didn't trust him, Mikki told herself that she did need him. As a bodyguard, nothing more. Besides, leaving him in that woman's clutches came under the heading of cruel and unusual punishment.

Clearing her throat, Mikki emerged from behind the stacks, her pad in hand. With a flourish, she tucked it inside her purse.

"Finished," she proclaimed. She thought that Shawn looked as if he wanted to kiss her. She swallowed and maintained a fixed smile.

Alicia looked deflated and shot Mikki an annoyed look as she drummed her fingers on the desk.

Mikki smiled innocently at her and turned toward Shawn. "Well, Boss, I think we'd better get back to the hotel. I need to transcribe my notes for you so that you can take all the glory in your byline the way you always do."

The relief Shawn felt at her arrival outweighed any annoyance he experienced at her blatant put-down of his work. He nodded at the librarian whose shoulders were slightly bowed in defeat.

Safe, he could afford to be genial. "Good day, Ms. Traherne. We'll be in touch."

"Please." The word was said longingly.

Shawn hustled Mikki out of the library and to his waiting car. "Was that really necessary?" he asked, opening the car door for her.

For the first time since this adventure had started, she was enjoying herself. Mikki got in and turned her face to his. With his eyebrows drawn together in annoyance, he looked almost unbearably handsome. A heartache looking for a place to happen, she decided. "Was what really necessary?"

He closed the door but stayed where he was. The window on her side was missing. "That crack you made about my byline."

So, he was sensitive about his work. At least that much was human about him. It made her feel a shade better about their partnership, although for the life of her she wouldn't have been able to explain why.

"Look." She watched as he came around the other side. "I could have just left you there. The thought did enter my mind. Be grateful that I'm the honest type."

Shawn got in and started the car. "I am, Mikki, believe me, I am."

Mikki turned just then to see that Alicia Traherne was watching them through the side window as they drove away. The expression on the older woman's face was thoughtful. Mikki wondered if there was anything more on her mind other than Shawn's departure. She couldn't help but think that there was.

"Well, did you find it?"

Mikki turned around in her seat and looked at Shawn. "Yes, I found it."

Shawn felt as if he were pulling the words out of her mouth. "And you took it."

"Yes." She sighed. "I took it."

Taking the book really bothered her. Maybe he had somehow stumbled upon the last honest person, he mused with a smile. He had become accustomed to bending rules in his line of work, bending them in order to get the final story, the news-breaking exposé. Maybe he had been living with the end-justifies-the-means dictum a little too long. There was a time, he recalled, when he hadn't believed that. Mikki took him back to that time.

"Mikki." His voice was so gentle, it made her look up in surprise. "I'll bet you anything you want that no one in this town even knows there *is* a German dictionary in the library, much less has any desire to actually use it. If it'll make you feel better, I promise I'll buy one as soon as we hit Houston and I'll mail this book back. Is that all right?''

She was about to agree when the rest of his sentence hit her. "Why are we going to Houston? According to the letter, the diamonds are in Borachon."

They drove past the local mechanic's shop. The large sign, listing to the left, proclaimed Ed's Ga ag in fading red letters. There seemed to be no activity. Shawn wondered if the man had finished repairing his car yet. He had promised to have it ready today, but Shawn had misgivings. "I live in Houston."

Mikki tensed as she looked at him suspiciously. Now what was he up to? "I have no desire to see your etchings, Gallagher."

"That's good, because I have no intentions of showing them to you. But I do need to check on a couple of things and call my editor."

It still didn't wash. "I thought we were in such a hurry."

"We are." He turned to look at her. "To leave here. But Houston's on our way to the border. You don't know your territory, do you?"

He was being smug again. She forgot any charitable thoughts she might have been entertaining about him. "Sorry, I haven't slept with my Rand McNally lately."

He couldn't let the opportunity go by. "Who have you slept with, lately?" He kept his tone casual, but when he asked, he realized that he really did want an answer. He should have been forewarned then, but the trail was much too interesting for him to take note of a danger sign.

Where did he get off asking things like that? He had only kissed her once. He had no right to her past. No one did. "That is none of your business."

No, it wasn't. He knew that. So why was he asking? Because he wanted to know, know a lot of things. He thought it was only his reporter's instinct, but that excuse didn't carry much weight anymore. "Just making conversation."

She reached into her purse and pulled out a mint. She needed a moment to cool off. As an afterthought, she offered him one. "Talking about the weather is making conversation, Gallagher."

"Thanks." He popped the mint into his mouth. It tasted tangy, like her kiss. He wanted to kiss her again. "That's much too boring a subject for someone like you."

He needed to be put in his place, and she was beginning to despair that that would ever happen. But she was determined to go on trying. "Someone like me is going to sever all relations with someone like you if you don't keep this partnership on a strictly professional level."

He cocked his head. "Another ground rule I take it?"

She moved back in her seat until she was almost pressed against the door, remembering the last time they had discussed ground rules. She felt the spring dig into her back and stiffened slightly.

"Yes."

Shawn turned his attention back to the road, having noted her retreat and guessed what she was thinking. "Don't worry, Mikki, I never drive and kiss at the same time. I need my hands for both."

As he drove up to the hotel, he saw two men leaving it and thought that they didn't look as if they belonged. They had an unsavory look about them. He wondered what they were doing in Mission Ridge.

"Thank God for small favors." She sighed, trying to find a position that didn't hurt or snag at her clothes. She couldn't. "I hope your car's more comfortable than this one."

"You'll get to find out on the trip to Houston."

She had a nagging suspicion that that wouldn't be the only thing she'd find out on her trip to Houston if she wasn't careful.

When they walked into the hotel, Harold looked up and immediately took a defensive stance. Shawn glanced over his shoulder instinctively, but there was no one behind them. Why did the clerk look so jumpy?

"We'll be checking out this afternoon," Shawn told the man.

Harold nodded a little too vigorously and scribbled a notation beside each of their names on the register. He started to speak, then stopped before the first word was formed.

Shawn noticed the hesitation. "Is there something on your mind?"

"No." Harold shook his head, the red fringe of hair around his balding head fluttering in the breeze his gesture had generated. "Just hate to see paying customers leave, that's all."

That wasn't what was on his mind, but Shawn let it go. It was probably nothing. "C'mon," he said to Mikki, "we have to pack."

"No one put you in charge, Gallagher. You don't issue orders." Shawn paused, waiting. "All right, we'll pack, but only because I agree."

"And you are so agreeable," Shawn muttered under his breath, but loud enough for her to hear.

Just as Shawn started up the stairs, the desk clerk asked nervously, "Did those two guys ever find you?"

Mikki felt Shawn tense beside her and wondered if someone was after him. She wouldn't doubt it. Probably a pack of irate husbands.

Shawn turned around slowly. There was no one in Mission Ridge who would be paying him a social call. He'd done his interviewing before Mikki had arrived in town, and there had been no one who sounded as if they had anything to add. Besides, he was sure that the clerk had to know everyone in the small town. If Harold didn't refer to the men by name, that meant that he didn't know them. Why were two strangers looking for him?

Unless it had to do with the diamonds. Shawn looked at Mikki. He had a hunch. And hunches were something he had learned early on never to ignore. He walked over to the desk. "What two guys?"

Harold cowered a little. The look in his eyes was uncertain as he spoke. "The ones who said they were friends of yours. Asked if I'd let them stay in your room until you got back." His voice rose, gathering strength. "Of course I told them that was out of the question."

"Of course," Shawn echoed. The frightened look was gone as Harold laid his hand rather unsubtly on the counter. He obviously expected to be paid for keeping the men out. Shawn dug a five-dollar bill out of his pocket and slid it along the counter, unwilling to put it in Harold's outstretched hand.

Mikki looked at Shawn. He was certainly acting very oddly. Just what did she know about this man? Had she thrown her lot in with some sort of fugitive? For all she knew, he really *wasn't* who he said he was. All she had was his word that he was a journalist. "Were you expecting anyone?"

Slowly, he shook his head. "No."

Mikki began to get a strange, nervous feeling in her stomach. "Maybe they were just two locals, wanting to talk to a 'big-time' Houston reporter."

"No, they weren't from around here," the clerk said, overhearing her. This information only managed to heighten Mikki's anxiety.

"Don't look so stricken," Shawn whispered into her ear. "It's okay."

But she didn't believe he really meant it. She saw his jaw tighten slightly.

Shawn leaned over the counter. His proximity served to intimidate the clerk, even though they were about the same height. The similarity ended there. Shawn was broad and muscular while the word *emaciated* described Harold perfectly. "Did they leave right away?"

"Why yes. That is, I—I suppose so." The man's confident tone began dissolving. "Actually, I went on my break just about then.'' His hand hovered over the phone. ''But I could call Amos. He's my nephew, he relieved me. He's just in the back—'' Harold's voice rose higher and higher as he spoke, finally cracking.

Shawn shook his head. He thought of the two men he saw leaving the hotel. It was probably them. That raised more questions than it answered. ''There's no need. If they want me, they'll find me.''

There was something very fatalistic about the way he said that, Mikki thought. Maybe he *was* a fugitive. Just her luck.

The clerk looked more than eager to agree. ''They said they had to talk to you.''

''Thanks for telling me.'' Shawn looked at Mikki's face and saw the wariness in her eyes. There was no need to worry her. Yet. ''Nothing to worry about,'' he assured her.

Mikki didn't think he sounded all that convinced himself, but she let the matter drop. It made no difference to her how many men were after him.

No difference? But she was with him. *That* made the difference. If they were after him, they'd be after her, as well. She couldn't afford to let that happen.

As soon as they reached the second-floor landing, Mikki turned to Shawn with her hand out.

''Do you want a tip, too?''

She frowned. Didn't he take any situation seriously? ''No, I'd like to see some I.D., please.''

Shawn looked at her, puzzled. ''This is a strange time to play policewoman, Mikki.''

''Not so strange.'' Her hand remained stretched out. ''How do I know you are who you say you are?''

''What brought this on?'' He saw her skeptical expression. ''Oh, that?'' He nodded down the stairs.

''Yes, 'that.' If you are who you say you are, why are there people after you?''

''Since the people in question are men, I haven't the slightest idea.'' He produced his wallet and flipped to his license and his identification card from the newspaper. He held them up for her benefit. "There, satisfied?"

Mikki took the wallet from him and looked down at the photo, debating the authenticity of the cards. "They could be fake."

"They could be," he agreed philosophically. "But they're not."

She hadn't the vaguest idea why she believed him. But she did. Mikki closed the wallet and handed it to him. "Women always run after you?"

Shawn slipped the wallet into his back pocket. "Excuse me?"

She hated herself for asking and even more for repeating it. But she had come this far, she might as well go the distance. "You said that since they were men, you didn't know why they were after you. I'm asking you if you have to beat women off with a stick wherever you go."

"Why, Mikki." Shawn laughed as he opened his door, then turned toward her. "I just love it when you get jealous."

Mikki made no answer. She merely stared past his shoulder, dumbfounded.

"Don't look now, Ms. *Wintermeyer*, but your mouth is hanging open."

She went on staring. "Don't look now, Gallagher, but everything you own is hanging open."

"What?"

In reply, she pointed into his hotel room. Shawn swung around.

The room was in utter chaos. The mattress was stripped and flung to the side. Drawers were opened, their contents dumped on the floor. Not a single thing in the room was where it had been when he had left it earlier.

"Not very neat, are you?"

Shawn waved for Mikki to be quiet. He slowly swept through the tiny room, cautiously checking out the interior of the closet and then the bathroom.

Mikki was positive that her heart didn't beat the entire time.

There was no one in the room.

Shawn looked around at the shambles, too stunned to register any anger yet. "Looks like whoever it was left." It was one hell of a mess.

Mikki walked in, picking her way around the single overturned chair. "This happen to you often?" She masked her mounting fear with irony.

Shawn looked at her, wondering if he was getting himself into something that was really dangerous. He knew that he hadn't trod on any toes lately. It had to be something associated with her. Her question brought a smile to his lips. "Not since my fraternity days."

"Animal House?" She could see him in a rowdy fraternity. Panty raids, turmoil, that seemed to be his style all right. He had certainly caused her enough turmoil since she had met him.

"Phi Beta Alpha." He began picking up the things that were closest to him, attempting to restore order. "Mind lending a hand?"

"Maid service doesn't come with this arrangement, Gallagher." But even as she said it, she was picking up one of his T-shirts. "Red?" She held it up.

He took it from her and dropped it on the box springs, not bothering to put back the top mattress. "I like bright colors."

"Uh-huh."

"Mikki." His voice had lost its bantering tone and had become sober.

She preferred it when he was being obnoxious. It didn't make her quite so nervous. Not life-threatening nervous anyway.

"I think we had better be on our way. Now." He unearthed his suitcase and threw it on top of the box springs as well. Quickly, he began packing, haphazardly piling things in.

She chewed on her lower lip and saw the flash of desire in his eyes. She stopped. They were in apparently too much trouble to add more to it. "All right. I'll just go back to my room and—"

But he stopped her wrist before she got out the door. "No." Shawn grabbed her wrist.

The touch of his skin against hers restrained her more than his grasp on his wrist. She didn't like that. She didn't want to react to him. Not on any level.

"Rule one," she called out, raising her wrist slightly. He let go. "Why can't I go back to my room?"

"Our decorator friend—" Shawn gestured around the room to get his point across "—might be waiting there."

Slowly it began to penetrate. Her and not him. "You think this had something to do with me?"

"Or the diamonds."

Mikki sighed. He was probably right. Again, damn him. "But my things—"

"We'll get them together, and then we'll get my car and get the hell out of here."

She nodded, running her hands along her arms. A sudden chill had come over her that she couldn't shake. "I think I like the sound of that."

He heard the touch of fear in her voice and stopped. This time, when he took her hands in his, she didn't pull away. The look in his eyes held her fast. He wasn't being the roguish seducer now. Just another human being who understood. Mikki allowed herself to relax a little. "I'll take care of you, Mikki."

She summoned bravado from somewhere. If she didn't, she knew she would have melted against him. She could feel the need.

"There are many ways that could be taken."

He laughed and shook his head. She was something else, all right. And he was beginning to like the difference. Maybe too much.

"C'mon." He put his arm around her shoulders. "I'll walk you to your room."

## Chapter Six

Any hopes Mikki had been entertaining that the ransacking was not related to her and the diamonds vanished as soon as Shawn cautiously opened the door to her room. It was a mirror image of his own.

One hand gripping the doorjamb for support, Mikki stood silently staring at the shambles within her room. As in Shawn's, not a single item had been left untouched. Everything had been gone through. Lamps were overturned, drawers were pulled out. Her clothes were scattered all over. She felt violated, violated and angry. Hands clenched at her sides, Mikki forced herself to steady her breathing.

Moved by what he took to be her fear, Shawn slipped his arm gently around her shoulders. "If you want, I'll pack your things for you. Let me get you a cup of coffee from the restaurant. You can wait for me in the lobby while I finish up here."

Mikki slowly moved her head from side to side, so frustrated that she could hardly speak. Her anger reached a slow, red-hot boil. How dare they invade her privacy? How dare they fling around her belongings like that?

"No thanks, Gallagher. My things have obviously been handled enough by strangers for one day. I'll do my own packing." Her voice was low, the pent-up rage at having someone sweep through her personal effects this way unmistakable.

She walked into the room and began picking things up. "What kind of people would *do* such a thing?"

Any doubts he may have had, any fear that he had teamed up with a woman given to fainting and weeping were permanently extinguished. He saw the wrath in her eyes. She was feisty, he'd give her that. And rather magnificent in her fury. Instinctively he knew he'd never want to be on the receiving end of it.

"Unscrupulous people. The world is full of them, Mikki. I deal with them all the time." Despite her insistence that she could handle everything, Shawn scooped up a heap of her clothes from the floor and deposited them on the bed. "Who else did you tell about the diamonds?"

Mikki tossed a pair of jeans onto the bed. He was implying she was at fault for this! "Absolutely no one. I'm not stupid."

He knew how people talked and wound up saying things they hadn't meant to. It was only human nature. And she was only human. He thought of the way her mouth had felt beneath his. Very, very human. "You told me," he pointed out.

That wasn't her fault, either. Spinning around, she waved a finger at him, her anger exploding. "Under duress. And—" she balled one hand on her hip "—I wouldn't have if you hadn't gone through my purse."

He covered her waving finger with his hand and pushed it away from his face. "Lucky for you I did."

"Yes, 'lucky.'" The word was heavily laced with sarcasm.

Only time would tell if she was "lucky." Maybe he was exactly what he seemed to be, a harmless, charming opportunist with a silver tongue who would soon be out of her life. And maybe he wasn't. But in either case, she needed to keep him in sight. Especially if he was something other than what he seemed, if he *was* out to trick her out of the diamonds. She'd already seen how he operated. Smooth and gregarious with the librarian. Tough and direct with the desk clerk. He was a man who knew how to get what he wanted. As far as she was concerned, it was always best to keep the enemy out in the open where you could watch him.

As she picked up a blouse from the floor, she saw that Shawn was holding aloft a pair of very flimsy robin's egg blue panties. The expression on his face was that of intrigued amusement. She would have liked to put a good-sized dent in that grin.

"Give me those." Mikki snatched her panties away from him. She wasn't about to add fuel to his fantasies. "I can pack my own underwear, thank you."

He would have needed an overcoat to protect him from the frost in her voice. "You wear these?"

"Yes, I wear them," she snapped, balling them up as she threw them into her suitcase. Mikki raised her chin belligerently. "What's it to you?"

Shawn grinned. "I'm not sure. Yet." Mikki's face flushed crimson.

He liked the fact that she blushed. It meant that she wasn't nearly as tough as she acted. There had been innocent wonder in her kiss. He felt certain it was genuine. It had tempted him all the more. Then and now. The pink hue highlighting her cheeks meant that Mikki was reacting to him despite all her protests to the contrary. Exciting, yet innocent. It was a combination that would have once sent him quickly on his way because it spelled trouble. Instead, it was reeling him in.

"Don't tax your brain too much, Gallagher. There isn't going to be a 'yet' for us." She needed to say that, needed to hear it said out loud. Because even though she was trying to convince him that their relationship would never become intimate, Mikki no longer was all that certain she wasn't lying to him and to herself.

Anything but a temporary, businesslike relationship between them would be all wrong for her. Shawn was just passing through her life. She knew that. Just passing through like all the other people had before him. All the foster homes, all the families that she wasn't part of. There was no use wondering what it would be like to be loved by him, to have him hold her and make the world spin away. For him to be hers.

It *wouldn't* happen and that was that.

She had no place in her life for anything but temporary alliances. She had accepted that fact of life a long time ago. If she yearned, once in a while, for something permanent to touch her life, well that was just her own weakness. Permanent relationships weren't for her. They didn't work out, no matter how much she wanted them to. Hadn't she had her affections rejected often enough to teach her that? She wasn't going to open the doors and be subjected to that risk, that hurt again. Things would be played out on her terms or not at all.

She was thinking about something. And it hurt. He could see it in her eyes. Shawn wondered what it was and if it had been triggered by something he had said. He didn't want her to hurt. But he knew that if he asked, if he offered to listen, she would only close up. Shawn decided that the best way to get her mind off it, whatever "it" **was**, was to change the subject to something they were both involved in. Consciously involved in.

"We're going to have to skip going to Houston."

Mikki folded her sweater carefully and placed it on top. She raised her eyes to his. "Why aren't we going to Houston?"

"Why, Mikki—" he snapped her suitcase closed for her "—you *did* want to see my etchings."

She spied a shoe she had overlooked and stooped to retrieve it from under the bed. Rising, she kept it in her hand as she answered him. "Not in this lifetime." Her meaning was very clear.

Mikki reopened her suitcase and tucked the shoe under her sweater. She surveyed the suitcase's interior. It contained almost half of her worldly possessions. Not much to show for twenty-three years, she thought. With a sigh, she lowered the lid and snapped the locks closed.

Mikki raised her eyes to Shawn's and realized that he was waiting for her to continue. "I don't like being taken for a ride, Gallagher. I like to know where I'm going. At all times."

And I don't with you, she thought suddenly, wishing his eyes weren't quite so green and compelling. I don't know where I'm going with you on any level. Except that it leads to nowhere eventually.

"All right, let me map it out for you." He sat down on the bare mattress, fingering the handle of her suitcase. Mikki tried not to stare, as she imagined those same fingers moving like that along her body. A small, incredulous smile lifted the corners of her mouth. She was letting her mind get carried away. But sexual fantasies were difficult to control. Actions, however, were different. Those she could control. Easily, she hoped.

Shawn noted the smile and wondered what was behind it. "Someone is very anxious to find something one of us has. My guess, and it doesn't take a sage—"

"You'd be the one to know about that."

He ignored her comment. "—is that it's probably the diary." Mikki looked over her shoulder at the purse she left on top of the bureau. It would be best if she kept it with her at all times. Deliberately, as he spoke, she moved over to the bureau and picked up the shoulder bag. "And the sooner we get to Borachon, the better. From the looks of the map, it's located on this side of the border. I figure if we start out today, we might be able to get there in a couple of days or so. Watching our back, it might take longer. I don't want to waste any time." That out of the way, he rose. "Got everything?"

She looked around, then nodded hesitantly.

"What's the matter?"

"I hate leaving the rest of the room looking like this—"

So, neatness counted. Bits and pieces of her personality were being revealed, and he was putting together a picture of the whole woman. It didn't fit with the blasé way she was trying to portray herself.

"Don't worry about it. I've already given that vulture at the front desk fifty-five dollars more than he deserves. It'll go toward cleanup. C'mon." Shawn picked up her suitcase and began walking out. "I've still got to get my gear together."

She followed in his wake. "As well as your act," she added.

He waited until she was through the door, then shut it behind her. "My act, Mikki, is as together as it's going to get."

"Thanks for the warning."

Though usually entertaining, her flippancy was wearing on him. He felt impatient to get to the real woman, the woman behind the quips and the bravado. He wasn't sure what he was going to do when he finally found her. He only knew that he had to.

"Tell me something, Mikki, do you ever let your hair down?"

Mechanically, she ran her hand through her hair. "It is down."

Shifting the suitcase to his other hand, he led the way down the hall. "You know what I mean."

"If I do—" Mikki spared him a glance "—I'm ignoring it. C'mon, let's go to your room."

"Ah, Mikki." He deliberately put a leer into his voice. If she could play games, so could he. Besides, it helped to reduce the hum of sexual tension that was growing between them. "I've been waiting a long time for you to say that."

Mikki stopped at his door, her hand on her hip. "Gallagher—"

"I know, I know," Shawn pushed open the door to his room and looked around. "Rule One."

No one had entered while they had been in the other room. He gestured her in, then followed. Quickly, he closed the door, then locked it. Mikki swung around when she heard the lock being turned. "For our protection," he told her, then purposely drew closer to her. "Any chance of repealing Rule One?"

Her eyebrows drew together over darkening eyes that enticed him. "When hell fr—"

"—eezes over." He dropped her suitcase on the floor. "I've got the picture."

Mikki began gathering his things together. "Make sure that you do."

The problem was, Shawn reflected as he packed, he did have the picture and it was on his mind constantly. That her image actually interfered with his usual instinct for survival, his usual way of functioning, surprised him. Though he had always loved women, delighting in their company and the pleasure of their bodies when it was to their mutual enjoyment, no woman had ever gotten under his skin. At least not the way this one had. And no woman had ever interfered with his thinking processes before. He found that because of her, he was having difficulty concentrating, on his series, on the diamonds. On anything. Yet there seemed to be nothing he could do about it. It had begun the moment he had seen her, and it had exploded when they had kissed. He kept telling himself that he eventually would work this all out of his system, but everything he did only seemed to embed his obsession with her all the more.

* * *

Packed within ten minutes, they drove over to Ed's Garage. The car Ed had loaned Shawn went protesting, bucking and wheezing all the way.

"Tell you one thing," Mikki began. They took a turn and the hanging glove compartment door swung dangerously close to her knee. She shoved it back. "I'm certainly not going to miss this car." She was starting to have her doubts that it would even get them to the garage. "Hey, Gallagher, I just had a thought. If the mechanic's spare car is in this kind of shape, just how good to you think his work is?"

He had to admit she had a point. "I'd rather not think about that, Mikki. I like getting chills down my back only when I'm holding a woman in my arms, not contemplating misfortune."

She blew out an angry breath. "Is that all you think about? Women?"

"No." Shawn thought of the exposés he had been privy to, the things he had seen that a man shouldn't bear witness to. The sorrow. The pain. The evidence of man's inhumanity to man. Things that stripped a man of his soul until there was nothing left for him to believe in. "But it's certainly all I'd like to think about."

There was something there, in what he had said, in the *way* he had said it, that spoke to her. A need. For a moment, Mikki thought of reaching out, of touching, soothing. But that wasn't her any longer, remember? she scolded herself. She wouldn't be pulled in that direction, only to have her feelings used against her. She shut out the look in his eyes and the empathy for him that rose up within her.

Mikki looked over to her left. "Is that the garage where you left your car?"

She pointed to the sign that proclaimed Ed's Ga ag. The other two letters had long since fallen off, and obviously Ed thought it too much of an effort to replace them. It was a good tip-off about the character of Mission Ridge, Shawn thought.

"That, Mikki my dear, is the *only* garage in town. Or 'gag' as the case may be." Shawn pulled the car up before the partially opened garage door. The Cougar backfired, then trembled to a halt. "I don't know whether to turn off the ignition or shoot it to put it out of its misery."

"Just turn it off. At least you'll be putting me out of my misery."

Shawn grinned. She had fed him another straight line. "All in good time, Mikki. All in good time."

Mikki was beginning to believe that if she turned to the word *egotist* in her German dictionary, there wouldn't be an appropriate foreign term for it. It would merely say, "See Shawn Gallagher."

She quickly got out of the car. "What's the mechanic look like?" Mikki scanned the area and saw a few men milling around.

"You'll know him when you see him," Shawn assured her.

They made their way into the garage. The interior was dark and dreary, filled with cars that were partially stripped, their hoods or doors yawning open, waiting to be fixed.

Mikki realized that she was walking very close to Shawn by choice and that, after the incident in the hotel room, she was feeling jumpy. So much so that when she turned and saw the lumbering giant coming at her, she stifled a yelp and tugged on Shawn's sleeve.

Shawn turned, his body tensed. It relaxed when he saw the approaching man. "I see you've found the mechanic." Her eyes, opened wide in wonder, made her look both innocent and sexy. It was hard not to think about kissing her. It was getting harder not to think about that all the time.

"Him?" she whispered. The man, dressed in bib overalls, looked more suited to be a farmer, plowing the north forty when the tractor broke down. Only the permanently oil-stained color of his hands hinted at another vocation.

"Him."

The mechanic's frame filled out the doorway and blocked the incoming sun, such as it was. He had a wide, bright face that broke out into a broad, sunny smile, displaying a double row of even, white teeth.

"Mr. Gallagher." For a big man, he moved easily. His outstretched paw swallowed up Shawn's hand as he pumped it up and down. "Glad to see you."

"So I gathered." Gingerly, Shawn withdrew his slightly crushed hand, avoiding Mikki's smirk. "Um, Ed, is my car ready?"

Ed looked pleased at the question. "Yep, just like I promised. "C'mon." His hamlike hand beckoned them toward the back.

Ed opened the door of the navy-blue Jeep Cherokee. The Jeep stood in the only clear spot in the backyard. The rest of the place was filled with piles of junk and parts of decaying automobiles that had given up the ghost.

Mikki circled the vehicle as best she could, taking care not to step on a fender that blocked her path. She frowned. "That's your car?" She had expected something flashier and far less practical. He didn't look like a man who would own a Jeep. She had been looking forward to riding in a luxury car.

Shawn recognized disappointment when he heard it. "My other car's a Ferrari." He laid a comfortable hand on the Jeep's hood. "I just go slumming and rescuing beautiful women in my Jeep. It's also good for going up the sides of hilly terrain."

Whenever she began to forget, he was always there to remind her that she would be only one of many passing through his life. "So are goats."

Shawn cocked his head, amused. "Is there a comparison in this?"

"Figure it out for yourself." She turned her back on him and looked at Ed. He stood beaming at her. She wondered if he ever thought of anything but cars. "Does it run all right?"

"Good as new." With a surprisingly gentle touch, he patted the car's rear.

"How good was it when it was new?" Mikki asked, not convinced.

Shawn looked inside the Jeep to make certain that the keys were in the ignition. They were. "You are a distrustful soul, Mikki."

She didn't bother looking in his direction. "I've always had to be."

He was beginning to believe that that part was true. Shawn paid Ed quickly, and then he and Mikki transferred their luggage to the back of the Jeep. He slammed the door and looked at Mikki.

"Ready?"

She nodded, climbing into the passenger's side. "I've been ready for a long time."

"So have I." Shawn got in. "I'll see what we can do about it later."

Mikki sighed. Maybe it was a phase he was going through. A very long phase. Mikki settled back against the seat, relieved that it was much more comfortable than the other car had been.

Of course it was all because of the diamonds, she thought. If he could find a way, she was sure that he'd separate her from her diary and the dictionary, both of which she made certain to keep always in her possession. Until then, he'd go on, pouring on the charm. As long as she had the diary and kept Shawn in her sight, everything would be all right.

Mikki crossed her arms in front of her, closed her eyes and told herself to relax.

Shawn pulled out onto the street, turned the Jeep south, and they were on their way.

They drove in silence for the first few miles. Shawn had turned on the radio, and a potpourri of Country and Western tunes filled the air. He saw her frown slightly to herself. "I take it you don't like Country and Western music?"

She shrugged. "I don't like crying-in-your-beer music, no."

"There's a lot to be said for catharsis. Getting sadness out of your system." He should talk, he thought. But at the moment, he was trying to find a way to get beneath her barbed-wire barriers.

He wondered what she was thinking, but knew better than to ask. He wasn't in the mood for one of her snappy answers. At the moment, he was trying to untangle the riddle in the letter and come to grips with his own uncomfortably confused reaction to Mikki.

He wished he could get the impact of that damned kiss out of his mind.

And the hunger out of his body.

He was going to have to do something about that. Soon. But not, he knew, if she didn't want him to. Though he wanted her and found his need growing at an alarming rate, he had never forced himself on any woman. He had never had to. Usually, the opposite was true. All he had ever had to do was look mildly interested, and the rest took care of itself. He wasn't about to establish a precedent. Not if he wanted to live with himself.

He shut the radio off in the middle of a vocalist's sob. "Have you been able to make any sense of the letter yet?"

He startled her. She'd been lost in her own thoughts, wondering what lay ahead, wondering why of all the men in the world, she had to finally react to one who was absolutely wrong for her. He was an emotional drifter if she had ever seen one.

"Um, no." She pulled the letter they had found in the strongbox out of her purse and scanned it again quickly. Maybe reading it aloud would help. "It just says that he found someone with the same last name as their beloved relative, a man suffering from the same malady that the relative had. He left the man clutching the diamonds to his bosom, promising to wait until Alfred arrived." She folded the letter and tucked it back into her purse.

Mikki turned toward Shawn, and the wind blew her hair into her face. Combing it back with her fingers, she rolled the words over again in her mind. "I know there's a clue there, but what? No man is going to stand patiently clutching diamonds for someone else no matter how noble he is."

The wind still played with the ends of her hair, making her look like some sort of wild spirit. A wild spirit he wanted to tame, at least for a night. He nodded in agreement. "Nobility only stretches so far."

"What would you know about being noble?"

"Mikki, you wound me deeply. Don't you think I'm noble?"

She didn't have to look at him to know he was grinning. She uttered a short, deprecatory laugh. "You don't want to know what I think."

He turned toward her. There was nothing but a dusty road ahead and no danger of running into anything but more road. He could afford to look at her for a moment. "Yes, I do, Mikki. Very much."

His words, like a warm caress on her skin, unnerved her. Why was he doing this to her, messing around with her mind? Did he just want to bilk her out of the diamonds? Or did he get his kicks watching women melt? She wasn't about to melt, not where he could see her do it at any rate. Still, when she spoke, she didn't have full control of her voice.

"You wouldn't like it." Her voice quavered only slightly, but it was enough to betray her nervousness.

"I'll be the judge of that, Mikki. And I *am* going to know. I'm going to get to know all your secrets. It's just a matter of time."

She refused to let him in. The wall went up. Her expression grew hard. "So's dying."

Shawn resumed looking at the road. "Ever think of putting out a book with your cheerful little sayings? Might make a mint. You could call it Words To Be Depressed By."

She didn't like his mocking tone. He had no right to judge her. "You don't know anything about me, Gallagher."

"Then tell me." His voice was low, coaxing.

For a moment, she wanted to, she really wanted to. But what good would it do? It would just give him power over her. Nothing good had ever come from opening up. Mikki pointed to the road. "Just drive."

"Okay. For now. But our time is coming." Out of the corner of his eye, he saw her opening her mouth to retort. He beat her to it. "And it'll be a lot sooner than hell freezing over."

That tore it. He was egotistical, insufferable, and she was afraid that given enough time, he'd make good his promise. Because she knew that she had always needed someone in her life, would go on wanting someone in her life. And he wasn't the right someone. She'd seen his type before. If she had any doubts, there were his own words to go by. Women entered and left his life with regularity. He didn't want commitments. Probably broke out in hives at the mention of one. And commitment was what she needed. A secure, meaningful relationship. It was something she was sure he couldn't offer.

"You can drop me off at the next town, Gallagher." She saw him look at her but couldn't read his expression. She began talking faster. "I'll pay you for your trouble once I have the money, but I think that this partnership is dissolved."

Several moments went by, and she wished the radio was on, or the car was rattling or *something* would fill the silence. Finally, when he spoke, his voice was low and calm and all the more unnerving for that. "No."

"No what?" she demanded.

"No, Mikki, I won't drop you off."

"You have no say in it!"

"I think I do. I don't drop out of a person's life that easily." Which was a lie, but not in this case. Generally, he did. He breezed in and out, no ties, no need to feel obligated. But this was different. And he wanted to know why. Needed to know why. "You're a riddle, Mikki, an even bigger riddle than the one in Wintermeyer's letter." He nodded in the direction of her purse, which lay on the floor of the car. "And I'm not letting you off in the next town until I solve it. I told you once before, I never leave things half finished."

Mikki stared straight ahead. "You're insufferable."

"We've already established that. Don't worry, I'll grow on you."

"Like a wart," she retorted. She was afraid that he already had. Anticipation warred with panic. "Don't I have a choice?"

"Not for the time being. But don't feel bad. Neither do I."

She looked at him in surprise, then turned her face away. "All right. Drive."

"Yes, Ms. Wintermeyer."

"Donovan."

Her voice was faint, tight, barely audible. He turned to look at her. "What?"

"The name is Donovan." She refused to look at him. "Mikki Donovan."

A breakthrough. The first piece of the puzzle had been handed to him. Shawn felt like whistling, but knew Mikki wouldn't appreciate it. He switched to an oldies station instead. "This suit you?"

"Yes." Her lips hardly moved.

"Okay, partner."

"Temporary partner," she reminded him.

"Right."

## Chapter Seven

"I don't see what you're complaining about."

Shawn pushed the hotel door open with his shoulder as he carried both of their suitcases into the small, homey looking room. The place was part of a chain of inexpensive but comfortable hotels that threaded throughout the country. Shawn had a certain fondness for them.

He deposited her suitcase on the bed and, still holding his own, he turned to look at her. "We have separate rooms, although I still think that it's a waste of money."

Mikki didn't answer immediately. Instead, she walked over to the adjacent wall. There was a closed door in the center. She pointed at it accusingly. "We have *adjoining* rooms." The man probably knew how to pick locks in his sleep.

This was going to take more than a moment. He set his suitcase down at the foot of the bed. The grin he gave her was slow, and lazy, and incredibly sexy. "Don't trust yourself?"

The bastard! Did he think he was that irresistible? What made it worse was that there was more than a kernel of truth in his implication—although she'd die before letting him know.

"It's not *me* I'm worried about." Too restless to sit, Mikki prowled around the room. There wasn't much room to prowl. "I don't see why we had to stop and book rooms in a hotel anyway."

He wondered if she got a kick out of being difficult. She did it so well. Shawn walked over to the window and pulled back a corner of the beige drapes. "In case you haven't noticed—" he gestured outside "—it's dark out there."

"You're afraid of the dark?" He had an ulterior motive, and she wanted no part of it. The sooner this was over, the better.

"I'm afraid of what's *in* the dark."

She folded her arms across her chest expectantly. This had better be good. "Such as?"

He let the drapes fall. "Such as the men who redecorated our rooms back in Mission Ridge. Men like that use the dark to their advantage."

Mikki arched an eyebrow, still unconvinced. "They're not the only ones."

She was his match all right. "If you're referring to the adjoining rooms—"

"Yes, among other things."

"I was only thinking of your safety."

"Is that what you call it now?"

Shawn grew serious. "Whoever ransacked our rooms might not have decided to call it quits. With even half a brain, they're going to come to the conclusion that if they didn't find anything in our rooms, then one of us has it on his person." His eyes swept over her. "I don't want them hurting you."

The last part surprised her. It sounded so genuine. The look in his eyes suddenly made her feel weak. She would have given anything to believe him, to be *able* to believe him.

But she knew better.

"You don't want them hurting the diary." She ran a nervous hand through her hair and began twisting a strand of it. Suddenly aware of what she was doing, she stopped. But her nervousness was conspicuous. "Right now, I feel a lot more threatened by you than I do by some nebulous characters who might just have turned out to be run-of-the-mill thieves and nothing more."

The room was small, and there wasn't much space left over after a bed, a chair and a desk were crammed into it. She needed to move around and couldn't. A few steps had her at the window. She played with the drapes, trying to close them properly. A five-inch space remained between the two sides. With an impatient sigh, she turned around.

Shawn blocked her way. He placed his hands gently on her shoulders. He was unnerving her. He knew it. Just as he knew that being here like this with her was unnerving him. "I'm harmless."

Everything about him belied the statement.

She sucked in her breath before she managed to find the strength to back away. Her eyes stayed on his, waiting for a false move. Possibly his, possibly hers, she wasn't certain just yet which of them she distrusted more, which was why she needed distance between them.

"I don't think so."

"Mikki—"

There was something in his tone that she knew was meant to break down her barriers even further. It was working and it scared her. She had struggled so hard to build those barriers, to keep the hurt away, to convince herself that she didn't care. Mikki took another step back and found the bed hitting the back of her knees. "I have work to do."

He looked at her, puzzled. "Work?"

"The diary, remember?" She raised her purse aloft for his benefit. He had noticed that she kept the strap on her shoulder at all times. Another indication that she didn't trust him. "The dictionary we stole?" Mikki let the purse fall back against her hip. Shawn looked amused. "What are you grinning about?"

"That's the first time you used the word 'we.'"

He would pick up on that. We. It had a nice ring to it, but a false one. "Don't get used to it."

She deliberately circumvented the bed and crossed to the tiny writing desk. Fishing the two books out of her purse, she placed them both on the desk next to each other. His shadow fell on the desk. Mikki stiffened.

He saw her back straighten in anticipation when he came behind her. "What are you afraid of, Mikki?" It took a great deal to keep the anger, the impatience out of his voice. Slow and steady, that was the only approach to take with her. After he had solved the puzzle, he'd decide if it had been worth the effort. Although he thought he already knew the answer to that one.

Very carefully she turned around. There was very little space between their bodies. Mikki wished the room was bigger. "Getting hoodwinked by a fast-talking, good-looking guy who slides in and out of places liked greased lightning for one."

Lightly, he played with one of the wisps of hair that framed her face. "That is part of my job."

She licked her upper lip. It was unbearably dry. "Sliding?"

He wanted to follow the path of her tongue—and lay new trails of his own. For now, he knew he couldn't.

"I'm a reporter, Mikki, not everyone wants to tell me the truth when I ask them for it. Like you." His hands dropped to his sides. If he continued touching her, touching any part of her, he'd be tempted to kiss her again. Any contact with her, however fleeting, managed to arouse him. She was becoming more habit-forming than the coffee he craved in the morning.

He was probing again. She didn't want him to probe. She had given him her name, and that was all she intended to give him. She didn't even know why she had confided that much. "You haven't called your editor yet," she reminded him, trying to divert his attention. "Why don't you go into your room and do that?"

Shawn knew when to back off. But each time, he did so after gaining a little more ground. His eyes teased her. "While you slip into something more comfortable?"

He was incorrigible. But this time, she had to laugh. Maybe she was getting used to his ways. "While I slip into the diary."

He glanced at the book behind her on the desk. "Tight fit."

"I'll manage, Gallagher." She pointed to the door. "Now go."

Obligingly, he picked up his suitcase and walked to the front door. "Yes, ma'am."

Mikki closed and locked the door behind him. Finally alone, she kicked off her shoes. She was tired and glanced longingly at the bed. But she was too keyed up to really sleep. So much had happened in such a short time. She wanted to sort it out. And she did need to make some headway with the diary.

She stretched, her hands linked together over her head. Her body felt as if it was at the snapping point. That, she knew, was Shawn's fault. And hers. By now, she should have far better control of herself. She thought she did have. But that was before she had met Shawn.

With a resigned sigh, she settled down at the desk to see what she could learn from the diary. She had already thumbed through it during the trip from Mission Ridge to the hotel. The writing in the diary was delicate and small, just as Klaus Wintermeyer's stitches must have been, she mused. The inside cover had declared this to be The Journal of Klaus Wintermeyer, Retired Tailor and had the date just beneath it.

From the moment she took in the first stroke of his pen she felt she knew him. Albeit clumsy and rambling, the thoughts he had committed to paper spoke to her. His feelings found kindred ones within her. This wasn't just an old diary written by a man who had lived a long time ago. It was written by a man who seemed to be able to put *her* feelings, however awkwardly, on paper. Klaus came to life for Mikki, more real than many of the people she had known. He was a sad, lonely man who had lost his wife and his dreams.

With her feet curled up, resting against each other under the chair, Mikki painstakingly began at the beginning again. He had started to write the diary on the ship that brought him to "a land where free to find my destiny I will be."

The diary showed that Klaus had desperately wanted to master the language of the country he was coming to. But there were many lapses into his native tongue. Haltingly, resorting to the dictionary time and again, writing down passages on the pad of paper the hotel had provided, Mikki pieced together the fear, the excitement of the ocean voyage undertaken in secret. She discovered that he had made the crossing in the belly of a freighter, too afraid to venture out into the open more than a few times, and always at night. She learned that even though he looked forward to his arrival in America, he was still anxious about it. He wrote that once he arrived at his destination, he'd be just another stranger in a strange land. Mikki smiled sadly to herself. It was the way she had always felt about being sent to another foster home.

But even beneath the sadness and apprehension, the words Klaus wrote had an underlying note of hope. Mikki understood that, too. She had gone on hoping for a long time after her parents had left her behind. It was all she had to cling to before she fell asleep at night, that tomorrow would be different, that tomorrow her dreams would come true.

"But they didn't, did they, Klaus?" she whispered softly, tears forming in her eyes. She closed the book and hugged it to her breast. "All that hope and there was nothing for you at the end, was there?"

He had knocked once, but there had been no answer. Only slightly concerned, he opened the door that adjoined their rooms, then stopped. She was bent over the desk, reading. He slipped in silently, wanting to catch her unawares, wanting to see her at work, her features unmarred by the tension that was always there between them.

Her head was bent slightly, her long straight hair pushed away from her face as she concentrated, exposing the delicate slope of her neck. He took in every detail. The way her head nodded as she read, the way her right foot moved in agitation along the sole of her left when she pieced together another passage. He wasn't certain how long he stood there watching her. He only knew that he was enjoying it.

But the quiet words and the sob that filled her voice as she said them pulled him to her.

"Mikki?"

Mikki jumped, dropping the diary to the floor. She swung around in her chair and looked at Shawn accusingly. She looked past him at the opened door.

Quickly, though she knew it was too late, she wiped the telltale tears from her cheeks with the palms of her hands. "I thought you said that thing was bolted." Attack was always the best defense.

"It was. On my side." But there was no flippant quip to match her words now. He crossed to her, picked up the diary and tossed it onto the desk. Then he put his hand under her chin, lifting it. "You're crying."

She jerked her head away. "I'm not crying," she retorted.

"All right, then there's a cloud raining on your face." With his thumb, he traced the path of one tear. "I don't like to see a woman cry."

"I thought you were supposed to be the big, bad, hardened reporter," she said sarcastically, embarrassed that he had seen her when she was so vulnerable.

"I thought so, too."

And he had been. Until he had met her.

Until he had met her, he had despaired that his work had permanently scarred him. It had robbed him, he thought, of the ability to feel. He had never experienced strong feelings for a woman, never had feelings of tenderness, much less love. He had thought his work had emptied him of all that. And then she came into his life, bringing it all out.

Shawn crouched down beside her, not about to be put off by her tone. "Mikki, what's wrong?"

For a moment, she couldn't answer. He was being too nice. She didn't know how to deal with him when he was being really nice. She preferred his come-ons and his banter. That she could deal with. Kindness just fed on her need to be held and comforted. She tried to cling to her barriers. But her barriers didn't only keep him out. They also kept her in. She couldn't reach out. "I always cry over German translations."

He rose to his feet, taking her with him. Though she struggled for a moment, he held her against him, stroking her hair and soothing her without saying a word. Mikki let herself relax for a moment and absorb the warmth, the comfort she found there. It wouldn't hurt if she gave in briefly. Nothing would happen.

Shawn avoided the temptation of laying his cheek against her hair. One thing would only lead to another. "Better?"

She could feel his heartbeat against her cheek. It was slightly accelerated. She tried to tell herself it didn't matter. But it did. "Yes."

Good intentions only went so far. "Mikki." Shawn raised her chin again, but this time he wasn't looking in her eyes to find an answer.

"What?" she whispered, her throat suddenly dry.

Did she have any idea how beautiful she looked? How desirable? It made him ache. "I'm going to kiss you."

"Is this something like a storm warning?"

"Something like that."

"Okay, I've battened down the hatches." Her attempt at bravado was only half successful.

His lips were only inches away from hers. "Don't count on it."

There was nothing she could count on, she realized, her fingers curling into his shirt, except that when he kissed her all bets were off. She was hurting, and she needed this, needed the shelter of his arms, the life-sustaining succor of having someone want her. If only for an instant, she was wanted. And she could pretend it was for all the right reasons, even though she knew it wasn't.

He was taking advantage of her. He knew it. She was far too vulnerable right now to resist what was happening. But her vulnerability had struck a chord within him. He wanted to protect her, to comfort her and to draw strength from the woman life had caused her to become. Most of all, he just wanted her. With such ferocity that it stunned him.

This was special. He'd allow himself a few moments of pleasure before he'd rein himself in. He didn't want to ultimately take, but to give. He wondered if she'd understand that. He knew he didn't. This was something very, very new to him.

His lips trailed over her face, softly kissing what he wanted to hungrily consume. But he reminded himself to go slowly with her, slowly even when everything within him cried out to be released, pleaded to be satisfied. He couldn't let himself hurt her. That was what mattered above all else.

He wouldn't be satisfied until she was. And that, he knew, would take time. He held her in his arms as if she were something precious, something that could shatter if he wasn't careful. But his mouth made love to her, while his body had to be held in check.

Mikki moaned his name as he kissed her throat, making the pulse there jump and vibrate. She forgot about Klaus, forgot about diamonds, forgot her name. All she could remember was that she had never felt this way before. The pain that had been her constant companion was there as he kissed her because it hurt to feel this way. But it also felt wonderful, impossibly wonderful.

She was hopelessly confused.

Her heart was hammering so hard, she felt dizzy, and when his mouth retreated, she held on to him for just an instant, trying to determine if she could stand on her own power, or, for that matter, if she ever could again.

It was an effort to stop, but he knew he had to. It was too late for him, but it was too soon for her. "I came in to see if you were hungry." There was a smile in his green eyes, not a teasing one, just a smile. "Want to get something to eat?"

She was grateful for the respite, grateful that he hadn't pushed. While she had no idea why he had stopped when he did, she knew that if he hadn't, she would have plummeted all the way. And then she would have fled.

Mikki sat down at the desk again and picked up the diary. Her hands were shaking. "Bring me back a ham sandwich and a soda."

He noticed the possessive way she hugged the book. "You're not coming?"

"No. I want to go on reading. Maybe I can figure out where Klaus hid the diamonds before we reach Borachon."

It was more than that, he thought. She was finding something in that book, something that troubled her. Something she wouldn't share with him. He wanted her to open up. He had never wanted anyone to open up as much as he did at this moment. Where were all his persuasive charms now?

"I admire a woman with a purpose." Quietly, he backed out through the open door.

"And with money," she murmured under her breath, getting back to the diary. She had to keep reminding herself that was all there was between them. She held the diary, so he held her. Nothing more. It was getting harder and harder to keep that in mind.

When Shawn returned twenty-five minutes later, he found Mikki still sitting at the desk. But her head was in the circle formed by her arms, her blond hair cascading around them. From the steady, easy breathing he heard, he guessed that she had fallen asleep.

He shook his head. "All work and no play isn't very good for you, Mikki," he said softly. He debated just leaving her there, then thought better of it. By morning, she was going to ache all over.

Shawn placed the bag containing the sandwich and soda he had brought back for her on the corner of the desk and then gently lifted her from the chair. She murmured something in her sleep and curled up against him. She weighed next to nothing in his arms, and he wanted to go on holding her all night.

"Sure do know how to get to a man, don't you?"

The scent of her hair filled his head and made his muscles tighten in response. "What am I going to do about you, Mikki? What the hell am I supposed to do?"

As if in answer to his question, Mikki turned up her face, her eyes still closed, and sighed, her breath feathering along his mouth. God, he wanted her. More than any other woman he had ever met in his life, he wanted her.

She was still asleep, but her mouth was so tempting that he bent his head and lightly brushed his lips against it. Mikki moaned and arched, her mouth avidly seeking his in sleep the way she hadn't let herself when she was awake.

Caught by surprise and driven by his own desires, Shawn allowed the kiss to flower and deepen. Passion flooded his body, turning it red-hot and demanding. He could feel his blood surging through his veins. Mikki's arms went around his neck, her mouth pressed against his urgently.

She stifled a squeal of surprise as her eyes flew open. Furious at what she assumed was a seduction in progress, Mikki pounded angry fists on his chest.

"What the hell do you think you're doing?" she cried hotly. "Put me down!"

"Okay."

Shawn dropped her unceremoniously on the bed. Mikki bounced once, then scrambled up off the bed and to her feet. Fighting mad, she pushed the hair out of her face and glared at him. "And just what did you think you were doing, Gallagher?"

"I was just putting you to bed." Why was she so angry? She had been the one who had kissed him. He had had only good intentions for a change.

"Yes, I know," she snapped.

Shawn was getting a little tired of all this, tired of his own emotions being tied up in knots and repressed, tired of her defensiveness. Maybe he should just concentrate on the diamonds and the chase and be done with it.

"*Your* bed," he shouted. "Look," he tried again, controlling his temper, "if we're going to be working together, I think a little trust is in order here."

"Maybe I could trust you a little more if I hadn't woken up to find you carrying me off to bed," she shouted.

His voice raised to match her own as he shouted back at her. "I found you asleep at the desk and was only trying to make you comfortable, knowing damn well that if I left you in that god-awful position, you'd be a hellish, crabby woman tomorrow. Even more than you already are."

That stung, although she told herself that she could expect nothing less of him. Or more. Mikki raised herself up on her bare toes. "I am *not* crabby."

"Then why are you shouting?"

Mikki lowered her voice. "Because you're driving me crazy." Frustrated, her mouth still warm from his, she began to pace. Anything to put distance between them. She was *not* going to give in. "All right, maybe, just maybe I find you attractive in a rough, Errol Flynn sort of way."

"Errol Flynn?"

"Old movie swashbuckler—and womanizer." She saw the interested look that entered his eyes. And the gleam.

"You're attracted?"

She had really put her foot into it this time. So much for using honesty as a weapon. "But it'll pass, like the flu."

He took a step closer to her. He wanted to see how far he could push her. "It'll pass faster if you've had your flu shots."

She was about to balance the distance by taking a step back, then decided to hold her ground. It was the only way. "I would prefer not to be inoculated, thank you. What were you doing in my room *this* time?"

He could have the most innocent-looking eyes when he wanted to. "I brought you back the sandwich and soda you wanted." He picked up the bag and handed it to her.

"Oh." He had stolen her thunder and she felt foolish. Not able to look into his face, she glanced down at the bag. "Thank you."

"You're welcome." He began to leave, then changing his mind, he turned. "Oh, and Mikki."

She looked up. "What?"

"Just this."

She had no time to react. He took her face into his hands and kissed her.

She dropped the bag.

The kiss that had begun when he was carrying her to bed needed further release, and she needed to be shown what there was waiting for them just beyond the edge of control. This time, he consciously tried to hold himself back from the brink as he put all the passion he felt into his kiss. Shawn was careful not to fall, careful not to be swept away by the sweetness, the raw passion that met him. He was just as careful to do what he could to make her yearn for more. The way he did.

When he raised his lips from hers, there was a dazed expression on her face, dazed and wanting. Had he continued, Mikki knew that she would have given in. Gladly. But he hadn't continued. He was just flexing his sexual muscles.

She could have killed him for it.

He stepped back and grinned. "Pleasant dreams," he murmured then, and walked to the opened adjoining door. He turned and winked before he passed through and shut the door behind him.

She heard the click as he put the lock into place. He had a lock and she didn't. He had control of the situation and she didn't.

Damn him!

Shawn was pulling his shirt over his head when he heard a loud whack hit the adjoining door. Mikki had thrown something at it. Several oaths involving the nature of his parentage accompanied it. Shawn was careful not to laugh out loud.

## *Chapter Eight*

The urgent pounding penetrated Shawn's brain, changing from an integral part of a hazy dream into reality.

Shawn opened his eyes.

Someone was knocking. On the connecting door between his room and Mikki's.

Shawn sat up and ran his hands through his hair, his mind still fuzzy from sleep. He picked up his watch from the nightstand. Six a.m.

Shawn swung his legs out of bed, trying to pull himself together. Normally, early morning was not his time of the day. He was not one of those people who could wake up and be ready to face the world within the first few minutes. He was a night person. Always had been.

"Gallagher, are you in there?" he heard Mikki's voice demand.

"Yeah, what's left of me." He passed his hands over his face, rubbing hard. It didn't help. "I'm not a pretty sight in the morning."

"Open the damn door!"

"You asked for it." He got up to unlock the door, then remembered that he was naked. Mikki might not appreciate the shock, he thought with a grin. He grabbed his jeans from the floor where he had thrown them last night and slid them on quickly, not bothering with the snap at the top.

When he finally opened the connecting door, Mikki darted into the room. She looked alarmed. A burst of adrenaline cleared away the last traces of sleepiness. Shawn caught her in his arms, a gentle but strong grip that telegraphed itself throughout her nervous system, telling her that he was there for her. She looked up at him, startled by the concern she saw on his face, by the fact that he was holding her, and by the fact that he was hardly wearing anything.

He misread her expression. "I believe Rule One is overruled in this instance. We covered that, remember?"

Her breath caught in her throat as her breasts pressed against his nude, hard chest. Her stomach began to churn. Nerves. Nothing but nerves, she told herself. "This isn't the time for games, Gallagher."

"It wasn't a game I had in mind." It had ceased to be a game somewhere along the line. It was real life now. His life. And it involved hers. Reluctantly, he released her, then ran his hand through his tousled hair again. "What's the matter?"

He looked over her shoulder into her room, but there appeared to be nothing out of place. Even her bed was made. The woman was hopelessly neat.

Mikki pushed the door shut behind her, then locked it, her heart still hammering hard. She didn't know if it was a result of what she had seen downstairs, or of what she had experienced just now. Adrenaline mixed with arousal, creating havoc and pulling her in two separate directions at the same time.

"This looks promising," Shawn murmured, his eyes indicating the locked door.

She pretended not to hear him. "I think we've got trouble."

The expression on her face told him that she believed what she was telling him. What sort of trouble? "Would you care to elaborate? I'm not up to Twenty Questions before my first cup of coffee." He wondered if room service was up yet. They had promised a continental breakfast with the price of the room.

Mikki tried to concentrate on something other than the fact that Shawn was standing in front of her minimally dressed. For a second, that wasn't possible. Her mind had totally gone blank as she stared at him. His jeans hung precariously low on his hips, looking as if they'd slide the rest of the way at the slightest provocation. His stomach was taut, the muscles above it hard and firm. A fine, light smattering of hair covered his chest, thinning down around his midsection until it became a single, soft line that snaked its way below the area covered by the jeans.

Mikki found that she had to remember to take a breath. She tried to remember what had prompted her to come rushing into his room in the first place.

"I, um—" She lost it. "Damn it, Gallagher, will you put a shirt on?"

"Anything you say."

He took out a fresh green jersey from his suitcase and slipped his arms into it, then pulled it over his head. The green shade brought out the color of his eyes. And the material clung to the contours of his chest, reminding her of the sculpted biceps and pectorals beneath.

This wasn't any better, she thought hopelessly.

"Okay, now what's this all about?"

She upbraided herself for gawking like a schoolgirl. This was serious. "I saw him."

Shawn stared at her. "Who—him?"

She didn't hear him as her thoughts poured out all at the same time. The agitation came back full force. It helped not to look at him.

"That is, I think I saw him. He was talking to the hotel clerk."

She moved to the window and looked out. They were on the second floor, and she had a clear view of the parking lot. But the man she had seen in the lobby wasn't anywhere to be seen. Was he still there?

Mikki turned back to Shawn. "It looked like he was asking questions."

Shawn felt as if he had been sucked into the middle of a conversation she was having with herself. "*Who* was asking questions?"

"The hotel clerk," she cried impatiently.

"The hotel clerk was asking questions of the hotel clerk," he repeated, totally confused. "He was talking to himself?"

"No!" She started to cross back to the window.

Shawn took hold of her shoulders to keep her in one place. "Mikki, I know I'm not too bright without caffeine in my veins, but would you like to take this from the top again?"

She closed her eyes, gathering strength. Wasn't he listening to what she was telling him? "I saw the hotel clerk downstairs."

He still didn't understand. Why should she suddenly get agitated about the harmless-looking man at the front desk? "So?"

"The hotel clerk," she repeated more emphatically, annoyed that he wasn't following her. Annoyed that she wasn't making herself clear. Words jumbled in her head. "The one from Mission Ridge."

Now her agitation was beginning to make sense. "You saw Harold?"

She pulled out of his grip and threw up her hands. " don't know his name."

He did. Shawn had an infinite capacity to remember everyone's name. "He was here?" Shawn tried to think

Had the man overheard something? It was possible. Anything was possible.

"Yes." Then her tone changed to self-doubt. "That is, I think so."

Shawn began to tuck his shirt in, looking around for his shoes. "All right, let's assume it was Harold. Did you overhear what he was saying?"

Helplessly, she shook her head. She hadn't gotten close enough. She had been coming out of the elevator when she had spotted the man. She had ducked behind a potted palm, afraid of being recognized. It had been too far away for her to make out anything but the buzz of words.

"Maybe it was just someone who resembled him," Shawn suggested. Or maybe—" he located his shoes under the bed and proceeded to dig through his suitcase for socks "—he was just visiting relatives."

They looked at each other. Neither one of them believed that. It was too much of a coincidence.

Mikki sank down on the bed. "How did he find us?" she asked quietly.

"I think that's immaterial. The point is, he did." Shoes and socks on, Shawn snapped the lid shut on his suitcase. "We're leaving here, Mikki. Now."

She didn't have to be told twice. "I can be ready in five minutes."

"Another one of your attributes. The list keeps growing." He kept his tone deliberately light, not wanting her to dwell on their being followed.

An absent smile crossed her lips. "Yeah." For both of them.

"This is the kitchen," Mikki hissed as they made their way quietly through the large room. They had come down using the back stairs and had cautiously walked through the hallway until they had reached the kitchen door.

The staff apparently hadn't begun working yet. It made things easier. He looked around as they made their way past the refrigerator. Then he waved her on.

"Being with you certainly is showing me a different side of life," Mikki whispered.

"Glad to hear it." By now, he knew what she was thinking. There was something rather nice about the predictability of that. "And if you're worried, I left a check on the bureau paying for our rooms."

"I know." He turned to look at her. "I saw it." He was much more honest than she had first thought. Maybe she hadn't made such a mistake, throwing in her lot with him. At least on a business level. "But that still doesn't explain why we're playing hide-and-seek in the hotel kitchen."

Shawn glanced around, but there was no one in sight. Their luck was holding. "We can't take a chance on having our friend from Mission Ridge see us leave if he's waiting out in the lobby."

She watched Shawn's back as he moved forward, then signaled for her to follow. She did, wondering what either one of them would say if they were discovered skulking about. Shawn would undoubtedly come up with something, especially if they were discovered by a woman. "You seem to know a lot about sneaking out of hotel rooms."

"Only what I've read about it." He took her hand, urging her to keep close. He carried his suitcase in his other hand.

"I guess I should be grateful you didn't insist on tying sheets together and lowering me out of the window."

"Not enough sheets."

They passed several long trays filled with breakfast pastries, doughnuts and individual cartons of orange juice. Shawn snared several doughnuts and a couple of cartons, stuffing them into Mikki's purse.

"Hey!" Dumbfounded, Mikki stared at the interior of her bag.

"Shh. We've paid for it. It's included in the charge for the room. A continental breakfast." He grabbed another doughnut, not certain when they would be stopping for their next meal.

"On the lam," she added dryly.

"I've always wanted my own gun moll. C'mon, before someone shows up."

Hurrying, they made it through the back exit and into the alleyway. A huge delivery truck was just pulling up. Shawn grabbed Mikki's hand and pulled her to the left.

Mikki stared at the back of the truck uneasily. "Now what?"

"The car's this way."

She sighed. At least he wasn't proposing that they smuggle themselves out in the back of a meat truck. She glanced at his face and realized that he was enjoying this. And, in a strange sort of way, she was, too.

They were in the Jeep and on their way down Route 59 in a matter of minutes.

Mikki slumped against the seat, then turned to look behind her, half expecting to see a car bearing down on them. There was nothing but the normal flow of early-morning traffic. She settled back. "Think that's the last we've seen of him?"

Shawn knew that there was no point in trying to sugarcoat things. "Mikki, I've learned that life is stranger than fiction, and I don't bet on anything but the worst case scenario anymore."

"Cheerful thought."

"Speaking of cheerful thoughts," he said, accelerating to go around a car that was traveling too slowly for him, "have you had any luck unraveling our riddle yet?"

She shook her head, then realized that he was watching the road. "No. Maybe it's not even in the diary, but I keep hoping that it is. It's the only thing we've got to work with."

He nodded. "Keep reading," he encouraged. His stomach rumbled, reminding him that he hadn't eaten yet. "Mind reaching into your purse and handing me a doughnut?"

She reached in, then groaned, holding the doughnut aloft.

"What's the matter?"

"There's white powder all over everything in here. You and your bright ideas."

He took the doughnut from her. "You'll thank me when you get hungry." He disposed of the doughnut in three bites.

Mikki shook her head in disbelief. Nothing seemed to affect the man's appetite. Her own stomach was tied up in knots, and the thought of food made her feel nauseated. There was a trace of white powder on his upper lip. She leaned over and wiped it off with the corner of her handkerchief. "I think you'd probably eat during the apocalypse."

He liked the feel of her fingers along his lips. "Probably."

Self-consciously, she withdrew her hand, aware of the way he was looking at her. Then, with a sigh of resignation, she began to empty out her purse on her lap, shaking out the fine powder that seemed to cover everything. She blew it off the diary and the dictionary, muttering a few choice words under her breath.

"Thanks."

Mikki looked at him. The word had come out of the blue. "For what?"

"For coming to me this morning. You could have just as easily gone off on your own."

"No, I couldn't."

"No?" Her blatant admission took him by surprise. Was she finally coming around?

"You had the car keys."

He should have known better. It figured. He was just coming to terms with the fact that this woman could really make a difference in his life, and she was treating him as if he were Jack the Ripper. The irony of it irritated him.

"Right."

She saw his jaw tighten. "Besides," she added quietly, "we are partners. We made an agreement. And I believe in honoring agreements."

His hands relaxed on the wheel. So it was just going to take a little longer, that was all. He could wait. After all, he wasn't doing anything except chasing after fifty-year-old diamonds and running from people who wanted to steal them. "So do I, Mikki."

She was beginning to believe him.

The terrain they traveled through was desolate, stark and lonely. The road stretched out for miles before them, unchanging in its flatness, almost hypnotic in its sameness. It made her sleepy. She wondered how Shawn could stand driving for so long. She closed the diary.

"Want me to take over?"

"I think you already have."

"The driving, wise guy," she clarified.

"Oh. No, I don't mind. I kind of like it. It relaxes me."

"It's putting me to sleep."

She looked around. There was nothing for miles in either direction. She knew there were towns and cities out there, thriving, bustling with people. But here, there were only the two of them. It made her feel closer to him, even though she knew it shouldn't. Almost against her will, little by little, she was relaxing her guard. "This is a great place to live if you like dust and tumbleweed."

"Where are you from, Mikki?"

She thought of giving him a vague answer, then decided that there was no harm in telling him the truth. "California."

He wanted more from her than that. "California's a big state."

She shrugged, looking straight ahead. She popped a mint into her mouth. "So's Texas."

All right, if that was the way she wanted to play it, he'd take the first step. "I've already told you that I'm from Laredo. I live in Houston now, but the old ranch house I grew up in is still standing on the outskirts of Laredo. I own it now. Nobody else in the family wanted to take care of it."

And he did, she thought. He was sentimental. Why did that make her feel like crying?

He had paused, but she hadn't filled in the silence. Determined, he asked, "Where are you from?"

"Here and there." Which was true. Then, because his eyes demanded it, she added, "I've got an apartment in San Francisco."

Progress. But not enough to satisfy him. A small taste wasn't enough for him when it came to her. "Grow up there?"

"No, Los Angeles." She turned to look at him. "I thought you weren't up to Twenty Questions before your morning coffee."

"For you, I seem to be making exceptions." He held up the orange juice container he had taken from the hotel kitchen. Although he craved caffeine, it would have to do for now. "Don't stop now, Mikki, we were doing so well."

But she didn't want attention thrown her way, didn't want him to know any more. Didn't want to see pity enter his eyes. Anyway, it was hard for her to share. She had shared willingly before, only to learn that it had meant nothing to the person before whom she was baring her soul. That *she* had meant nothing to the person before whom she was baring her soul. She didn't want to risk going through that disillusioning experience again.

"What were you working on in Mission Ridge?"

All right, if it was too painful for her to tell him about herself, they'd talk about him for a while. "A series on small towns in Texas."

That seemed like pretty tame stuff for an investigative reporter. She could see him exposing graft, or misused funds, or shoddy building materials and pay-offs. There was none of that in a story about small towns. Or was there? "What kind of dirt were you trying to expose?"

He laughed, mostly at himself for having thought the series would work. "No dirt. I was trying to find something noble, something I thought existed once."

She turned in her seat, caught by something in his voice. Wistfulness. "But you don't anymore?"

"No."

The sadness got to her. Somehow she couldn't picture him being sad. "Like what?"

"The fight for survival. The belief in Mom-and-Apple-Pie and a better tomorrow." He shrugged disparagingly. "Things I thought were there when I was growing up."

She could almost see it, feel it. It sounded so wonderfully normal. "You grew up with that?" It was her turn to be wistful.

Because she seemed to want to know, he told her. "That and four brothers and sisters."

"Older, younger?"

It was the first time he had heard eagerness in her voice. He wondered if she knew how hungry she sounded. It made him imagine the kind of life she had led. It made him want to hold her, instinctively knowing that his life had been far richer than hers. "All older. I was the baby of the family. The runt of the litter until I hit fourteen."

To look at him now she would have never believed it. The only way he could have qualified for the title was if everyone else in his family was gargantuan. "What happened then?"

"I filled out and shot up in six months."

And probably had to fight off women for miles around. She quickly dismissed a twinge of jealousy. "What made you want to be a reporter?"

He turned to look at her. The wind was whipping her hair around her face, but she didn't seem to notice. Her eyes told him that he had her undivided attention. He decided to be totally honest. He usually held back a piece of himself. But not with her. Not any longer. "My dad."

Everything he told her created a bittersweet feeling inside her, similar to yet different from how reading Klaus's diary affected her. Shawn's background made her feel cheated that there had never been anyone in her life to share things with, no one to care about what she made of herself. Still, she hung on each word he spoke, absorbing them all and wondering what it would have been like if she had had a similar life to look back on. "Was he a reporter, too?"

"A journalism teacher," he corrected. An image of his father came to mind. Tall, thin, kindly. The smell of cherrywood pipe tobacco clinging to his favorite cardigan. John Gallagher had never been too busy to listen, never too busy to care.

He had been lucky to have such a father, Shawn thought. What sort of father had Mikki had?

"But he'd always wanted to be an investigative reporter. He made it sound exciting, dangerous, thrilling. So I did it for him as much as for myself." Shawn shook his head, remembering. Looking back, he almost would have rather become a teacher himself. Hindsight was wonderful. "He wasn't missing much."

"Why?"

"Because standing behind his desk in that classroom, my father was in touch with the better parts of life. He got to see young minds unfolding. He got to glimpse hope for the future."

He was dissatisfied. Why? She would have thought his life suited him. "And you?" she prodded. "What did your work do for you?"

"It brought me in direct contact with people who sold out for a dollar, burned out for less and had no hope for the future. People who would sell out their friends and families for less than thirty pieces of silver." Bitterness entered his voice. "Every sensational story, every exposé showing the dirty side of life, I was there."

"And it got to you." She wanted to say something comforting, but nothing came. Startled, she wondered if she even knew how to comfort a person.

He thought of his disillusionment. "In spades."

"So stop."

He laughed. She had a way of cutting things to the bone. "Just that simple?"

"Why not?"

"Why not?" he echoed. She made it sound so easy. "Because I keep telling myself that I'm doing some good, that I'm showing people not to go into life blindly. That I'm exposing the grafters and the thieves." A jackrabbit ran into the road and then froze. Shawn swerved to avoid hitting it. "Damn things have no sense."

"He knew enough to run in front of your car instead of someone else's." When he looked at her, she waved her hand in the air. "You were saying?"

"Lately, I'm wondering if maybe I'm doing people a disservice, making them take off their rose-colored glasses."

"People should know what they're up against."

"People should have something left to believe in."

"Do you?" She needed to know the answer to that. She needed to know the answer to many things. She had begun by telling herself not to get involved, not to get to know the man. Suddenly she had an overwhelming need to know him.

Shawn began to answer, then laughed. "Mikki, I was going to pry your secrets out of you, not tell you all of mine."

She said nothing for a moment. And then she smiled. "I'm glad you did. It's nice to know you actually have a soul."

He could hear it in her voice, if not in the actual words. It was an offering of trust. By telling her about himself, he had made her less leery of him, less hesitant. The edge was off. If he didn't get much information about her for his trouble, he knew that he would soon.

"I never leave home without it." He nodded toward her purse. "Why don't you have a doughnut?"

"What happened to your appetite?"

"I thought you might want to eat something. I'm thinking of driving straight through to Laredo, picking up some groceries and then staying at the ranch house for the night."

This time when he proposed stopping for the night, she didn't even offer token resistance. It was too late for that. "How far is that from Borachon?"

He fished out the hand-drawn map she had given him and glanced at it. "With any luck, we'll probably be in Borachon by tomorrow afternoon."

There was that word again. *Luck.* Luck had brought the letter to her. Luck had brought Shawn to her as well. Or was it luck? She wasn't certain what to call it or what to think anymore. She did know what she was feeling, though. His story had broken down a barrier, just as Klaus's diary had. Klaus lived a more dramatic version of her own life. Shawn had lived the kind of life she had always wished for. A home, a family, brothers and sisters to play with and to tease. A normal life. Something that had been denied her for reasons beyond her control. The luck of the draw. Maybe this time, she thought, settling back in her seat with

# WOW!

## THE MOST GENEROUS
# FREE OFFER EVER!
## From the
## Silhouette Reader Service™

**GET 4 FREE BOOKS WORTH $11.80**

Affix peel-off stickers to reply card

## NO COST! NO OBLIGATION TO BUY!
## NO PURCHASE NECESSARY!

Because you're a reader of Silhouette romances, the publishers would like you to accept four brand-new Silhouette Special Edition® novels, with their compliments. Accepting this offer places you under no obligation to purchase any books, ever!

# YOURS

We'd like to send you four free Silhouette novels, worth $11.80, to introduce you to the benefits of the Silhouette Reader Service™. We hope your free books will convince you to subscribe, but that's up to you. Accepting them places you under no obligation to buy anything, but we hope you'll want to continue your membership in the Reader Service.

So unless we hear from you, once a month we'll send you six additional Silhouette Special Edition® novels to read and enjoy. If you choose to keep them, you'll pay just $2.74* each—a saving of 21¢ off the cover price. And there is *no* charge for delivery. There are *no* hidden extras! You may cancel at any time, for any reason, just by sending us a note or a shipping statement marked "cancel" or by returning any shipment of books to us at our cost. Either way the free books and gifts are yours to keep!

## ALSO FREE!
### VICTORIAN PICTURE FRAME

This lovely Victorian pewter-finish miniature is perfect for displaying a treasured photograph—and it's yours *absolutely free*—when you accept our no-risk offer.

*Perfect for a treasured Photograph*

*Plus a FREE mystery Gift! follow instructions at right.*

*Terms and prices subject to change without notice.
Sales taxes applicable in New York
© 1990 HARLEQUIN ENTERPRISES LIMITED

# WE EVEN PROVIDE FREE POSTAGE!

It costs you *nothing* to send for your free books — we've paid the postage on the attached reply card. And we'll pick up the postage on your shipment of free books and gifts, and also on any subsequent shipments of books, should you choose to become a subscriber. Unlike many book clubs, we charge *nothing* for postage and handling!

the diary in her hands again, luck would treat her differently. It would be good to her for a change.

She glanced at Shawn's profile as he drove. Maybe it was being good to her already. She had a feeling that time would tell. Soon. Very soon.

## Chapter Nine

She was too engrossed in the diary to notice it at first. Klaus was reminiscing about his childhood when he and his brother Alfred had been sent by their parents to spend summers with their *Oma*—their grandmother, Mikki penciled in—and had enjoyed being young and carefree. The entry went on for several pages and Mikki was enchanted with the love she found there. His grandmother was vacationing in Europe when she met and fell in love with his grandfather. Apparently she had left a profound impression on him and Klaus wrote glowingly about her in the diary. Mikki absorbed it and experienced it all vicariously. She juggled the diary on her lap as she regularly made use of the worn German/English dictionary.

Vaguely she realized that the Jeep had come to a halt. She looked up at Shawn quizzically.

"We're here."

He swung his legs out and walked around to the back of the Jeep. Three bags of groceries stood huddled together.

He had purchased them at a store that his parents had frequented when they lived here. It was a mom-and-pop store, and the owners always greeted him enthusiastically by name whenever he came by. They had looked Mikki over with unabashed interest. Shawn was the last of the Gallagher brood to remain unmarried. Mikki had taken their conspicuous curiosity all in stride.

He glanced toward her now. She was still sitting in the Jeep. He noticed that she had put away the diary and was looking at the house.

"It needs a little work," he acknowledged, apologizing for it the way one might for a favorite relative who had fallen on hard times.

"It looks just fine to me."

The note of appreciation in her voice pleased him. He hadn't realized until this moment that he wanted her to like the house he had grown up in.

The single-story, sturdy ranch-style house was typical in this area of the country. Its red clay-tiled roof was faded from years of baking in the sun and was chipped in a few places. The stucco walls had long since lost their snowy whiteness and were slowly turning a yellowish hue. Shawn kept meaning to paint the house himself, even looked forward to it, but there never seemed to be enough time. He supposed he'd have to hire a painter and hope for the best.

Love had lived here. It was the most beautiful home she had ever seen.

Mikki stepped out of the Jeep, then moved slowly to the rear to take out the final bag of groceries. Shawn noticed that she seemed to be hugging the bag to her unconsciously as her eyes devoured every detail, every line of the house. He wished he knew what she was thinking, but he was certain that what he saw in her eyes was hunger. It made him wonder about her all the more.

She lagged behind him half a step as he unlocked the finely carved front door, but then walked in without waiting for him to lead the way.

The house welcomed her.

There was no foyer, no place to feel separated from the rest of the house. The front door opened onto a large, homey-looking living room, done predominately in Western decor. She would have expected nothing less, she thought. He was Texan all the way, larger than life. The house suited him. Warm earth colors wove their way through the furnishings and the tapestries that hung on two of the larger walls. The vaulted ceiling, with its heavy, wooden beams, accented the space. The focal point of the room, however, was the flagstone fireplace and the huge portrait done in rich oils that hung over it. It was a family portrait. His family.

Mikki moved toward it like a piece of metal drawn by some hidden magnet, the groceries still clutched in her arms.

He didn't look at all like his father. Except, perhaps, around the eyes. Even at this distance, looking up, she could see the resemblance there. They had the same sensitive green eyes. Shifting the groceries against her, Mikki placed her hand on the mantle as she studied the painting, then belatedly looked at her fingers. There was no dust.

He said he lived in Houston. Was there someone else here, as well? She turned to see him standing in the doorway between the living room and the kitchen. "How long since you've been here?"

"A couple of months. I pay a woman in town to come in every couple of weeks to get the dust off the furniture and let some air into the house."

He had intended to walk straight through to the kitchen, but the way she was looking at the painting made Shawn pause. He remembered the day his father had made them all gather together for the portrait. It had been a cool autumn day. Lucky for him. He could have never withstood wearing a jacket if it had been hot. That had been nearly eleven years ago.

What did she see there that he didn't?

He crossed to her. "Here, let me have that," he offered, taking the grocery bag from her, juggling it with the others he already held.

She surrendered the bag without taking her eyes off the portrait. Seven people. They all looked so happy. So solid. Standing grouped before a huge coral tree, his father's hand hooked comfortably around his mother's waist. The other hand was resting on the wide shoulders of a dark-haired young man who stood taller than the others. He had his mother's coloring. And her smile. The others were fair, like their father. The runt of the litter he had said. Mikki smiled.

"Is that you?" She already knew. She would have known him anywhere.

"Which?"

"The one right next to the man with the gentle smile."

"Yeah, that's me. Handsome devil, eh?"

He expected a tart retort to that, but he didn't get it. "Handsome family," she answered, catching him by surprise. "Where are they now?"

He stopped a minute to think. "Kathleen's an attorney in Dallas. Bridgette's a geologist teaching at the University of Austin. Patrick and Ryan have a business in Galveston. Doing pretty well, too. Since Dad passed on, Mother spends her time visiting all of us."

She heard the affection, even though it was unspoken. God, how she envied him. "They've all spread out."

"Some," he agreed, shifting the bags to keep them from sagging. "We see one another around the holidays. It's Kathy's turn to hold the family gathering this year." He chuckled, knowing how much his oldest sister hated to cook. They'd all wind up pitching in, and she'd end up making the salad or something else equally as easy. Kathy took after their mother.

"Must be nice," Mikki said wistfully.

He was lost in his own thoughts. "What is?"

"To plan family gatherings." She realized she was saying too much and took back the bag she had surrendered to him. "C'mon, let's get these into the kitchen before you're tempted to eat them raw."

He led the way toward the back of the house. "Just set it down over there." He nodded toward the butcher-block table. "It'll take me about forty-five minutes."

She had assumed that he wanted her to prepare dinner. "You can cook?" She looked at him with interest. She could more easily picture him peeling back the foil on a TV dinner than wearing an apron and holding a spatula.

"I'll let you be the judge of that," he said with great confidence.

Mikki set the table, using stoneware dishes that had a glazed, blue-gray tint to them. As she placed the silverware at each setting, she tried to imagine what the meals in this room must have been like years ago, the sound of five voices vying for attention, shouting to drown each other out. She wished she could have been part of it.

She looked so preoccupied, Shawn left the pot he was tending to and walked up behind her. Effortlessly, because it seemed right, he put his hands on her shoulders and turned her around to face him. She was still holding a knife and fork in her hands. He took them from her and placed them on the table, then slipped his hands around her waist. He was both surprised and pleased that she didn't try to pull away. "You look a million miles away."

She knew she was on dangerous ground, that she was being careless, but here, in his house, it was as if she had entered a world of pretend. So she pretended. Just for a little while, she pretended that she was part of this world. It did no harm, she rationalized. Not to anyone. And it let her dream.

"Just wondering what mealtime was like around here when you were growing up."

"Bedlam. Pure bedlam."

"I had a hunch."

Because it seemed to please her, he elaborated. "The five of us yelling, fighting, my mother threatening to take a strap to us if we didn't settle down."

She had thought as much. "And your father?" she prompted, wanting the whole picture.

Shawn laughed. "Dad left all the discipline up to Mother. He just kind of sat back and watched us all, a little bemused by all the noise. I always got the impression he was studying us, the way you were in the living room before."

"I, um, always wanted a family portrait like that." And a family to fit into it, she added silently.

Mikki glanced over toward the stove, wanting to divert his attention to something else. "Aren't you afraid of burning your culinary masterpiece?"

He didn't even bother to look. He'd much rather look at her. She was a riddle, a mystery to him. There was so much more beneath the surface than she was willing to show him.

"No masterpiece." He smoothed a wisp of hair down at her temple. "Just chili."

She wished he wouldn't do that. When he touched her that way, she found she couldn't concentrate, couldn't use words to put him in his place. She was losing control. "Who taught you to cook, your mother?"

He laughed, then let her in on the joke. "My father. My mother had trouble boiling water and not burning it. He did most of the cooking, thank God."

She envied him the fondness that curved his lips and the memories that caused it.

He took the plunge. "What about your family?"

She straightened a little, the wary look returning to her eyes. "There's nothing to tell." Absolutely nothing, she thought.

Oh, but there was. Shawn's pride stung a little that she still didn't trust him enough to tell him about herself. Mikki was hiding something, and he'd have no peace until he knew what it was.

Doggedly, he was about to try another approach when the chili began to make tiny, bubbling noises as the mixture rose up in small peaks and erupted, like miniature volcanoes oozing lava.

Mikki pointed toward the stove. "I think your chili's trying to tell you something."

"Yes, that it's ready." He released her waist. Saved by the chili, he thought. "C'mon," he urged, "you're in for a treat."

"That's what they all say," she quipped.

He turned and looked at her. "Do they?" Her playful words made him think of other things. How many men had known her? How many had held her in their arms and gained the trust he could not seem to?

How many men had loved her the way he ached to?

He wanted to know, and yet he didn't if the answer involved a number larger than zero.

She saw the serious look darken his eyes and refused to be drawn in. "Yes. But you're the first I'm taking up on it. Serve your chili, Gallagher, before I hop in that Jeep of yours and look for a McDonald's."

He told her to sit down, and then he served her with a flourish.

"You know," she laughed, watching him, "I could get used to this."

Shawn ladled a second huge spoonful of chili into her bowl. "Yes," he said significantly, "me, too."

He was surprised at his own admission. Not that he hadn't thought of someday following in his parents' footsteps and having a home and family of his own. That was something he had always taken for granted. It was tucked away in the recesses of his mind. But in the last few years, what he had seen, what he had been exposed to had made him believe that having the sort of life his parents had shared wasn't possible. At least, not for him. A hopelessness, a despair for the human race as a whole, had seeped into his soul. And the women he encountered were never those beside whom he wanted to wake up year after year.

Until now.

She saw desire flicker in his eyes. Mikki swallowed, her throat dry, afraid she was reading too much into his words. She could let herself dream as long as she remembered that it was just that, a dream. She couldn't afford to let the lines between fantasy and reality blur. It was far too dangerous. And hurt too much.

"This is good," she commented as the spicy, flavorful meal registered slowly in her taste buds. "Really good." She dug in for another forkful. "You have possibilities, Gallagher."

Shawn sat opposite her in the kitchen. He had barely touched his own bowl. He was too busy watching her. "Yes, I know."

She arched an eyebrow. "Nothing like being smug."

"Not smug." But his tone was cocky. "I just know my capabilities."

Yes, she was sure he did.

After dinner, she helped him wash the dishes and then put them away. She took extreme pleasure in the nice, domestic scene. The flippant woman-of-the-world act that she always kept within easy reach dropped from her like the hard, binding cocoon from around a caterpillar. Except that she wasn't a caterpillar. Not anymore. For this evening, she was a butterfly, a beautiful butterfly, she thought, doing delightfully normal things.

Although she was still careful in her answers to him, she found herself relaxing. Shawn was good company. He was warm, witty, and yes, sensitive, with an anecdote for every situation.

He was a man, she thought, she could easily fall in love with. If that had been an option for her. But it wasn't. She knew it and kept herself aware of the fact all evening. But it didn't stop her from enjoying being with him.

She was like a completely different woman, Shawn thought, regarding her over the snifter of brandy that he held in his hand. Or maybe this was what had attracted him to her in the first place. He had seen this within her. Sensed it. Right now she was behaving like the woman he had instinctively known she was. The innocence he had detected in her eyes was not a lie. It was there in the way she spoke, in the way she asked him to tell her things about his family.

She seemed to want to know everything. Whether he had had a dog when he was growing up—he had. If he had fought with his brothers and sisters—he had. If he had been good in school—it was only when his back was to the wall.

Now more than ever, he felt a protective pull toward her. He wanted, he realized, to share all this with her, to share his life with her. Now and forever. His arguments, his thoughts, his adventures. His whole damn life. It was a heady, slightly frightening insight.

He wondered what she'd say to that. Probably tell him he was crazy and then run like hell.

In the hall, he heard the grandfather clock chime eleven.

"Well—" Shawn stretched on the sofa "—it's getting late."

"Yes," she agreed quietly, "it is." She didn't want the evening to end. But she knew it had to. Tomorrow, they would go back to being temporary partners again. Until they found the diamonds.

The diamonds.

She flushed guiltily.

He was just getting to his feet and offering her a hand up—the sofa had a way of engulfing people—when he saw her expression change. "What's the matter?"

She took his hand without thinking. It was a good grip. A strong grip. Yet his hand had felt so gentle on her face when he had kissed her.

She had to stop letting her mind wander.

"I haven't even worked on the diary tonight. I was supposed to get a lot more done after dinner." But instead she had opted to wash and dry dishes with him because she hadn't wanted to lose a precious moment of being with him, talking to him. When, how had that happened? When had her barriers crumbled so entirely?

It had to be the house, she thought. She felt safe here. And warm. She had to remind herself it was an illusion, this sense of safety and well-being.

He had trouble remembering the treasure hunt. And for his series, he had hardly written three words since he had met her. His editor would be far from pleased. It wasn't like him. "There's always tomorrow."

Mikki shook her head. "Some soldier of fortune you'd make."

He walked out of the room with her, the large dark brown tile beneath his feet registering the sound of each step they took. "I'm not a soldier of fortune. I consider myself a bodyguard at the moment. And an observer."

Her own thoughts were making her warm. "I thought you were in this for the story."

"That, too." *No, I think I'm in this for you. Because you've brought back a part of me I thought was gone forever.*

"Well, 'bodyguard,' this body would like to turn in." She looked around. There were several doors on either side of the long hallway. "Where can I—?"

"You can use my sisters' bedroom. I'll show you after I bring your suitcase in from the Jeep."

She nodded. For a moment, Mikki stood in the hall looking after Shawn as he headed for the front door. She didn't like watching him walk away from her. That was going to happen all too soon. Impulsively, she hurried after him.

He turned as he reached the porch. Her quick, light pace echoed along the tile, telling him she was following. "Afraid?"

She shot him a disdainful look. "I thought I'd get a look at the stars while I let you do the heavy work."

"Sounds like something you'd do," he murmured, knowing she was lying.

She wrapped her hands around the post and gazed out. The stars were out in force, thousands of them. The moon was full and bright and seemed to smile down on them. A peacefulness wove its way through her. She couldn't remember the last time she had felt this way. She looked over toward Shawn. If only...

No, there was no "if only's." There was just reality, she reminded herself. Reality was that she had a chance at something, however incredible. A fleeting chance, true, but a chance nonetheless. If that panned out, she could entertain other hopes. If it didn't, well, it wouldn't be the first time.

She watched as Shawn walked toward her, her suitcase in his hand. He had left his in the Jeep. Probably had clothes in the house from the last time he was here, she mused.

She wished things could be different. She wished *she* could be different. She wished that her belief in happily-ever-after hadn't been destroyed.

"C'mon—" he opened the door and held it for her "—it's this way."

He led her to a spacious, tidy bedroom and placed her suitcase inside the doorway. He didn't trust himself to enter the room. That was asking too much of him. All night long, he had resisted the temptation to kiss her, feeling that maybe he had been rushing her too much. That was his way, to go in and take. He had never been one to twiddle his thumbs, not even as a boy.

But that wasn't the way it would be with her. He wanted to give her gentleness. The longer he was around her, the more he was beginning to sense about her. She needed tenderness, never mind the brashness in her voice. She reminded him a little of the mare his father had brought home one summer. The mare had been mistreated, and it had taken a great deal of gentle patience on his father's part before she had settled down and trusted him.

Shawn laughed to himself and wondered how Mikki would like being compared to a mare. He had a hunch he knew how she'd react.

He shoved his hands into his back pockets, afraid of what he'd do with them if he left them free. "The bathroom's to your left. Call me if you need anything."

Mikki nodded in response.

He turned on his heel to leave. His own room was down the hall, and he had better get to it before he was tempted to stay.

"Um, Shawn?"

He only half turned. "Yes?"

She hesitated. "Thanks." It wasn't what she had wanted to say. She no longer knew what it was she wanted. Or maybe she did and it was confusing her so profoundly that she couldn't think straight anymore.

"Any time."

He was gone.

She expected him to make some sort of move toward her. Hold her. Kiss her. Something. It would have made things easier. It would have given her an excuse to give in to him. And to herself.

But he didn't make a move. He behaved like a perfect gentleman.

The bastard.

He was driving her absolutely crazy. She supposed that she should be grateful that he had left her alone tonight, but she felt oddly bereft. And restless. Exceedingly restless.

Maybe it was just the effects of the brandy making her feel this way.

And maybe, she thought sarcastically, the moon was made of green cheese.

Mikki picked up her suitcase and put it on the bed closest to her. She opened the locks, lifted the lid and drew out her nightgown. She laid it out, then closed the case and set it aside.

She turned around in the room slowly. It was a nice room. A wonderful room. The kind of room she would have died for as a child. It was wallpapered with a soft network of tiny pink flowers inching their way across a field of off-white. There were two single beds, identically covered with white eyelet-lace comforters. A nightstand, sporting a hurricane lamp with a delicate rose painted across it, stood between them. She could almost hear the whispers, the giggles that had passed between the two beds in the middle of the night, the secrets that had been shared. She felt happy just standing here.

She was dreaming again, she upbraided herself.

"What you need," she said aloud, "is to get your head together and your priorities straight."

She slipped her shirt off and folded it neatly before placing it on the other bed. Not having much had taught her to be careful with the things she did have.

"Maybe a nice hot shower would help." She caught her reflection in the oval mirror above the long, sleek bureau. Her face was flushed. That was Shawn's doing. "Or maybe you'd better make that a cold one," she amended with a self-deprecatory laugh.

He did have her blood humming. There was no getting away from that. But any dreams she had about Shawn Gallagher were only that: dreams. It was time she gave it up, forgot about misty fantasies that would never come true for her and concentrate on things that might. The diary and the hunt.

They were so close now. Shawn had said that Borachon was less than a day's drive away. She could actually be less than a day's drive from riches.

The excitement she expected to feel wasn't there.

All she could think about was Shawn. Once this was over, he'd be gone, too, whether or not they found the diamonds. She'd better hope that the treasure was there somewhere in Borachon and that this wasn't just a wild-goose chase. At least then she'd have something, something tangible to hold on to.

Instead of a shower, she'd be better off turning her attention to reading more of the diary.

With a resigned sigh, she reached for the nightgown she had laid out. Out of the corner of her eye, she thought she saw something move outside the window. Looking up, she realized someone was trying to break in.

Fear caught in her throat.

## Chapter Ten

No one had ever accused Shawn of being illogical. As a young man, he had carefully mapped out what he wanted to be in life and then had gone after it: good grades in school, because he wanted a scholarship; a scholarship, because he wanted to get a degree in journalism. When he had set a goal for himself to be the best investigative reporter on the *Houston Chronicle*, it had only taken him twenty-three months to achieve it. Everything had a plan. A beginning, a middle, and an end.

So why, when faced with this mercurial woman who shot straight from the mouth, pulled him headlong into a treasure hunt complete with ransacked rooms and flights into the night and made his blood run hot, was he so totally befuddled, so totally at a loss at how to understand her?

Why was she affecting him like this?

Where was his analytical mind now? Where was his ability to delve, to divide and conquer? She had conquered him instead, and he hadn't the faintest idea how to turn the tables on her. His charm and persuasiveness, the main tools of his trade when he was interviewing people, coaxing them into telling him things they would never dream of saying, had failed him here. She was immune to his methods. Worse than that, she seemed to be getting him to tell her things while offering him nothing in return.

She would make one hell of an investigative reporter.

And one hell of a woman to make love to.

He had to get his mind on something else or he wouldn't get any sleep tonight. His attention turned to the diamonds. He still doubted whether anything would come of it all. If he was honest with himself, he would admit that he had only thrown in his lot on this venture because of her. He thought that by joining her, he'd get to know her. He hadn't. Instead, he had become reacquainted with a part of himself he had thought was dead. But the more he felt for her, the more he realized that everything inside him wasn't dead. She made him feel alive.

His problem, as he saw it, was making her believe that.

Maybe when this was all over, whatever the outcome, she would be more relaxed, more receptive to opening up to him.

But what if there *were* diamonds? After they found them, would she take the treasure and disappear from his life forever? For the first time in a long, long time, he felt anxious.

Shawn blew out a frustrated breath and told himself that if he wanted to continue being a reporter on the *Houston Chronicle*, he had better report something. His editor was understanding, but there was a limit to that understanding. He'd have to get to that series he had promised to send in. His call to Cal had been short, telling the editor that he was onto something new. Cal had no way of knowing that what Shawn was "onto" was five feet six, sharp-tongued and had upended his star investigator's entire life.

Later—he'd write the article later. Right now, he had to—

Shawn had just tugged his pullover up over his head when he heard it. A blood-curdling shriek. It sliced through the stillness of the night like a razor-sharp blade, shattering it into a thousand pieces.

Mikki!

He threw the shirt on the floor and was already running out of his room, his bare feet hardly touching the cold, Mexican tile, before the fact that something had happened to her, here, in his house, had completely registered with his brain.

What could have made her scream like that? He had left her no more than a few minutes ago. Everything had been all right then. But it obviously wasn't all right now.

He swore under his breath. Why hadn't he checked out her room before leaving her? Because he had been in a hurry to get away from her, in a hurry to go before his desires got the better of him.

He had been a coward, and now Mikki was paying for it.

A second scream echoed through the hall, a raw edge of naked terror rimming it. Adrenaline pumping through his veins, he slammed his shoulder against the closed door and burst into her room. Mikki stood trembling by the bed, her eyes trained on the window. She was pointing toward it, terrified.

Shawn could only think of grabbing her, protecting her, doing whatever it took to make her feel safe. His arms around her, he looked from Mikki to the window. "What? What is it?"

"There, in the window!" He felt her shrink against him.

Shawn looked. The noise she had heard came again. A sharp, tap-tap-tapping sound. The huge, hulking shadow was still there, outstretched limbs scraping against the panes. But it wasn't a man.

Shawn held her, not knowing whether to laugh with relief, or shout at her for scaring him half to death. He did neither. He only held her. She was really frightened. "It's just a tree, Mikki."

"A tree?"

Her eyes were huge as she looked past him toward the window again. When she was younger, there had been that horrible fear of the dark that no one had ever taken the time to dispel. And there had been that couple in Pasadena. She had only stayed with them for three months before the courts had placed her somewhere else, but they had used her fear to make her "mind" them. They had shut her in closets for hours on end and told her frightening stories of monsters that lived only in the dark, stories that fed on her mind until she trembled and dreaded the approach of each night, convinced that she wouldn't live to see the next morning.

When she had looked and seen that huge shadow, the gnarled limbs tapping against the pane, it had all come spiraling back at her.

Mikki sagged against Shawn. "I knew that."

"Sure you did."

She tried to pull away then, embarrassed, annoyed at his words, annoyed at herself for being so childishly stupid. The evening had been so pleasant that she had allowed herself to relax. This was what happened when she let go of her emotions. The bad ones surfaced—her vulnerability. And the need to be loved. All the things that took away her shield, her barriers, that sapped her strength. And left her helpless.

Shawn wouldn't let her go. Instead, he stood there, holding her, stroking her hair and murmuring words she couldn't quite hear. The sounds were comforting. She let herself be held.

"I—I thought it was one of them, one of the men who ransacked our rooms." She laughed self-consciously, trying to make light of the situation. "Things always look scarier at night."

Shawn looked down into her face. The only light in the room came from the hurricane lamp. It glowed, giving her skin a golden hue. The ache inside of him grew until he was no match for it.

"Not all things." He traced the outline of her lips with the tip of his finger. They parted beneath his touch. "Some look even better."

She felt naked, exposed. The last defense she had was irrevocably shattered, crumbling in the face of his gentleness. Had he laughed at her, mocked her fears, she could have marshaled some restraint. She could have yelled, or resorted to something physical. Such as hitting him. She could have rallied.

But he was being kind again. She had no defenses against that. Only an enormous thirst for more.

"You don't fight fair," she whispered. She placed her hand on his chest, wanting to keep some barrier between them. She felt the beating of his heart beneath her palm. It was beating hard. For her. Everything inside her turned to jelly.

Lightly, he kissed her hair, and then her eyes, one by one. They fluttered shut as her heart quickened. "I don't want to fight at all, Mikki."

"Neither do I."

Her words were like the gentlest breeze upon his mouth, reaching into his system and holding him fast, seducing him. He brought his mouth down to hers. He meant to do it gently, and though he held himself back at the last possible moment, the contact was jarring to both of them. The hunger he felt, the need that had been eating away at him all day, all evening, was there for her to feel, as well.

She expected fear. Fear of pain and disappointment had always held her back. It wasn't there. The only fear she had was that he would stop.

She hadn't expected exultation, or triumph, but they *were* there, shooting through her veins, confusing her, exhilarating her. It was as if she were dying and being born again all at the same moment.

Mikki clung to his shoulders as he kissed her, clung because she was afraid that he'd back away and she knew that she would whither away to nothing like dust and blow away if he did.

But he didn't back away. He didn't stop. His mouth soothed and excited, bringing pleasure and pain, bringing her to the brink of a world she had always wanted to believe in but doubted it existed.

A world where she was welcomed. One for just the two of them.

Desires pounded through his body, hammering away, petitioning for release. He wanted her both physically and emotionally, yet he hesitated. This first time, he promised himself, would be different for her, different for him. It had to be. He would give her something to remember, so that all the other times to come would be because of what happened between them now.

Molding her to him, he skimmed the warm skin of her throat with his lips. He felt her pulse beat frantically, heard her moan his name. His fingers tangled in her bra straps and pushed them aside, freeing her shoulders for the onslaught of his lips.

He wanted to sample it all, to taste her secrets, know her flavor so indelibly that he would remember it until the last breath left his body. Until his dying day.

She arched against him, every fiber of her body, every nerve ending stretched taut, urging him on. Her breaths grew shorter and shorter each time she felt him touch her, using his hands and mouth to explore her body.

She couldn't get in enough air.

She couldn't get enough of him.

Now that it wasn't fettered by the shackles her mind had created, her body took over, responding automatically. He took and so did she. He gave and she offered. The gifts were treasured by them both.

At first hesitantly, and then with growing confidence, she allowed herself to touch him, allowed herself the pleasure of running her hands along his body. He was hard and muscular, a strong man, a powerful man. Yet he was so very gentle with her. And he had come to her rescue, to save her from whatever it was that had frightened her. Her hero.

Mikki felt herself falling in love, and there wasn't a thing she could do about it. Or a thing she wanted to do about it. At least, not for now.

And now was all there was.

She felt the hook and eye release along her back, felt her bra part slowly from her body. His hands were there to cover her, to knead her flesh and set her on fire.

Everywhere he touched, he brought her endless gratification. It was as if he was trying to put her pleasure before his own. And her pleasure *was* his own.

The hot, pulsating fire in his loins was growing in tremendous proportions, heightening with each innocent gasp she uttered.

"I want to make love to you, Mikki," he breathed against her throat.

"I had my suspicions."

But her quip was lost amid the sensations that bombarded her. She wasn't even sure she had said it aloud. Maybe she had only thought it. Everything was running together in her head like a multicolored fabric that ran in the rain. Except it was creating something far more beautiful than what was there before.

"With me, not to me," she corrected, forcing herself to think. She felt the soft chuckle against her breast as he raised his head to look at her.

He combed his hands through her hair, bracketing her face. "Always equal partners."

"Temporary partners."

The words came out in a breathless rush. She needed to say them, to remind herself that what was happening here tonight did not have Forever stamped across it. She wanted to let him know that she didn't expect anything more than what was given. The coming together of two people, coming together just the way their shadows were entangled on the wall.

*No, not temporary,* he thought. But he would have to show her the way. And take care not to get lost himself. He meant to please her, to release the throbbing demands within his own body. He hadn't meant to get pulled in so hard, so fast that his own head was spinning, his own bearings were blurred.

But he had suspected all along that it might be like this. He wasn't disappointed.

For a long time, he made love to her only with his mouth, tantalizing her, no, tantalizing both of them. He enjoyed heating her body, getting her ready for another part of the journey. Taking the fear he sensed within her away from her.

With impatience shredding his resolve, he fought vainly to curb his hands and keep from ripping the rest of her clothes from her body, a body that was made for loving. He couldn't wait any longer.

"How can you wear jeans so tight?" he asked in exasperation when they wouldn't slide easily down her hips.

"They weren't tight this morning." Her hands pushed his aside and, moving her hips in a way that made Shawn's mouth go dry, she shed her jeans the rest of the way until they gathered at her ankles. "It's the chili. I'm expanding."

He stopped and laughed, though an insistent pain gnawed at his belly. "You're incredible."

Her eyes were smoky, her hair loose and mussed around her shoulders. Only a tiny swatch of material remained on her body. The blue lace panties he had held aloft only the other day. She looked like Botticelli's *Venus Rising from the Sea*. Except that Venus could never make him feel the way Mikki did, could never make his muscles tighten and jump until he thought they'd snap.

"Words, Gallagher," she whispered, her arms outstretched. "Show me."

His body took on the imprint of hers as he pulled her against him. Together, touching, kissing, seeking completion in each other, they fell onto the bed, entwined. His mouth never leaving the softness of her skin, he shed his own jeans.

He sought and found every single erotic point of her body.

His body hot against hers, Mikki moaned and let herself go, sliding into the molten river of passions met and fulfilled. This wasn't something she consciously knew how to do. These were primal instincts releasing signals that guided her and showed her the way. She moved in a rhythm she heard in her head and felt in her body, vibrating against him with increasing frequency.

She had absolutely no idea that she was driving him to the brink of madness.

He cupped her breast in his hand, bringing it to his mouth. He touched the tip with his tongue. She jerked and shuddered, her fingers digging into his shoulders. His tongue savaged, taking possession, branding. Her skin was slick, as emotions poured out of her that had been too long locked away.

Never, not in her wildest dreams, had she ever thought it would be like this. Not like this. Her fingers tangled in his hair, dragging his mouth back to hers. The length of his body slid along hers, making her tremble in anticipation. Her breathing was so ragged, she wondered if it would ever be normal again.

And still there was more. So much more he had to show her about herself. Sensations exploded within her, leaving her weak, seemingly sated, until his hands began to weave their magic again. And then it would start again, layer upon layer of endless pleasure.

He rolled himself on top of her, marveling at the way her body accepted him, beckoned to him, as if it had been created just for this moment. Bracing himself on his elbows, he framed her face in his hands. Her blue eyes were dark, unfocused, her thin lips parted, inviting his.

He felt her body tense slightly as he began to enter her.

"Are you afraid?"

"No," she lied. She was, just a little, but there was no one else, would never *be* anyone else, to whom she would want to offer this gift.

"I'd never hurt you, Mikki."

"I know," she whispered hoarsely, searching her mind for something that was just out of reach. Oh, yes, she remembered. Something he had said to her in another lifetime, when she had thought herself whole without him. "You said you'd never do anything I didn't want to do."

"And?" He teased the corners of her mouth with his own.

"I want to." She drew a jagged breath, her breasts rising and falling against his chest. "Now."

He slipped into her and felt the resistance, but it was too late for him to stop. Her arms went around him, holding him as the pain gave way to almost unbearable pleasure that filled her head and took her soaring, moving more and more urgently until the final pinnacle was reached and exploded, leaving her incredibly weak. And happy.

She didn't want to move, not now, not ever. Her fingers slowly glided along the ridges of muscles along his back, savoring every ripple, every contour, every sensation over again.

When he shifted, she murmured a protest, but he changed his position until she lay against him, her hair spread out along his chest, her cheek against his heart. There was guilt to be dealt with. "Mikki, I had no idea. I didn't know."

Don't say you're sorry. Please, please, don't say you're sorry. "And I thought it was in all the papers. Some reporter you are."

He raised her head until he could see her eyes. Her mouth might say things, but it was her eyes that told him the truth. "If I had known—"

"What?" she asked defensively. "You wouldn't have made love with me?"

He smiled at her. "Don't give me that much credit for restraint. I'm not superman." He played with a strand of her hair, marveling at its silkiness. "But I would have been more gentle."

Her eyes teased him as she tried to hold back a smile. "You mean that was rough?" It had been the most wonderful experience of her life.

"No, but your first time—"

Words failed him. She had been a virgin, and he had been her first. That was a heavy responsibility. And yet, though he knew it was a sign of male pride, he liked that, liked being her first.

He wanted to be her last.

"I shouldn't say this, because it'll give you an even bigger ego than you already have—" she ran her hair along his lips, tickling him, tantalizing him "—but it was wonderful." She kissed his mouth, first lightly, then with more urgency. "Really wonderful."

Greedily, he moved his mouth over hers, surprised at the sudden renewed energy that was already taking hold of him. His arm tightened around her. "Who are you, Mikki Donovan? Really."

She looked down at his chest. He deserved to know the truth. At least, some of it. After all, he already had her soul. She shrugged, trying to sound nonchalant. "Nobody."

He cupped her chin and lifted it. Did she really believe that? How could she? "No, that's not true. You're someone very, very special."

She felt her limbs grow weak and then dissolve. "You're just saying that because you want to make love again."

"Yeah, that, too."

This time, he rolled her on top of him as the passion and longing erupted again.

The pearly light of dawn was streaking the sky when they lay together in contentment again. Softly, he glided his fingers along her hair. "Tell me things, Mikki."

"How about those Houston Oilers, eh?"

He couldn't help laughing. "God, you're crazy. I mean something more personal."

She knew what he was looking for. And she wasn't ready yet. Some things were still too painful to share. "I thought we were doing pretty good with body language."

He let his fingers dip and skim along her curves, naturally seeking secret places that had become his in the course of the night.

"There's that, too, but I want to *know* things about you."

She moved only slightly, but he took it as a sign of withdrawal. "There isn't anything to know."

He dropped a kiss on her hair. "Unless you really did rise up out of the sea like Botticelli's Venus, there is something to know."

Mikki raised her head and looked at him. "Botticelli's Venus?" She rested her chin on the hand she placed on his chest, intrigued and more than a little pleased, even though she knew it was vanity. No one had ever even told her she was pretty, much less said something like that.

Shawn sifted a long, silvery strand through his fingers. "Yes, there's a resemblance around the hair."

Mikki smirked, pulling back her hair and tucking it behind her ear. "If I remember the painting correctly, she was a redhead with a lot more hair."

He gathered her closer and was glad when there was no resistance. "She was also a lot less feisty."

Mikki cocked her head and looked at him. "Dated her, too, did you?"

He laughed, then grew serious. He thought of what he had taken so carelessly. It still bothered him. "Mikki, didn't anyone ever—?"

She could tell by his tone what was on his mind. Funny, how she had gotten in tune with him so quickly. "Still hung up on that?"

But he had to know, to understand. "I can't believe that no one had ever tried—"

She shook her head. "I never said that."

Now he was totally confused. "But—?"

"It isn't that no one tried, Gallagher. I just never let anyone succeed."

"Why?" he pressed.

She moved her shoulders in a half shrug. "Because there was never anyone I wanted to be that close to."

"And now?"

She glanced down at their bodies, still warm, still touching. "I'd say this was close, yes." She raised her eyes to his face in a movement so patently seductive that he was lost before she had even completed it. "Wouldn't you say that?"

"I'd say that and more."

She placed a finger to his lips. "Don't."

She didn't want to hear empty, conciliatory promises that would never be kept. It was enough that she had this, a memory to treasure, to keep with her forever. She looked toward the window. The tree that had frightened her so terribly now stood like a harmless wooden sentinel. "It's almost morning."

"Almost."

"I think we'd better get a little rest if we're going to find the diamonds today."

She was withdrawing again, but she had given him enough of herself for one night, he thought. He gathered her hair in his hands, his fingers molding themselves against the back of her head, urging her closer. "Soon."

Her eyes sparkled. "Soon?"

"Well," he speculated, bringing her mouth to his, "maybe not so soon."

## Chapter Eleven

The warmth of the rising sun caressed his face as he lay half-asleep, facing the window. Shawn woke up gradually. First came a hazy, contented feeling of well-being. Then came the recollection of what had happened the night before. Crystalline images of their lovemaking floated through his brain, teasing him into a wakeful state of arousal. Murmuring a term of endearment, eyes still closed, he reached out for Mikki.

And found nothing.

Turning to face the middle of the bed, he discovered that was all he was facing. The middle of the bed. Rumpled sheets and a pillow still fresh with the imprint of her head were the only signs that last night hadn't been a figment of his imagination.

"Now what?"

He sat up and looked around. The clothes he had stripped off her body last night were gone. As was the purse she had left draped over the back of the door.

Was she gone, as well?

The bedroom door was closed, and there was no noise coming from the bathroom. No running water from the shower, no light sounds of movement. Nothing. She wasn't here.

Something was wrong. His pulse quickened, muscles tightened. Adrenaline began to charge through his body. This sixth sense he had developed was what his editor called a nose for trouble. Premonitions occurred just before things went sour. Like that time he had gone undercover at the toxic chemical plant when— This wasn't the time for a trip down memory lane. He had to find her. Though the woman in his arms last night had been soft, passionate and incredibly vulnerable, he had absolutely no idea what she was capable of. That was part of the excitement about her and right now, part of the trouble.

After throwing the covers aside, Shawn dragged on his jeans and hurried to the door. As he crossed the room, he stepped on something small and soft. Bending down, he picked up the panties he had pulled off her last night. One side of the lacy undergarment was torn, a testimony to his eagerness. He smiled, remembering how she looked wearing only these. And then how she looked when he had removed them. Tentacles of desire shot all through him, as strong and binding as the nylon cords of a parachute.

Impulsively, he stuffed the panties into the pocket of his jeans. He'd buy her a dozen more to replace these. If she was still here.

He caught the scent of the light perfume she wore as he walked out of the bedroom. Even if she was gone, her trail was still warm.

Very warm. He found her curled up on the sofa in front of the fireplace in the living room, her feet tucked under her bottom, an old family album spread out on her lap. She was poring over it intently, as if she was trying to commit the images to memory. It touched him and aroused his curiosity, as well. He had seen her looking just that way when she had first gazed up at his family portrait. What was it she was searching for so eagerly?

On bare feet, he walked up behind her. "What are you doing?"

Convinced that he was still sleeping soundly, she jumped when she heard the sound of his voice. She had awoken early, unable to get more than a couple of hours of sleep. What had happened last night had been too much for her to assimilate so quickly. She had needed time, time away from him to sort things out. She couldn't think with him lying there, nude beside her, asleep, his arm tucked casually yet possessively around her waist. It had all seemed so natural, so right.

But she knew that it wasn't.

Mikki tried to regain her composure and appear non-chalant. Wasn't that how women were supposed to behave the morning after? No big deal, right? Except that it had been, to her.

"Trying to get a handle on you."

Shawn lowered himself into the small space between Mikki and the corner of the sofa. His thigh brushed against her. He almost pulled her to him, then thought better of it. There was something in her manner that told him to restrain himself. He felt her shift away. It was a slight movement, but it was enough.

They couldn't be back to square one again. Or could they? "I thought you did a pretty good job of that last night."

"I'm serious." Unsure of her emotional stability if she was to look at him, Mikki kept her eyes on the album and continued thumbing through it.

"So am I." He raised the hair away from her neck and touched his lips to the tender skin he had discovered there the night before.

Mikki held herself still, controlling the shudder that threatened to vibrate through her. Last night had been a mistake, a glorious, wonderful mistake. She had to remember what was real and what wasn't. The diamonds and what they could secure for her—a house, if not a home—were real. What had happened last night had happened dozens, maybe hundreds of times before for Shawn. It didn't mean anything to him beyond the momentary pleasure he had attained. She couldn't let it mean anything more than that to her, either. He already knew how inexperienced she was. She didn't want him to feel he owed her anything for last night. Pity was the last thing in the world she would welcome or tolerate from him.

Nor did she want him to think that she was that easily possessed. Possession without commitment would make her feel like some sort of unwanted pet.

Trying to be casual about it, Mikki moved farther along the sofa, away from Shawn, then turned to face him. "You were right."

"I usually am." *Except, maybe, about you. What was wrong?*

Mikki tapped a photograph she had been looking at. "I meant about being a funny-looking little runt."

For a moment, he let her retreat. He leaned over to look at the picture she had singled out. It was one taken about twenty-five years ago. He was sporting an awful haircut his Uncle Bruce had given him while he was practicing to become a hairdresser. His uncle had gone on to sell real estate, a much wiser choice, considering his questionable aptitude in the tonsorial arts. Admittedly, Shawn looked as if he should have been wearing a sign that read *Send this Boy to Camp.*

Shawn reached over and turned the page. She was smirking. "Okay, what did you look like at six?" he challenged.

The smirk vanished and was replaced by an expression he recognized was meant to put distance between them. Another barrier.

"I don't remember," she replied, the tone of her voice striking a melancholy chord.

"There must have been pictures." He tried to read what was going on in her mind but couldn't.

"None that I recall."

He wouldn't let it go. This was it, he thought. This was the key she wouldn't let him have. The key that unlocked the door she kept barricaded. "Families always take pictures."

Yes, if you had a family, she thought. "Mine didn't. It was against their religion," she added flippantly. She remembered reading about a tribe of Indians who steadfastly refused to have their "images captured." "They didn't take pictures because they felt it would trap their souls," she said cryptically.

Was that it? thought Shawn. Had she grown up in a family that repressed the natural exuberance that was so much a part of her? There was only one group he could think of that may have shunned Mikki's brand of vitality.

"You're Amish?"

She wished he'd stop probing. She had given him more than she had planned to already. "No, just hungry."

Mikki snapped the book closed and put it back on the coffee table. Her purse, he noticed, was there. Obviously she still didn't trust him. He felt his hurt turning into a brooding anger.

"Let's eat."

He swore under his breath. "That's my line."

"Then say it." Mikki rose to her feet and turned to leave.

He stretched out legs and barred her way. "Later."

He wasn't going to break her down. She had already let him in as far as she was going to at this point. What did he want from her, anyway? She had given him more than any other man, more than she could really afford to give.

"Now."

"Mikki," he said evenly, "I think we need to talk."

She turned to go the other way, but he grabbed her wrist. Furious, without understanding where the full extent of her anger had come from, she swung around. "What do you call what we've been doing?"

"Shadowboxing."

Still holding her by the wrist, Shawn rose and gazed down at her, looking for answers in her eyes. What he saw was anger. And fear. Of him? Or of herself?

"Gallagher, let go of me." She yanked her wrist free, then massaged it. "I'm not up to an investigative reporter's questions this morning."

He wasn't about to let her talk her way out of this. He wanted to know what was tormenting her and why what had happened between them last night seemed now to frighten her so much. He knew why it frightened him. Because he had come face-to-face with what he wanted, everything he wanted, and the realization that it was his, finally, had caused a momentary panic. That sudden panic that came before an irrevocable step was taken. If there was a problem, he wanted to know what it was. He wanted a chance to resolve it. But she was running away from him, from it. From them.

"How about a lover's questions?"

Mikki's chin shot up pugnaciously. There was a strange blend of fear and arrogance in the gesture. He was nearly tempted to take a swing at that pretty little chin. She was pushing him to the limit.

"Last night doesn't mean we're going steady." She didn't want to hear empty promises, or words brought on by any residual heat from last night. She had slipped, but she hadn't fallen. She was trying to regain her balance on the tightrope she walked, and he was pushing her by saying things she knew he didn't mean.

"Okay." She looked as if she was getting ready to leave. He kept one hand on her shoulder. "What did last night mean?"

"To whom?"

"To you, damn it. I already know what it means to me."

Yes, a good time. An interlude. "It meant you were a lot more even-tempered in the dark than you are in daylight. Go get your coffee, Gallagher, and lighten up. We've got diamonds to find."

"Mikki." He tried again, amazed at his abiding patience. "I know what you're doing."

She did her best to put on an innocent expression. "Then why are you asking questions?" She wanted him to lose his temper and give up.

Patience was getting very, very ragged. "I've never felt like hitting a woman before, but you just might be the exception." Her chin went out farther, matched with an I-dare-you gleam in her eye. He drew a deep breath, his grip on her shoulder tightening. "Mikki, why the hell are you doing this?"

She spread her hands wide. He wasn't going to make her cry. He wasn't. She had a lovely memory of last night, and that was all she was going to have. She knew it; he knew it. She couldn't let herself go any further and build castles in the sky. He wasn't going to drop down on one knee and propose or pledge his undying love. He was reacting to the afterglow of last night's lovemaking. Maybe even trying to secure his position for several more nights. She didn't know. But he couldn't begin to guess what was stirring inside her. Or know that she had fallen in love with him. She had to take things at face value, and she was doing her best to do just that. Why was he trying to get her to say more? To feed his pride?

"You just said you knew."

For a moment, her eyes betrayed her. He had a glimpse of the frightened child inside the woman who was determined to brazen it out. "Mikki, you're running."

Purposely, she looked down at the floor. "My feet are planted firmly on the ground."

Completely frustrated, he gave her one good shake. "But your soul is running."

"Gee, I'd sure like to stick around and hear how this all comes out, but I don't have the time," a strange voice said.

Mikki jerked, startled, and Shawn uttered an oath as they swung around to see a shabby-looking, tall, thin man standing approximately five feet away from them. In his hand was a gun. It was aimed right at them. "Get your hands up! Both of you."

In a quick, reflexive movement, Shawn reached out to take Mikki's hand, then pushed her behind him. He meant to shield her with his body if he had to. She felt a twinge of shame for having put him through hell a moment ago. But she had been going through hell all morning long, trying to file away feelings that she knew would eventually spell her doom, were she to let them take over.

She glared at the intruder. "What are you doing here?" Mikki demanded.

The man sneered. "Holding a gun on you."

"I like a man who believes in simple answers," Shawn said dryly. His mind raced, searching for a way out of this. He came up empty. "How about another one? What the hell do you want?"

"The map, pretty-boy." Another man emerged from the kitchen and joined them in the living room. "We want the map to the diamonds." Behind him, the kitchen window hung open.

Mikki's eyes were wide. How had they known? "How many more of you are there?" With a skill learned long ago, she kept her true reaction carefully hidden. Otherwise, they'd know that her nerves were ready to snap.

"Why?" The second man leered, his eyes sliding over her. "You have something in mind?"

Not if you were the last man on earth. "I just want to know how large a can of Lysol I'll need."

Was she trying to get herself killed? "Discretion," Shawn warned, leaning toward her, "is the better part of valor, Mikki." Her mouth was going to get them into more trouble than they were already in, he just knew it.

"We'll have a philosophical conversation later, Gallagher, after you get rid of this vermin." They were after her map, and though she was afraid, she was also very angry.

Shawn looked down the barrel of the first man's gun. "Just what is it you'd like me to do, Mikki? I left my bullet-proof chest in my other shirt."

The two men exchanged looks. "I don't know about her, Gallagher," the gun man said, "but I'd like you to cut the garbage and give us the map."

It didn't take much to piece things together. "You were the ones who ransacked my room." Since Mikki thought she had seen the desk clerk following them, as well, Shawn wondered where the third man was. But there seemed to be no one else in the house.

"And didn't find the map." Impatience was crackling the edges of his voice. He slowly cocked the gun. "Now where is it?"

For a second, Shawn followed Mikki's lead, brazening it out. "What map?"

Instead of answering immediately, the man moved around the sofa and aimed the gun straight at Mikki's head. "The one you're going to give me or if you don't, you can watch her get splattered all over your sofa."

"It's in her purse." Shawn nodded toward it. Mikki shot Shawn a dirty look. He was giving away *her* map. "Think for once in your life," he snarled. Was money all that mattered to her? He couldn't believe that. "It's not going to do you any good if you're 'splattered.'"

"Smart man," the gunman muttered. He grabbed Mikki's purse and began to rummage through it. "Hey, look at this." He took out the diary.

"That's mine!" Mikki lunged. Shawn grabbed her and then released her, raising his hands again as the man turned the gun on him.

"Give it to me, Neil," he instructed his partner. "If she's that upset about it, it's gotta have something to do with the diamonds."

"Hey, don't use my name on a heist, *Rick*," the man named Neil said spitefully to the gunman.

Mikki began to think maybe these two weren't quite the professional holdup men they'd like them to believe. Still, they did have a gun. She watched, outraged, as Neil thumbed through the diary. Moreover, she felt violated. The diary was hers now. Reading Klaus's diary had gone from an exercise in trying to find out where the diamonds were hidden to something far more intimate. And that man's dirty hands were all over it. She could hardly stand it.

And then she saw Neil's eyes shift to her. The small slits in his round, melon-shaped head made her want to shudder with revulsion. She didn't. She kept her ground. If he expected her to plead for mercy, he was going to be disappointed. As he loomed over her, she could smell his rancid breath. Mikki braced herself to go down fighting. She'd be no match, but she'd leave her mark on him, if it came to that.

Rick looked up from the diary. Shawn made himself ready to protect Mikki, despite the gun aimed at them.

Slipping the book into his pocket, Rick nudged Neil aside with the barrel of the gun. "We don't have time for that." Because the other man had the gun, Neil began to move off sullenly. "Find something to tie them up with."

Neil glared defiantly. "Like what?"

"Rope, belts, spaghetti. How the hell do I know? What do you usually tie people up with?"

Neil had the appearance of a man whose last floor was pretty vacant. "I don't usually tie people up." He looked meaningfully at Shawn. "I shoot them."

"Take the drapery cords." Shawn pointed to them at the side of the windows.

Cursing loudly, Neil pulled the drapery cords off roughly. The light blue drapes swung loose, taking some of the sunlight with them.

"That was a big help," Mikki snapped. "First you hand them the map, then you help them tie us up." She winced as Neil jerked her wrists together and bound them behind her back.

"We're still alive, aren't we?" Shawn pointed out.

"My hero," she muttered in disgust. Neil pushed her down onto the floor, and she yelped in surprise.

"Now you, tough guy." Neil laughed as he said the latter. Tying Shawn's hands together, he shoved him down onto the floor beside Mikki and then bound them together, taking great care to make the knots tight.

With a triumphant laugh, Rick pulled the map out of Mikki's purse. "Okay. I got it." He tucked it into the diary, then slipped it back into his pocket. "Let's go." He saluted Shawn and Mikki with the tip of his gun. "Nice doing business with you folks. Have a nice day."

And then the two intruders disappeared through the front door. It slammed in their wake.

The house was still except for the sound of Mikki's ragged breathing. She was madder than hell. At the thieves, at the world. At herself. "Shawn?"

He half turned to her, although the cords made it difficult. Was she afraid, he wondered. "Yes?"

"You're a lousy bodyguard."

He should have known better. The lady was as tough as nails. At least, on the outside. "We haven't lost yet."

She yanked at her ties. They wouldn't give. She exhaled loudly. This was no time for misguided optimism. "I'd say that losing the map, the diary and the letter and being tied up like Thanksgiving turkeys on the living-room floor comes pretty close."

"There's got to be a way out of these ropes." He strained and tugged. The ropes held. "Of course," he muttered, struggling, "I could be wrong."

She could either give up and let those two run off with what in her mind had become rightfully hers, or she could do something. In the worst of times, Mikki had always refused to give up. This situation was no different. "Maybe if we lined up." She angled her body closer to his. "I'll do yours, and you do mine."

He chuckled, following suit. "That sounds kinky."

"Gallagher, you might have heard them break into the house in the first place if your mind had been above your belt instead of below it."

He refrained from reminding Mikki that she hadn't heard them breaking in, either. "I didn't hear you complaining last night."

That again. She definitely wasn't in the mood to talk about that now. "Let's leave last night out of it."

He had had enough of her evasiveness. "Maybe you can, but I can't."

Something in his voice made her pause. She stopped working on his ropes. "Why?"

She was exasperating. "For the same reason I didn't want him shooting you."

She knew what she *wanted* to believe, but that was a far cry from reality. "Does this have some kind of macho reasoning behind it?"

Shawn gave up. She was impossible. "Mikki, stop talking and work on my ropes. I want to get my hands free so I can strangle you."

For some reason, she wanted to laugh. Maybe she was losing her mind. She struggled to keep her tone belligerent. "We'll discuss it after we get those guys and get my things back."

"We'll discuss a lot of things then," he promised meaningfully.

"Deal." She had no idea why she was overcome by an anticipatory thrill. She was only setting herself up for a fall, and she knew it. "Now concentrate on these ropes, Gallagher, or there'll be nothing to discuss except our funeral. By the time your cleaning lady gets here, she'll find two dead people tied to each other for all eternity."

"About the last part—" he began, then stopped as he heard the noise. "Oh God."

She tried to turn toward him to determine what it was he had seen. "What?"

He knew the unique sound his Jeep made when it was being started up. He was hearing it now. "I think they're taking the Jeep."

It seemed they were going to be stranded as well as tied up. "Why are they taking your car? They must have had a car of their own. How else could they have gotten here?"

"Mikki, I'm not omniscient. I don't know," he snapped, then relented. There was no point taking his frustration out on her—although she did add to it. "Look, I'm sorry."

"Yeah, me, too." She bit her lip. About a lot of things, she added silently. "Do you think you can get out of those?"

One of the things he liked best about her, he thought, was her ability to bounce back. He resumed twisting and turning his wrists, although the rop_s were cutting into them. He remembered that his sister had picked out these drapes and the cords that went with them. He'd have to have a few words with Kathleen—if he ever got the chance. "Did the Lone Ranger ever fail Tonto?"

"That depends." Her own cord wouldn't budge. The rope burns on her wrists were stinging.

"On what?"

"On which one of us is the Lone Ranger."

He sighed. "They should have never given women the right to vote. Okay, you can be the Lone Ranger," he conceded, purposely keeping up the banter. He didn't want her to think of what could have happened to them. To her. "You'd probably look better in the tight pants."

"It's a toss-up."

"Thanks."

"Anytime."

And I plan to take you up on that, Shawn thought.

Finally, after twenty minutes, he managed to work the cords off one hand and then yanked them from the other. With a triumphant, colorful expletive, Shawn rose to his feet. "That guy must've been a Boy Scout. These were damn hard to get out of."

Mikki turned toward him expectantly, but Shawn headed for the telephone. She stared at him incredulously. "Aren't you forgetting something?"

"Oh, yeah." Shawn crossed back to her, but instead of untying her, he dropped a kiss on her lips.

Mikki was dumbfounded. "I didn't mean that. Aren't you going to untie me?"

He thought of leaving her in that condition a minute longer to pay her back for what she had put him through this morning. "Say please."

"Gallagher!"

She looked as if she could spit fire. That's what she was, all right, he decided, a blond spitfire.

"Close enough." He untied her, then became serious. "Just because I untied you, I don't want you to get any ideas."

She took the hand he offered and got to her feet. "Meaning?" What was he driving at?

"Meaning I want you to wait here."

She stepped over the cords and kicked them out of the way. "While you do what?"

He rubbed his wrists to get his circulation back. "I'm going after them."

Mikki picked up her purse and looked inside, as if she was hoping that the diary had miraculously reappeared. It hadn't. "I'm not good at keeping the home fires burning." If he thought for a moment that she was going to stay behind, he was in for a surprise.

Shawn shook his head. He knew she wouldn't agree before he had said it. But he had to try. "You have to be reprogrammed, woman."

She slung the purse strap over her shoulder. "Not by the likes of you, Gallagher."

"We'll see."

Mikki ignored the look he gave her. "Just tell me the rest of your plan."

"Plan?"

What did the expression on his face mean? "What are you going to do once you catch up to them?"

His temper was growing a little short. Did she think he really *was* the Lone Ranger? "I'm working this out as I go along, okay? You sure you won't stay behind?"

"I'm sure."

Shawn drew the curtain aside and looked out the window. There was another car in the driveway, but it wasn't his. From the looks of the old heap, the tires had been slashed. He let the curtain drop back into place, then turned to look at Mikki. She might think she was invincible, but he knew she wasn't. He wouldn't be able to bear it if something happened to her.

"I saw this John Wayne movie once where he punched the heroine in the jaw right after that line—for her own good."

Mikki leveled a warning gaze at him. "Don't even think it."

He reminded himself that her spirit was one of the things he liked about her. "What am I allowed to think about?"

She looked out through the curtain. The sun was already high. And hot. "How we're going to get those guys on foot."

"We're not."

Was he really giving up? Well, he might be ready to, but she wasn't. "Gallagher, if you think I'm going to let those men run off with my map and my diary without—"

She had called it her diary. A slip of the tongue or something more? He filed that away for future examination. "I can get us a car."

Her mouth dropped open. But only for a second. "Well, why didn't you say so?"

"Because you wouldn't let me get in a word edgewise, that's why." He crossed to the phone to call his neighbor.

For a moment that he would long cherish, Mikki said nothing.

## Chapter Twelve

It took them thirty-five minutes to walk to the neighboring ranch house and ten more minutes for Shawn to secure transportation.

That gave those two despicable men a little more than an hour's head start, Mikki thought. Actually, sixty minutes didn't make that much difference as far as finding the diamonds was concerned. She hadn't been able to figure out the clue in the diary as yet, and the map didn't tell them where the diamonds were buried. She doubted whether those two oafs could find the diamonds in a year, much less an hour. What really concerned her was getting the diary back.

As Shawn was thanking his neighbor, a moon-faced, jovial-looking man named Hank, for the loan of his car, Mikki quickly got in on the passenger side of the gleaming, metallic-blue pickup. She wished he'd hurry up. The more she thought about the theft of the diary, the angrier she got.

Mikki rolled down the window. "C'mon, Gallagher. We're losing precious time."

"Eager little thing, isn't she?" Hank nudged Shawn, giving Mikki a wistful look. "But then, you always had all the luck." Shawn made a noncommittal noise as he climbed into the driver's side. Hank slammed the door behind him. "Have her back by nightfall."

Shawn nodded. "Will do." He only hoped he would be able to keep his promise.

Hank smiled at the pickup and patted the hood, then stood back. He waved at Mikki as Shawn started up the engine. She returned his wave mechanically. "Why are you promising him to have me back by nightfall?" It seemed a little odd to her that Hank should care what time she was back.

"Not you, the pickup." Shawn put it into gear and drove carefully out of the driveway. He kept Hank in his sight by using the rearview mirror, stepping on the accelerator only after the man had retreated into his house.

"Okay." She accepted that. "And why did he refer to the car as an eager little thing?"

Shawn laughed. He knew she wasn't going to like this. "That was you."

Mikki sat up, indignant. "Me?"

"You said we were losing precious time." His innocent expression was getting a little difficult to maintain.

"I was talking about following those two rats. Heaven only knows what they'll do to the diary when they find that they can't read it." Her eyes narrowed. "What did you tell Hank?" she asked suspiciously.

"That I was borrowing his car to go on a picnic with you." He glanced over and saw her eyes growing wide. "I told him my car broke down just after I convinced you to go out with me and you had your heart set on being out with me in the great outdoors."

It wasn't that simple, not knowing Shawn. "So he thinks—?"

"Yup."

So that was why Hank had been grinning so broadly. "You swine."

"Well I couldn't very well tell him that I wanted to use his car to chase down two men who broke into my house and stole a map to the whereabouts of fifty-year-old diamonds, now could I?"

She hated that patronizing tone. "No," she said grudgingly, "I suppose not." They jolted and bumped along on the road. The pickup, Hank had said, wasn't quite broken in yet. Mikki frowned. "You didn't have to say that, though."

"First thing that came to mind."

Women were probably always on his mind. "I guess you've had lots of practice." She rolled down the window all the way. Lack of humidity or not, ninety-three degrees was hot.

"Excuse me?"

"Taking women out for the day and running out of gas—oh, never mind."

She knew she'd only get into trouble if she went on. She had no business being jealous of faceless women who had come before her—and would no doubt come after her. She told herself to concentrate on the theft of the diary and the map and forget about what had happened the night before, but it wasn't easy, especially not with his standing next to her. She was beginning to feel claustrophobic.

All right, Shawn thought, if she was determined to think of him in that light, he'd play it up. "I never run out of gas, Mikki."

She stared straight ahead, swallowing a two-syllable expletive she had on the tip of her tongue. He was an egotist, an insufferable egotistical maniac. She should have her head examined for even wanting to be with him, much less entertaining the idea of a more permanent relationship.

Purging her feelings, she returned to the subject that had put them on this winding road. "Can we make good on your promise to have the car back by nightfall?'' She felt badly about having lied to Hank.

"We're going to give it a good try. If we don't, he'll understand." Shawn hoped that Hank would understand and that he could return the pickup in the same condition he had taken it in. "Hank and I grew up together. He owes me a few favors." He thought of one instance in particular. "Some rather *large* favors."

She turned, curious. "He's the same age as you?" The man they had left behind was paunchy and looked at least ten years older than Shawn.

"Yeah, why?" He studied the road. There was nothing out there, Shawn thought, wondering where the two thieves were and what he and Mikki were going to do when they caught up to them. He kept his thoughts to himself.

Mikki shrugged, shifting. Her foot hit something hard. Using her toe to move the object out into view, she saw that it was a tire iron. What was it doing out here? She thought those kinds of things were kept in the trunk. "He looked a little ragged around the edges, that's all. I thought he was older than you."

Shawn made a little mental calculation. "No, actually, I'm older than he is. By five months." He thought of Hank. He *was* a little ragged around the edges. "That's what comes of picking a mate that you spend all your time arguing with." Shawn grinned, remembering. Hank and Ellen had gotten into an argument at their wedding reception. "He calls it 'a continuous difference of opinion.'"

Mikki became quiet. "Don't think much of marriage, do you?"

"I haven't thought much about it at all, no." Which was a lie, but he was certain that if he said that something had clicked into place last night when they had made love, he'd frighten her off.

"I see." She looked out the window and nodded. She had guessed right about last night. God, sometimes she hated being right.

The land before her stretched out endlessly, long and lonely. There was nothing but flatlands for miles as far as the eye could see. Flatlands and dust. Those men were out there somewhere. Armed. Mikki looked back at Shawn. "Shouldn't we have a gun?" A distant rumble of thunder gave emphasis to her question.

It was times like these that he wished he had let his father teach him how to shoot. But, unlike his brothers, he had had absolutely no interest in hunting. "We should, but we don't."

She stared at Shawn in disbelief. "You don't own a gun?"

"No." Why did she sound so surprised?

"But you're a Texan."

He was surprised that she had such a stereotypical view of things. "And since you're a Californian, where's your surfboard?" Before she could argue with him, he added, "This is 1991, not 1891. You've been watching too many Westerns, Mikki."

She bristled at his put-down, especially since it contained more than a germ of truth. "I just thought it would be a smart thing to have one, especially since they do."

"It would be," he conceded. "If I knew how to use one. Not so smart since I don't."

"You can't shoot?"

"Oh, I can shoot all right. I just can't hit anything."

"Terrific," she muttered, sliding down in her seat. She leaned her elbow out the window and felt a drop or two of rain. It dried instantly as it hit her skin. She craned her neck to look at the sky. Here and there, the sky was slowly beginning to turn a darker shade of blue. In between the clouds, the sun still shone brightly.

"Next time, get Wyatt Earp," he suggested. "Until then, you're stuck with me."

Mikki looked at his profile. No, stuck wasn't exactly the word she'd use, she thought, softening. She remembered how he had moved in front of her when the gunman had burst in on them. Shawn had meant to protect her with his body. She could have done worse than to get mixed up with him. Much worse.

"How are we going to track them? They're driving a Jeep, not a lame horse over the sand."

Shawn laughed, shaking his head. He had a live one on his hands. "Just how many Westerns *have* you watched?"

Why did he keep harping on that? "A lot, okay? Why?"

"It shows." The road curved ahead, though the scenery didn't vary. So far, they had only passed three other cars, all going in the opposite direction. He wondered about their odds, but there was nothing else they could have done. "Anyway, to answer your question, I think it's safe to assume that they're on their way to Borachon." He remembered the hand-drawn map. "We'll just take the shortest route and either overtake them, or meet them there."

She thought of the two men. She wasn't sure which one made her flesh crawl more. "Sounds like a social tea."

"Later we can have it out with them at the O.K. Corral if you're a hankerin' for some mean shootin'."

Mikki frowned. "Are you always this sarcastic?" Without waiting for an answer, she turned her attention to the road. The land, she decided, was colossally depressing.

Her feelings were hurt. He hadn't meant to do that. She was more sensitive than he had thought. The word *vulnerable* played through his mind again. She had seemed so defenseless when he had rushed into her room last night. "Mikki, I didn't mean to hurt your feelings."

"You didn't."

He had, but she wasn't about to admit how thin-skinned she was at times. She had grown up watching Westerns whenever she could, sneaking out of her bedroom after everyone was asleep and turning the set on, keeping the volume so low that it was hard to hear. She'd loved watching those old movies, imagining herself back in times when things were simpler, freer. It had been a wonderful retreat into a world of fantasy. She didn't care for his making fun of it, or of her.

They drove in relative silence for another hour. The clouds hung in, but there were frequent bursts of sunshine that seemed to say there'd be no storm today. The only conversation that passed between them was vague and noncommittal. It was as if they were feeling each other out. It was hard for Mikki to imagine that they had been in bed together only a few short hours ago—or was that a lifetime ago—entwined in each other's arms, bringing each other pleasure.

That had involved a world of make-believe, she told herself, just as the Westerns she had watched as a child had. The truth of the matter was that they were just two strangers caught up in an adventure, nothing more. The lovemaking had just been a part of that adventure. At least for him. Every way she turned, things kept reminding her not to blow that part out of proportion. If she did, she'd only be hurt and disappointed, the way she always had been before. Then it had involved wanting to be part of a family. Now it seemed the stakes were much higher and the accompanying disappointment all the more—

She squinted, leaning forward. She thought she had seen something. Shawn saw her go rigid. "What's the matter?"

"Up ahead." She pointed to his left abruptly, accidentally poking him in the face. "Oh, sorry. Over there. Do you see something?"

"No, and one inch higher and I never would again. Be careful." She was serious, he realized. It was probably just another car. "What did you see?"

"I don't know." Mikki kept squinting, trying to make out something. "I think—Shawn!" She grabbed his arm excitedly, as if doing so could make him see what she did. The pickup swerved to the right.

"Watch it," he warned.

She didn't hear him. "I saw something bright flash over there."

Shawn looked in the direction she was pointing and saw nothing. It was probably her imagination, but he decided to humor her. "Okay, let's check it out." He turned off the road and followed the bumpy terrain, guiding the pickup to the left. He didn't think they'd find anything, but it was worth a try.

As they drew closer, he realized the flash that Mikki had seen might have been the reflection of sunshine on a windshield. The Jeep's windshield.

"It's them." Mikki's voice was a low, excited whisper that got to Shawn at an incredibly fast speed. He wished they were out for a joyride instead of doing what they were doing. "Cut the engine."

The two men, standing beside the Jeep, were too far away to hear them. But not too far away to see them if they happened to turn around. There was no shelter anywhere.

"Yes sir." He turned the engine off. "Shall I send the scout back to warn the cavalry?"

He was making fun of her, but she didn't care. All she could think about was getting Klaus's diary back. Klaus hadn't wanted it to fall into the wrong hands, and there weren't hands that were more wrong than these, she thought.

"Wake up and smell the coffee, Gallagher. We *are* the cavalry."

When this was over, he'd see to it that she never got in front of another television set again. "Yeah, right."

She began to get out of the truck, and Shawn grabbed her wrist. "What do you think you're doing?"

"Shouldn't we try to get the drop on them?" she asked impatiently. Didn't this man have any imagination?

"Mikki, think." In case she was so excited that she was incapable of being sensible, he continued to hold her by the wrist to keep her from running off and doing something stupid—like getting herself shot. "They'll see us before we get within twenty feet of them. If they weren't arguing—"

he glanced at the men and saw the angry gestures they were making ''—they would have spotted us by now.''

''Okay, what do *you* suggest?''

''I don't know.'' He contemplated the situation. ''Give me a minute.''

She sighed, held in place by his firm grip. He was right. But they had to do *something*.

The argument between the two men was obviously getting rather heated as they watched both men gesturing more and more angrily. The shouting was almost audible.

''They don't seem to be getting along any better than we are,'' Shawn observed.

She gave him an annoyed look. If he couldn't come up with a plan, the least he could do was refrain from making comments such as that. ''They're probably having a falling-out over the diamonds. Or maybe they can't read the map. I think I saw this in a Western once,'' Mikki murmured. ''They started out by scaring off the horses.''

Westerns again. ''They don't have horses,'' Shawn pointed out patiently.

Mikki shrugged. ''Small point. Think we can get our hands on the Jeep?''

''Not without being seen.''

''Well,'' she said, as she considered the odds, ''there's only two of them.''

The woman definitely needed help. Just his luck to have fallen for a crazy woman. ''There's also only two of us.''

''So?'' She watched Shawn's eyebrows rise in exasperation. ''We can rush them.'' Shawn opened his mouth to protest, but she wouldn't let him. ''It'll work. They're not expecting us,'' she insisted.

''Mikki, when this is all over, I'm confiscating your remote control.''

''All right.'' She folded her arms across her chest. ''What's your swell idea?''

''I don't have one,'' he answered grudgingly. ''Okay, we'll rush them.'' He should probably have his head examined, he thought, but the idea did bear merit, especially since the two men were busy arguing. They had to keep the element of surprise on their side, and any moment now, one of them would turn and see them.

Shawn turned the ignition back on.

She had been all set to leap out, but Shawn was still holding her wrist. "What are you doing?"

"Since they have a gun, I'd feel a lot better if we rush them in the pickup. That'll put the odds in our favor so that we can 'get the drop on them.'"

She grinned. The idea had a lot of potential. Then she remembered the way Hank had patted the hood lovingly before they had pulled out of his driveway. The truck didn't even have a thousand miles on it yet. "What if you wreck Hank's truck?"

It was a calculated risk. They had no other choice. "Then Hank won't owe me any more favors, and I'll owe him a pickup."

Shawn gunned the engine, revving it once, and then drove straight for the arguing drifters.

Mikki watched in fascination as they drove toward the men. Rick looked as if he was about to swing at his cursing partner when they both turned, alerted by the sound of the truck. The two men had just enough time to dive away as the truck came barreling between them. Rick ran to the Jeep, undoubtedly to get the gun.

Shawn jammed on the brake.

"Stay in the car," he ordered as he dashed out after Rick. With luck he could get to the man before he had a chance to retrieve the gun. Shawn wasn't certain, but he thought he heard Mikki yell after him. It was the battle cry he had become familiar with: "When hell freezes over."

Rick was just scrambling out of the Jeep, gun in hand, when Shawn grabbed him by the collar. The two men grappled for possession of the small revolver and went down.

Sparing Shawn a single worried glance, Mikki jumped out of the pickup clutching the tire iron. She intended to do whatever it took to keep Neil out of it. The one thing she had always hated about early Westerns was that the heroines had always cowered, waiting for the men to take charge and come to their aid. They never lifted a finger to help, even if the hero was being beaten to a pulp. Mikki believed in sharing the load.

Neil was staggering to his feet, grunting in angry surprise. He never made it. Just as he looked up in her direction, Mikki sent the tire iron crashing down on his head.

"One down," Mikki muttered, feeling more than a little satisfied.

She turned quickly to her left to see how Shawn was doing. He and Rick were still fighting. Mikki winced as she saw Rick land a punch on Shawn's jaw. The blow went right through her. Getting a grip on the tire iron, she hurried over to them. The rain started in earnest, though it was evaporating before it even hit the ground. Both men were getting filthy, rolling around in the dirt.

Mikki stifled an exasperated cry as she nearly hit Shawn. Each time she raised the tire iron to swing at Rick, they rolled in a different direction.

"Damn it, Gallagher, hold him still," she ordered, trying to get a clear swing.

"This isn't exactly fun for me, either," Shawn yelled, swallowing a curse.

Just then, Rick managed to roll over on him, getting the upper hand. He pulled his gun free from Shawn's grip and aimed at his head. Horrified, Mikki swung with all her might. Rick slumped off, unconscious.

Not wasting a moment, Shawn struggled to his feet. He shook his head, dazed. The rain, mingling with the mud on his face, washed the dirt away. Shawn looked at Mikki accusingly. "When you hit him that thing could have gone off and blown my head off."

Mikki didn't want to think about that. She pushed her bangs out of her eyes with the back of her hand and surveyed the damage. "But it didn't."

Prudently, he took the tire iron from her. "Where the hell did you learn how to swing like that?"

She hurried over to the Jeep and looked in through the window. The diary was on the front seat. She sighed, relieved. She lost no time snatching it up and then tucking it inside her blouse.

"The orphanage." The words slipped out without thought. Startled, she looked quickly over at Shawn, hoping he hadn't heard. One look at his face told her that he had.

So that was it. Pieces of things she had said earlier fell into place. "Orphanage, huh?" He kept his tone casual as he picked up the fallen gun and tucked it into the back of his jeans. It was something he had once seen a TV detective do. He had no other place to put it. "You ever get adopted?"

"No." The word was uttered defiantly.

Shawn slipped his hand around her shoulders and hugged her close. "With a swing like that, small wonder. I'd have been afraid to take you in myself." But in his heart, he knew he already had—in a manner of speaking. "C'mon, let's see if we can tie up these bad guys, partner."

Mikki blinked against the rain, which clung to her lashes. She looked at the fallen men. "What are we going to do with them once we tie them up?"

Shawn pulled out a coil of rope from the back seat of his Jeep. "I'd like to leave them out here." Shawn rubbed his jaw. For such a skinny man, Rick had packed quite a wallop. "But I've got a thing about polluting the environment." He began tying Rick's hands behind his back. "Best thing to do is to take them in."

"We'd have to press charges." Which meant another delay, but now that she had the diary back, the idea of waiting a little longer didn't concern her. Mikki grabbed a length of rope and did the honors on Neil. The man groaned, and she tensed, ready to hit him again if necessary. But his eyes never opened.

"Breaking and entering and car theft should be enough to keep them for a while," Shawn said and then muttered under his breath upon discovering a gaping hole in his jeans just above his knee. "Let's see what we have here." Shawn lifted a wallet out of Rick's pocket. In it were three separate licenses. "Rick Chandler. Or George St. Claire. Or Doug White." He held them up for Mikki. The pictures were identical. "Take your pick."

Mikki pulled Neil's wallet from his back pocket. There were four I.D.'s in his, all different. "Same thing here. I'd say they embarked on a life of crime long before they ran into us, wouldn't you?"

"Two guys with seven I.D.'s between them have to have a list of priors on them." He tucked Rick's wallet into his jacket pocket.

Mikki cocked her head. "Priors?"

"Oh, I forgot. They don't talk like that in Westerns."

She doubled her fist and punched him in the arm, then regretted it when he winced.

"Gotcha!" He laughed, then pulled her into his arms. This was totally insane. It really was like a scene out of one of those movies she seemed to thrive on. They had charged the "bad guys" and won. He hadn't felt so alive and content in a long time. Barring the other night, of course, he thought fondly.

"Smile, when you say that, partner," she warned, playing along.

"Only if you kiss me."

She looked down at the unconscious, bound men on the ground. "We have an audience."

He brushed some of the dust from her face. "They're unconscious."

"You talked me into it."

She felt giddy and told herself that one kiss was harmless. It wasn't harmless. One was too much, and a thousand weren't enough. They all intoxicated her. Because they were his.

Mikki arched her body into his, forgetting the men at their feet, forgetting everything but the feel of his mouth on hers. She was going to miss this when it was over, she thought sadly. And it would be over. All too soon.

Reluctantly, Shawn released her. "We'd better be getting these desperados into town, ma'am, to make the world a safer place to live."

"Will you stop that?"

"I'll think about it." He glanced at their prisoners. "Meanwhile, we'd better get these men to jail."

Making certain that the men were still securely bound, he loaded them onto the back of the pickup, swearing under his breath.

"They're a lot heavier than they look," he told Mikki. "I'll drive the pickup. You take the Jeep."

She was already on her way. "I'll follow you."

The rain was letting up. His eyes, lashes bright with raindrops, teased her. "Is that anything like covering me?"

She stopped and debated her answer. "That, and the fact that I don't know the way might have something to do with it."

They killed the better part of the day at the police station, swearing out a statement that in the long run proved to be unnecessary. While running the two men's aliases through the computer, it was discovered that both were wanted for a number of offenses. Running illegal aliens across the border topped the list.

When Shawn and Mikki finally left the station, the sun was coming back out. But it would be setting again in a couple of hours. The day had taken on a shade of gray.

"I'd say that they are out of our hair for a long, long time," Shawn said to Mikki as they walked toward the parking lot.

She was grateful for that. "Can't say I'll miss them."

"There's nothing standing in our way now." The thrill of the chase had dampened somewhat for him. He was now far more interested in the woman than the diamonds. Would she go once they found them, he wondered.

Why did his words make her feel so sad? "Nothing but knowing where the diamonds are hidden," she agreed quietly.

He put his arm around her as they walked to the two vehicles. "You'll figure it out, pard. I've got faith in you."

Shawn drove the pickup back to Hank's house, and Mikki drove the Jeep. Hank had a few choice things to say about the dirty condition of his beloved truck and a few questions to ask about the sudden resurrection of the Jeep.

"I'll tell you all about it in the morning," Shawn promised, easing himself out the door. "Right now, we're kind of tired and hungry, not to mention dirty."

Hank gave Shawn the once-over. "I'll say. You two roll around in the dirt?"

"Only him," Mikki said cheerfully as Shawn edged her over and took control of the wheel.

Hank scratched his thinning hair. "Whatever turns you on."

Mikki laughed as they drove away.

"That wasn't necessary," Shawn said.

"Yes it was." She felt very smug. She had the diary, the letter, the map—and Shawn—at least for another day. "That pays you back for this morning—letting Hank think you were off on a joyride with a woman of easy virtue."

"I can't help what Hank thinks."

"I don't think Hank looks as if he can come up with those thoughts without a little help." She saw that Shawn was taking the road that led back to his ranch house. "Where to now?"

"I think I'd like to put on some clean clothes and get something besides doughnuts and coffee into my stomach before continuing the search." He glanced toward her. "How about you?"

She thought of his house. She had felt safe there. But she wasn't. Not from him. Not from herself. She knew if they went there, they'd probably stay the night. It was getting dark. Starting out early the next morning was the only wise thing to do. But if she stayed, she knew that they'd wind up spending the night together. And that wasn't wise.

Impulsively, she made up her mind. "Fine with me."

## Chapter Thirteen

Shawn walked into the house and shut the door behind Mikki. "With those two locked up, things should go a little more smoothly for us."

Us. Funny how the term had irritated her so much only a couple of days ago when he had used it in reference to them. Now she felt comfortable with it, warmed by the very sound of the word.

"I don't know." She dropped her purse, with the diary safely tucked inside, onto the sofa. It seemed such a small, natural thing to do, yet it carried such great significance for her. It meant, for however short a time, that she belonged here. "We've still got to untangle the meaning behind the clue in the letter. We have no idea where those diamonds *are* in Borachon." Or if they still are in Borachon, she added to herself. "And," she said, crossing to him, "I still can't get over the uneasy feeling that we're being followed."

Shawn noted that she no longer felt the need to keep her purse at her side. She was finally beginning to trust him. It hadn't been easy for him, but his patience was paying off.

He draped an arm over her shoulders. "That's just your imagination."

She didn't like having her instincts dismissed so lightly. He made it sound as if she saw ghosts behind every bush. "I don't have an imagination," she retorted, which wasn't true but she didn't want to give him something else to be amused about. "I see only reality, and what I do and the way I think is based on logic and practicality."

"Oh?" He arched one eyebrow in disbelief. The lady was protesting too much. He refused to let her distance herself again by picking a fight. "And what was the practical reason for going to bed with me last night?"

"I was cold."

"No, lady—" his eyes seared into her, drawing out all her secrets "—you were red-hot."

Mikki pressed her lips together. "Think a lot of yourself, don't you?"

"Not half as much as I think of you after last night." Maybe by bringing up the intimate moments they had shared, he could get her to open up again, to drop the facade she seemed to want to hold on to so desperately.

It had the opposite effect. His words were making her uncomfortable. She believed in never putting herself in a position that potentially could hurt her. She believed in never showing vulnerability. Last night she had done both. She didn't want it thrown up against her.

Letting out an exasperated oath, Mikki started to turn away, but he wouldn't let her. He took her hands, gripping them in his. "You might even be able to believe what you're saying, but I don't." She yanked, but couldn't get her hands free. He was determined that she hear him out. "You can lie to yourself, Mikki, but you can't lie to me."

"What's that supposed to mean?" she challenged, knowing he was right. And afraid of the truth.

"Last night was more than just two people wanting warmth, more than just the mindless mingling of two bodies." He looked into her eyes. There was fear there. Why wouldn't she set it free? "You'd feel a whole lot better, Mikki, if you opened up."

She withdrew her hands and looked away, but he wouldn't leave her alone. She felt his hands on her shoulders, not pushing, not turning her to face him, but just there. He deserved an answer. She owed him that.

"I don't think I know how to open up anymore," she said quietly, facing the darkened fireplace. She glanced up at the portrait. She could reconstruct it with her eyes closed now. A family. She'd never be part of that, part of anything. Always on the outside. "When you're an orphan, loving is something you forget how to do. There's no market for it," she added dryly.

He heard the hurt in her voice and ached for her. How many times had she been rejected? He hated them all, all the people who had turned their backs on her, all the people who had forced her to form this scar tissue around her heart.

Gently, he turned Mikki around to face him. She believed what she was saying, he thought. It was there in her eyes. Didn't she know it wasn't true?

"You don't forget how to love, Mikki. It's something that's born in you and stays with you."

"Maybe," she answered, her voice low, "it's something that dies in you, as well."

Shawn held her close, stroking her hair. "The woman I was with last night hasn't forgotten a thing about loving, about sharing."

Mikki stiffened. She didn't want him to know how much their lovemaking had meant to her. That was private. And he had had so many women. "That was—"

He held her away from him in order to see her face. "Just physical?" he said, completing her sentence. "No, I don't think so. Give me a little credit for knowing the difference, Mikki.''

He knew too much, saw too much. He was going to be her downfall, she thought with rising panic. Every time she felt good about a situation, about a relationship, it turned sour. She didn't want to destroy the memory of last night by having her affections ultimately rejected.

Pressing too hard would yield just the opposite of what he wanted. There was nothing to do but bridle his impatience, but, God, it was getting hard.

Knowing that she was at her most relaxed when they were sparring, he shifted gears.

Shawn took a step away from her and began shedding his clothing. Mikki watched him toss his jacket on the floor, followed by his shirt and his boots.

Just because they had made love once, did he think she was going to be that easy the next time? ''Just what do you think you're doing?''

''I decided that, thanks to those doughnuts at the police station, I'm a lot dirtier than I am hungry.'' He unnotched his belt. ''So I'm getting ready to take a shower.'' He stopped just short of unzipping his jeans and took a strand of her hair in his fingertips. ''You could probably use one yourself.''

''You say the sweetest things.'' She slapped his hand away.

''We could, in the interest of water conservation, take a shower together.'' He leaned an arm on either side of her, folding his hands behind her head.

Mikki pretended not to be affected by the sight of his bare chest, tried not to look at the well-developed muscles that rose and fell with his breathing. And not to let her pulse rate increase. ''You're having a drought?''

He put on a solemn expression. ''Worst one in fifty years.''

''It just rained.''

He shrugged, undeterred, "Dry rain. Probably didn't even make a drop in the bucket."

His eyes were doing it again, she thought. They were making love to her without his laying so much as a finger on her. "If you're not careful, Gallagher, I'll tell you where you can put that bucket."

Shawn sighed, withdrawing his arms. "Okay, we'll shower separately."

Mikki tried not to smile. He was one of a kind, all right. An ever-changing package of surprises. "Good idea, Gallagher."

"If you say so," he said, giving in for now. He pointed down the hall. "You'll find extra towels in the linen closet if you need them."

She nodded. They parted, each going their separate ways. She entered the room where they had spent the night. With a sigh, she shut the door behind her. Her pulse was just now settled down to its normal rate. For a moment, she stood, leaning against the door, absorbing it all. The sheet was still rumpled, just the way she had left it. Just the way *they* had left it.

Bits and pieces came back to her. She let the memory engulf her. There was no need for imagination here.

Mikki roused herself. She couldn't just stand there, rooted to the floor, daydreaming. Briskly, she checked the bathroom, found the items she needed to take her shower, and stripped off her clothes. Unlike Shawn, she folded them neatly in a pile on the hamper.

Stepping into the pink-tiled shower stall, Mikki adjusted the water temperature until it was as hot as she could physically endure. The spray hit her body with force, attacking her aching muscles, kneading out the kinks. It felt good just to absorb the heat and let her muscles turn to mush.

She sighed, bowing her head and letting the water hit the back of her neck and shoulders, her hands braced on either side of the faucet.

Mikki began to relax. After what they had been through today, she needed to unwind a little. It really had been, she thought with a slow grin, a little like something out of a Western. Now that the danger was over, she could enjoy the excitement of finding the diamonds. It seemed as if there had been nothing but excitement since Shawn had entered her life.

She slowly rotated her shoulders, letting the force of the spray spread to another part of her body. Mikki thought longingly of a hot bubble bath but knew that was out of the question. She didn't trust Shawn to stay away long enough for her to indulge herself. When it came right down to it, she wasn't certain she'd put it past him not to come in while she was—

"Hi, I guess I got finished first. Need any help?"

Mikki shrieked, jumped back and hit her head against the side of the faucet handle. Water and hair ran into her eyes as she glared over her shoulder. "What the hell do you think you're doing here?"

Shawn stood holding the shower door open, dripping wet and wearing a mint-green towel. The towel was slung around his neck.

"Being helpful." There was no disguising the appreciation in his eyes as they moved over her lightly. And thoroughly. His mouth turned dry as desire tightened in his belly and spread to his loins. "I thought I made myself clear."

"You'll make yourself dead if you don't shut that door and—behind you, Gallagher, behind you," she cried as Shawn tossed the towel aside and stepped into the shower with her.

He peered over his shoulder at the object in question. "I did shut the door behind me." A playful grin was on his face as he turned back to her. "Nice fit in here, wouldn't you say?"

"No, it's not a nice fit, and I meant shut the door with you on the other side of the door." She gritted her teeth, trying not to let embarrassment get the best of her. "Outside."

"Oh. Too late."

The look he gave her told her that he could see through her protests. And he was right. They were wearing thin fast, as was her resolve. She wanted to make love with him again. And again. She wanted to do it as many times as there were opportunities. She craved memories, lots and lots of memories to fortify her when eventually she would be on her own again.

But she wasn't about to make it too easy for him. "You're impossible, Gallagher."

"No I'm not." He lowered his head until his mouth was inches away from hers. "I'm very, very possible." With the water still spraying against her back, he touched his lips to hers and sent an electric charge vibrating through her. "Try me."

Her laugh bubbled up from deep inside as his arms tightened around her, pressing her against him. "I already have." She felt herself floating away as he kissed the hollow of her throat, rediscovering the vulnerable spot he had found last night. "Shawn, please, I haven't washed my hair yet."

He was aware of water and the cool, delicious taste of her skin as he kissed the side of her neck. "That's okay. I don't mind."

"But I do." Two more seconds and she knew she wouldn't mind anything.

"Okay." Releasing her, he took a half step back. "I'll do it for you. I'm pretty good at it."

Jealousy sliced at her. "You've probably had a lot of practice." How many others had stood here with him, sharing such intimacy?

"Yes."

Mikki felt something sharp and painful go through her. She told herself she had no business being jealous. He had a life of his own, as did she.

"I wash my hair everyday."

Was he laughing at her? "I meant other women."

Shawn smoothed the hair back from her face as steam, both man-made and otherwise, began to engulf them. It was a beautiful, angelic face, with fine bone structure and classic features. He had always been a sucker for class and the kind of eyes so blue you could swim in them. But never, he knew, to this extent. "No," he murmured aloud, though the words were to himself, "this is a first."

She knew he could be lying, but she didn't care. For now, she'd believe him, just as she'd believe that what was happening between them would last far longer than the steam that was clouding up the stall.

Shawn reached for the bottle of shampoo that stood on the window ledge overhead. Uncapping it, he poured a handful into his palm. Devilishly, he raised and lowered his eyebrows like a mad scientist about to embark on an experiment. "Okay, lean back your head."

"Am I going to regret this?"

"Never," he promised, his voice softening.

She knew he wasn't talking about the shampoo. She only wished that it was true. But regret was only a heartbreak away.

Mikki closed her eyes as she felt the cold shampoo penetrate her wet hair and coat her scalp. And then his fingers massaged the lather in ever so slowly. Mikki felt herself melting as the erotic sensation worked its way through her body. Her breathing became more labored, and she struggled to keep from slipping away.

"Are you sure you've never done this before?" The words came out in a sigh. He was much too good at this to be a novice.

"Never."

She opened her eyes to see the grin that went with the denial, but it wasn't there. She knew suddenly that he was telling the truth, and her heart almost burst. It was a small, silly thing, but this was a first for him, just as her making love with him had been for her.

Mikki rested her hands on his waist, thrilling to the feel of him. "You do this very well."

"Maybe I'll open up a shop." Now he was grinning, and she grabbed the body scrubber and hit him with it, splashing water everywhere.

"Just for that—" He pushed her head under the shower head, rinsing off the suds. She sputtered, surprised.

"Why you—" She twisted around, ready to take a swing at him.

He had anticipated her. Catching her hand, he held it overhead as he pulled her against him. "I guess I'll just fall back to the tried-and-true method of shutting you up." And before she could respond, he covered her lips with his own.

Mikki was surprised that the water running from the shower head didn't just evaporate on contact with her body. The fire he created within her sizzled along her skin, its searing tongues licking through her. She held on, pushing him closer against her, trying to absorb every movement, every contour. His body pressed tightly against hers, and she could feel every inch of his hard, demanding body. It made her hunger for more of what she had tasted so generously the night before. The thought that he wanted her echoed through her mind, overwhelming her. His mouth strayed to her shoulders, and she could feel his tongue gliding along her skin. She shuddered. Her fingers tangled in his wet hair, bringing his mouth down to hers.

The water worked to cool the heat of their bodies but did nothing to cool the passion that flamed beneath. His hands now moved over her body with the ease of loving familiarity. He knew her secrets now, knew where to touch, to probe to make her his alone. As his fingers slowly slid along the soft, inner core of her femininity, he heard her moan. It echoed within his own chest. He was both jailer and prisoner, arrow and target. Whatever he did for her, he did for himself because her passion kept him bound to her.

It had never been like this before. He knew it would never be like this again. Not with anyone else. And he never wanted it to be.

"We're wasting water," she murmured against his mouth, trying hard to hang on to a thread of rationality. But she was getting swept away by feelings that were too powerful to control.

"I'll send the water company a bonus," he promised, covering her face with a network of kisses that made her tremble. She longed for fulfillment, yet wanted this to go on forever. "And an apology," he added.

Passions rose, needs met them. Desires fed on one another, entwined as surely as their bodies were. Shawn slipped his hands around her waist and lifted her, never stopping the onslaught of his lips to hers. Mikki arched until he could fill her. His name echoed in the small room, cried out in rapture as she accepted him, her mind spinning out a million miles past any galaxy, past any home base. Her fingers dug into his shoulders as their bodies moved in ever-increasing, perfect harmony. She sucked in her breath, and then he snatched it away from her as his mouth devoured hers.

He couldn't get enough. Dear God, it was both worse and better than before. If he had ever thought that he could get away, he knew now he was trapped. If the first night had seemed a fantasy, this, he knew, was his reality.

He needed her. Wanted her. She had broken open something inside of him, a thin, but impenetrable wall that had been relentlessly growing since his very first days on the *Chronicle*. The years that followed had buried his soul. She had brought it back to him.

And he loved her.

The realization, strong, overpowering, and very real, humbled him. His arms tightened around her as they took each other to the highest peak and then slowly, languidly, descended to earth again. He whispered her name softly, knowing that he would never know another this way.

Mikki sagged against him, her head dropping to his chest. Droplets of water clung to the light matting of hair. She thought she had never felt anything so soft, so wonderful.

The water from the shower head was still spraying against her, a thousand tiny needles breaking across her skin. She roused herself as the impression penetrated her mind. "What happened to your water shortage?"

"It was canceled." Though he was spent, the sensation of her body against his was infinitely soothing. It only served to convince him further that this was right.

His heart was beating hard against her cheek. She smiled secretly to herself. "I'd sure hate to see your bill next month."

"Whatever it is, I'll pay it. It was worth it." He lifted her chin. Her eyes were unfocused, the pupils large. Her lips were blurred from the imprint of his. "Worth anything they want to charge me."

Lightly, he brushed his lips across hers, then reached past her head and shut off the water. He knew if he kissed her again, they'd never get out of the stall. It had its merits, but if he was going to make love to her again, he wanted to do it where he could stretch out next to her, where he could stroke her body and watch the waves of desire building just for him.

Shawn felt excitement rising again and forced himself to think of something else. For now. "C'mon, I'll dry you off."

Mikki looked down at her nude body. She knew it was silly, but she felt awkward now that the heat of passion had passed.

He saw the blush rise to her cheeks and loved her for it. "Pink is definitely your best color."

Shawn laughed softly to himself. Opening the shower door, he felt her shiver slightly as cold air mingled with hot. He pulled the towel from the rack on the opposite wall and wrapped it around her, fashioning a terry-cloth sarong.

Then he took a towel for himself and draped it around his hips.

Mikki thought he looked impossibly sexy.

"Hungry?"

One appetite temporarily sated, she discovered another building. "Yes." She wrapped another towel around her wet hair.

"I've still got some chili left over from yesterday."

He beckoned to her as he began to walk out the room and down the hall.

His room was in the opposite direction. "Aren't you going to get dressed?" she asked, following him into the kitchen.

"Why?"

He grinned rakishly over his shoulder. Mikki told her heart to stay still.

"You'll only have to take them off me. Although," he considered, facing her, "there is something to be said for that." He raised her hand to his lips, then kissed the center of her palm. Incredibly delicious sensations bounced all through her like a tiny, directionless rubber ball. "I like the feel of your hands on my body."

She took his comment and hugged it to her, then stored it away like a precious treasure. That's what it was to her, a cherished, precious treasure.

"Go heat up the chili," she whispered, her voice smoky with emotion.

He planted one tiny kiss on each of her shoulders. "That's not all that's heating up."

He was teasing, but she loved it. She knew she should get dressed. She knew she should be getting to the diary. There was no other way to find the diamonds unless she deciphered what she read there. But even her need to assimilate the details of Klaus's last adventure, of his struggles in the remaining few months of his life, had been superseded by what was happening to her here and now.

She swallowed hard. "Go cook."

"Yes, ma'am."

Towel tucked firmly around her, Mikki set the table, just as she had the day before. But yesterday she had tried to conjure up what life had been like in this room long ago. Tonight, all she could concentrate on was what it was like now.

Shawn stood at the stove, his chest and feet bare, a towel clinging precariously to his middle. It was a domestic scene, a scene out of a newly minted union. It was a scene she had never dreamed she would ever be part of. Yet here she was, setting a table while he cooked, sharing tasks, sharing food.

Sharing love.

Or what passed for it, she thought, trying to anchor herself to reality. She knew she couldn't get totally carried away. That as long as she remembered it was make-believe, it was all right to pretend. But she caught herself pretending very, very hard. And wanting the fantasy to go on forever.

## Chapter Fourteen

He made love with her again. Right after dinner. The dishes remained on the table where she had placed them, totally forgotten. The towels they had worn lay in a tangled heap on the floor, discarded in the heat of the moment. The evening had melted into night, filled with sensations and feelings, filled with needs satisfied, then raised again, harder, stronger, more demanding with each resurrection.

She didn't know it would be like this, had never dreamed it could be like this. There had been no hint, not in anything she had so intently watched flickering across the television screen as a child, not in anything she had fantasized about. She had discovered a certain power in lovemaking. She had power over Shawn, just as he had over her. It was an equal partnership, each craving to give, each wanting to take. The thought made her smile. For as long as it lasted, she was going to make the most of it.

In the wee hours before dawn, Mikki stirred against him, reveling in his warmth. His arm was thrown over her protectively in sleep, cradling her to him, his hand resting possessively on her thigh. Her body fit so well against his. In any position, she thought with a fond smile.

She shifted very slowly, keeping his arm where it was, until she could look at him. Fading moonlight cast long, thin yellow fingers through the room. His thick, black hair seemed even darker, like the inside of midnight. It was mussed around his face, giving him a wild look. His jaw didn't seem quite so hard and chiseled, but it still reflected the strength within the man. His mouth, with its slightly larger lower lip, bore witness to the sensuality and sensitivity she had uncovered.

Even if they did find the diamonds, discovering them would pale compared with what she had discovered here. He had managed to get to her, had tempted her until she had permitted herself to respond. And it had all happened so quickly. She still felt that the end result would be the same, that this would end, but it was so good, so wonderful now.

Whatever happened tomorrow, she thought, she had this tonight. At peace, she drifted off to sleep.

It was morning. Time to get up. Soon. Shawn moved to gather Mikki against him and found nothing to hold. He awoke quickly, struck with the feeling of déjà vu. Her side of the bed was empty.

Annoyed, confused, he bolted upright, then slumped against the carved headboard, the blanket pooling around his middle. This time was different. She was in the room, dressed in an old bathrobe she had found hanging in the closet. It draped over her hands and hid her body completely, teasing him. Her legs were tucked under her as she sat curled up on a chair by the window. The diary was in her lap, and she was reading. The dictionary lay on the windowsill.

He stayed where he was, quietly studying her. She moved her head as she read. Her long, shiny hair kept falling in her face. Impatiently, she tucked it behind her ear where it would only work its way loose as she worried a strand, searching for the right word to explain a passage she didn't understand.

She reminded him of a child concentrating on a difficult homework assignment. He felt the pull, strong and demanding, coursing through him. But while it was insistent, it was cushioned with a gentleness. Something new. He could have said that he was merely feeling protective of someone who had had a hard time in life. But it would have been a lie. He was in love with her the way he had never expected to be. When he had envisioned the woman who was to share the rest of his life, he had figured on someone warm and sweet. And rather docile.

He grinned, running his hand through his hair. That definitely did not describe Mikki. Loving Mikki meant being ready to go toe-to-toe with her at the drop of a hat. It meant never knowing what would come next. Excitement. Carnival balloons. Yelling and hurt feelings and impossibly wild nights in bed.

It was more than he had ever dreamed of or hoped for.

Mikki frowned, pulling the dictionary over and flipping through it. This meant so much to her, he thought. The lure of diamonds had affected men and women everywhere, tempting them until they finally lost sight of themselves and those they loved. Kingdoms had been won and lost because of the quest for riches, as had been men's and women's souls. People did strange things when money was concerned. It was their god, their lover, their everything.

Was Mikki like that? When they found the diamonds—if they found the diamonds—would it change her?

He didn't think so. Technically, he had only known her for a matter of days. But somehow, he *knew*. She wanted the diamonds not just for the money, but because they would fill an emptiness in her life, an emptiness *he* was determined to fill.

"I thought you were gone again."

She looked up, startled by the sound of his voice. When she had checked only a few minutes ago, he had been sound asleep. She couldn't sleep once dawn had lit the room. A restlessness plagued her. She had always been one to go forward and meet her destiny, and the diary contained her destiny. So she had left the shelter of his body and had applied herself to figuring out the mystery of the journal. She hadn't gotten very far.

"Again?"

She looked at him quizzically. The morning sun now filled the room. His beard was just coming in, dark and heavy, to match the texture of his hair. She remembered the feel of it on her face last night. She would remember everything when this was over, every sight, every sound, every touch.

He nodded. "Like yesterday morning."

She still didn't understand. "I was in the living room yesterday."

He let it go, finding it simpler just to agree. She couldn't have guessed at the strange panic that had seized him when he had thought she had left his life as suddenly as she had entered it. He had trouble understanding that himself. He wasn't a man to panic. But then, he wasn't a man to do many of the things he had done—until she had come into his life.

Shawn moved the covers aside. As he did, Mikki looked back down at the diary. She was still shy, he thought, finding it touchingly sweet and at total odds with the woman he had lain with in the night. Although, he mused, he had caught a moment's hesitation in her eyes before she had returned her attention to the book on her lap.

For her sake, he pulled on the jeans he had left outside her bedroom door. Her bedroom. How quickly things had attained her brand, he thought. Such as him.

Snapping the jeans closed, he crossed over to Mikki. "Making any progress with that?" He tapped the top of the diary.

"A little." She sighed and massaged the bridge of her nose. A small, nagging headache was building behind her eyes. "It'd be a whole lot easier if he'd stuck to writing it all in English."

A strand of her hair was caught beneath the collar of the bathrobe. He tugged it out. "Life isn't easy," he commented absently.

Mikki laughed shortly. "You don't have to tell me that."

What was she feeling? What had she felt when she was growing up?

"Mikki?"

Another confusing word appeared in the middle of a perfectly good sentence. She sighed and began thumbing through the dictionary for the umpteenth time. "Hmm?" It would have helped matters greatly, she thought, if he'd stop fiddling with her hair and making her mind wander. *H* came before *I*, not after it.

"How long were you at the orphanage?"

She looked up sharply, then lowered her eyes to the dictionary. The letters became a blur. "Long enough."

It wasn't an answer. Cupping her chin in his hand, he raised her head until he could see her eyes. "Don't shut me out, Mikki."

The smile was small and sad. She looked toward the bed behind him. "I didn't think that was possible." Not anymore.

"I don't mean physically."

She closed the diary. Her fingers drummed nervously on the worn cover. "Just what *do* you mean?"

He crouched down so that his face was level with hers. "Damned if I know." His mouth caressed hers.

Was the first kiss of the morning the sweetest? Or was it the last one at night? She didn't know, but she would have liked to have taken a survey, starting and stopping with him.

"If we start again, we're never going to get anywhere."

He laughed, rocking back on his heels. "That is a matter of opinion." But he rose to his feet again.

Food was always a good diversion as far as he was concerned. "Want breakfast?" she asked.

"Sure."

By now she knew how to read that look in his eyes. "The kind you put on a table, Gallagher."

He put his hand on the small of her back, lightly guiding her to the bed. "Hmm. I've never done it on a table before." As he spoke, he tugged at the sash around her waist.

The robe fell, gathering around her feet. Mikki laughed and gave up. The headache that had been building miraculously faded away.

Breakfast waited.

When they finally got around to entering the kitchen, Mikki offered to fix breakfast, but Shawn told her to go on with her reading. She didn't know if that meant he enjoyed cooking, or that he wanted to hurry with the hunt since they had already lost so much time. But she took him up on the division of labor, and while he was doing something at the griddle that created a delicious aroma that wafted through the air and tortured her empty stomach, Mikki went on with her translation.

Klaus Wintermeyer. She had learned a great deal about this man who had been a stranger to her only a few days ago, whose last thoughts she held in her hand. Mikki glanced over her shoulder toward where Shawn stood working at the stove. She had learned a great deal about him, too. Both men had taught her about herself in different ways. Her hunger to learn about his life showed her that she still wanted to connect with a family, no matter what she told herself to the contrary. The need, the yearning, would always be with her, buried or exposed. It existed. Reading about Klaus's life, his loneliness, his memories of his family life, filled a void for her.

Shawn filled a larger void in her life. He made her *feel* love, something she thought she was no longer capable of feeling. She didn't fool herself into thinking this could go on forever, but for a few short days in May, he had made her feel protected, alive, in love. She blessed the whimsical gods of fate that brought them together.

The diary. Get your mind back on the diary, she admonished herself.

With a sigh, she went back to reading. And struggling. The more Klaus wrote in the thin journal, the more he lapsed into his native tongue. The going was slower and slower. Except for the passage in which he talked about his grandmother, she found that he—

Mikki stopped and blinked. Of course. That was it! How could she have been so stupid?

"Shawn!" She jumped up from the table, nearly colliding with him and the two plates full of hotcakes and French toast he held aloft.

Shawn took a steadying step back. "Hey, easy. If you were that hungry, I would have made something that took less time."

She shook her head emphatically. "Put all your appetites on hold, Gallagher. I think I've found it."

"Found what?"

Blowing out an impatient breath, she searched the front of the book for the passage she wanted. Shawn placed the two plates on the table and crossed to the pantry for some syrup. Finding it, he turned back. Mikki was shoving the book into his face and pointing at a page before he reached the table.

"Here!"

Still holding the syrup, he scanned the page and saw nothing that should have gotten her so excited. "Here what?"

"Don't you see?" Mikki looked back at the passage. It was right there. She pressed the book against her as she looked up at him in wonder. Was he blind?

"All I can see is you holding a book against your chest." He took the book from her. "I'm getting very jealous of an inanimate object."

"Gallagher," she cried, exasperated. He wasn't trying. "It's Jeremiah."

"What's Jeremiah?" Talking to her at times was like running through a maze. Backward.

"You're not paying attention."

He sat down at the table and began helping himself to breakfast. If she was going to be babbling nonsense for a while, he would need to fortify himself for it.

"I'd stand a hell of a lot better chance if you were speaking English."

She took two deep breaths and blew them out slowly, like a woman in labor trying to get control before it was wrenched from her. She was letting things get ahead of themselves. The technique worked. A little.

In a calmer voice, she tried again. "Klaus wrote in his journal about his beloved grandmother. Her last name was Jeremiah."

He did make a mean hotcake even if he did say so himself. He realized that Mikki was waiting for him to make a comment. "Odd German name."

"It's not German." He still didn't get it. Well, why should he? It had taken her a long time, hadn't it? And she was more deeply involved. "She came from America. But that's not the point."

There was excited tension in her voice. Shawn put down his fork. "What is the point?"

"Don't you see?"

"No."

"That's the name we're looking for." She came around to his chair and placed the book on the table next to his plate. She jabbed at the name on the page. "Jeremiah.

That's the name Klaus was referring to in the letter. The same name as that of their 'beloved relative.' All we have to do is find someone in Borachon whose last name is Jeremiah.''

He was skeptical. ''We're still talking fifty years here, Mikki.''

She retrieved the book. ''Okay, someone who had a relative named Jeremiah. Fifty years isn't that long.'' She sank down on the chair next to him. ''George Burns is ninety-something.''

He hadn't gotten as far as he had in his profession by letting excitement cloud his thinking. ''And Elvis died at forty-two.''

She cocked an eyebrow. ''You're determined to be a pessimist about this, aren't you?''

Yes, if it takes you out of my life, he thought. No, nothing was going to take her out of his life, he decided. Not if he had to bind her to his side with Super Glue until he convinced her to stay of her own free will. If that failed, he'd buy more Super Glue.

''I'm determined to eat first,'' he said easily. ''You should, too, to keep your strength up.'' Her eyebrows raised higher. He knew what she thought he meant. ''I didn't mean that. I meant that it's going to be a busy day today if we're going to go into Borachon. Finish your breakfast and I'll get some supplies together.''

Mikki could hardly believe it. They were less than a day away from ''more riches than to tell you I can.'' She remembered Klaus's wording fondly.

And then a strange sadness seeped into her, warring with the excitement. They were near the end of their goal. Maybe the mystery would be unraveled today.

And what of tomorrow?

Shawn would have his story and a share of the diamonds. Once afraid that he was after it all, she now wanted to give him half. It was only fair. But then what? Then there would be no more need for them to stay together. She had her apartment in San Francisco, he had his in Houston. Half a country away. It might as well have been half a world away. There would be no more reason, no excuse for her to be with him or he with her.

It would be over.

Finished eating, Shawn took his plate to the sink and left it there. Cleanup was something to put off as long as possible. He moved over to the pantry to see what provisions they would need for an expedition that might be over within the day or take a couple of days at most.

He was being optimistic, he thought, believing that they would find the diamonds and soon. Another new one on him. Having her here did that. Being with her did that. Feisty, argumentative, she still filled him with optimism. She might say she dealt only in reality, but if she did, where did she get all that endless hope from? He half expected her to introduce him to a mutt named Sandy and start singing about "Tomorrow."

He saw her as she was. Not as she saw herself, but as a woman with limitless love to give, unending hope to draw upon. A woman the world could not beat into the ground no matter what it did to her. He saw her, quite simply, as his salvation.

He pulled out a couple of cans of pork and beans, several packages of Ring Dings and the last of the fruit they had bought at the store. The pastries had been his idea, the fruit hers. They complemented each other, he thought, placing the items on the counter next to the pantry.

And they'd need water. He wondered where he had stored some of his camping gear. He walked by the table quickly and noticed that she had finished eating, but was still sitting there, staring into space, her head propped up on her hand. She was frowning.

"What's the matter?"

"Hmm?"

"You're frowning. Did you make a mistake about the name?" He looked at the diary.

She wondered if she had. Maybe if she hadn't told him the name, if she hadn't been so excited about finding it, she could have been able to put off the inevitable for a few more days.

No, that wasn't right. She couldn't hold him back any longer. They both had lives to get on with. Hers would only be emptier, that's all.

"No." She sat up and smiled at him. "I'm just excited."

"You could have fooled me."

And me, she said to herself. She never would have expected to approach fortune with such leaden feet.

## Chapter Fifteen

"**Y**ou were saying?" Shawn asked as he brought the Jeep to a complete halt.

They had stopped in the center of Borachon and sat looking around the long, wide street. Nothing moved except for the tumbleweed that was doing lazy cartwheels down the middle of the street. The town was located exactly where Klaus's map had said it would be. But that wasn't the problem.

Mikki gripped the top of the windshield as she stood up. "It's a ghost town."

There was no arguing with that. From the condition of the surrounding buildings, Shawn judged that it had been one for quite some time.

"So much for finding someone whose name is Jeremiah clutching anything."

Stung, momentarily wrestling with defeat, Mikki turned to Shawn. "Why didn't you tell me?"

He was annoyed at the accusation in her voice. "Tell you what?"

"That it was a ghost town."

"Because I didn't know." It wasn't his fault that this was a dead end. "Look, I'm not familiar with every town and hamlet in Texas. In case you hadn't noticed, Texas is a pretty big state."

"But you grew up not that far from here," Mikki pointed out, trying to come to grips with her disappointment.

There was no point in losing his temper. The look of defeat in her eyes made him feel guilty at having raised his voice.

"Not that far as the crow flies. If the crow is driving a Jeep, it's a lot farther." He looked at his watch. "It took us over four hours to get here. As a kid, if I couldn't get somewhere in an hour on a bike or a horse, I didn't want to know about it."

"Sorry," she muttered, shoving her hands deep into her jeans' pockets. "I just can't believe we came all this way for nothing."

Shawn put his hand on her shoulder and played with a strand of her hair. An image of her in the shower came back to him. "Oh, I wouldn't say nothing." If it hadn't been for the diamonds, there would never have been a reason to join forces.

She flashed a vacant smile at him and climbed out of the Jeep. Since she had come all this way, she wanted to look around. Maybe there was something here that would spark an idea. Maybe she should reread the diary and the letter.

Borachon had been one of those typical towns that sprang up during an oil boom and then slowly died out. In a way, it reminded her a little of Mission Ridge, except that Borachon hadn't been nearly as modernized. It looked like a town that had been dead for a hundred years. But fifty years ago, it had to have been alive.

Or did it?

She rolled the thought over in her mind. It could have been a ghost town then. Maybe Klaus had come here after it already was a ghost town to bury the diamonds. It could have happened that way.

Restless, she began to walk toward one side of the street. Mikki frowned, thinking. Klaus hadn't used the word *buried* in his message to Alfred. But maybe that had been just to throw people off. She sighed, dragging her hand through her hair. It was certainly throwing her off.

Shawn came up behind her. She didn't even notice. Her mind was racing around, trying to catch hold of a thought. "I can hear the wheels turning in your head."

She turned on her heel to look at him. "Do you think the diamonds might still be here?"

There was that hopeful glimmer in her eyes again. The woman never gave up. He hated to be the one to rain on her parade. "Anything's possible." But his tone was highly skeptical.

Slowly, she scanned the rows of closely grouped wooden houses. Each had once been someone's pride and joy. Now they were deserted. Windows were broken, doors boarded up, a sad testimony to dreams that had gone bad. Was this what Klaus had seen when he came here so long ago? Would she find any evidence of that at the end of the diary?

"Maybe he buried it in someone's backyard," she guessed out loud.

But whose?

Shawn shook his head, thinking back. "That wouldn't match what he said in the letter, remember? He supposedly left the diamonds with someone clutching them to his bosom."

The wind was beginning to pick up, coming from a northerly direction. It played with the dust and swirled it around. He wondered if it would get worse. If it did, they'd be forced to take shelter here for a while. Remembering

Mikki's reaction to the dark shadows cast by his tree, he reckoned she probably wouldn't care for that.

Mikki continued to roam along the long street that had obviously been the town's main business area. A building that had weathered the years better than the rest caught her eye, and she stopped in front of it. The window bore the words Borachon Gazette. Had the editor hung on until the end, chronicling the death of the town? There'd be no one to tell her.

"Fifty years is a long time to clutch," she mused, echoing his earlier sentiments.

Shawn's gaze shifted from the *Gazette's* window to Mikki's profile. He thought of last night and this morning. "Not if you have the right inspiration," he murmured under his breath.

They passed a saloon. The swinging doors had long since fallen off. The door that was used to lock up the establishment for the night stood rigid, its hinges having rusted years ago. Mikki couldn't resist walking in, curious, hopeful, not knowing where to go and not wanting to give up.

In a way, it looked just as she would have imagined. The interior was laden with dust. Cobwebs were everywhere. Spiders seemed to constitute Borachon's population now.

Mikki looked at the mirror that hung over the bar. The glass was dingy and covered with grit and grime. She couldn't make out her own reflection. The only illumination in the long, silent room where men had once drunk, commiserated and laughed, was sparse. It came in through the broken windows.

She walked around slowly, absorbing the emptiness, then stopped at a table. A bottle and glass stood in the middle. Someone had forgotten them. Perhaps he had been the last to leave, wanting one more drink to toast the town. She ran her fingers along the neck of the bottle. "God, it looks so sad."

Shawn stood behind her, his hands on her shoulders. He could feel what she was thinking. It was as if she sensed the

ailure that was here, the lost dreams that had made an en-
ire town clear out. Was it the fact that she had been re-
ected as a child that made her understand this sort of thing
o well?

"Ghost towns usually do. The only thing worse are towns
hat are dead and don't know it yet." He thought of Mis-
ion Ridge and the others like it.

There was a noise at the far end of the bar, by the door.
Trying not to be alarmed, Mikki moved closer to Shawn,
her eyes fixed on the door. All morning long, she had had
n uneasy feeling that they were being followed.

A kangaroo rat scurried by. Mikki let out a sigh of re-
ief, and Shawn laughed. She realized that he was holding
her close.

"Of course, ghost towns do have their uses in bringing
eople closer together."

An impatient, embarrassed look crossed her face as she
moved away from him. She hated being taken for a fool,
ven if no one was pointing a finger at her. Mikki couldn't
et over the feeling that they were being followed, and that
was what had made her jump. But she didn't want to say
nything to Shawn. He'd only make a comment about her
magining things again. Maybe he was right and she was
magining it.

She bit her lower lip, thinking. "You're not trying, Gal-
agher."

He gave in to the expression on her face and pulled up a
ickety chair. A possible fortune in diamonds was worth a
ttle cerebral effort. One leg of the chair tottered danger-
usly as he slowly lowered his weight on it. He leaned his
rms across the back gingerly. "Okay, let's look at this
hing logically."

She heard another noise. This one sounded more like a
iss. A snake? The visibility in the saloon was poor, with
orners hidden in the dark. If she was going to be attacked
y desert creatures of all sizes and shapes, she wanted a
ghting chance to see them first.

"Could we look at it logically outside?" She failed to suppress a shiver that went through her.

He saw how her eyes darted about as she spoke. "Afraid of ghosts?"

Mikki was already moving toward the door. "Let's just say I'm afraid of things I can't see."

Again he thought of that first night, when she had screamed because of the shadows cast by a tree.

"Sure." He rose and took her hand. The chair collapsed.

He gave it one final glance before following Mikki outside. "You just might have saved me from a nasty fall."

And set me up for another, he thought. But that was already history. There was no point looking back at that. He had fallen for her that first night, and there wasn't anything he could do about it, even if he had wanted to. Which he didn't.

Light encompassed them. "Okay, how could Klaus have been so certain that the man—"

"Or maybe a woman," Mikki interjected.

"Or maybe a woman," he allowed, "would truly be honest enough to wait for Alfred to come by and claim the money?" He followed her as she walked along the opposite side of the street. Maybe she'd work this thing out of her system and they could go back. "That seems like an awful lot to ask of a ma—a person."

She grinned at his correction. He was trying, she'd give him that. That and much more. She considered the point he was making and agreed with it. "I certainly wouldn't trust anyone with such a treasure unless they were dead." She flashed him a dazzling smile. "Present company excepted, of course."

He was about to turn toward what looked to have been a blacksmith's shop when he stopped and looked at her. "Say that again."

"Present company excepted, of course." The thought made her smile. She knew she could trust him, and that meant a great deal to her.

"No, no, the other part."

"What other part?" She didn't understand what he was driving at. Out of the corner of her eye she caught a movement behind the blacksmith's shop and turned to look, but there was nothing there. Probably just another desert animal. She longed for Fisherman's Wharf. She knew how to deal with two-legged animals. The four-legged kind made her nervous.

"The part about being dead."

Because he was being so adamant, she thought it through. "I said I wouldn't trust anyone with that kind of treasure unless they were dead," she repeated slowly, reconstructing her words.

"That's it."

"It is?" She still didn't follow his thinking. Shawn took her hands in his. He could feel his enthusiasm beginning to build. Maybe this wasn't such a wild-goose chase after all. "What sort of 'malady' did dear, sweet Grandmother Jeremiah have?"

Mikki thought. "Klaus didn't mention one. By the time he wrote about her, she was already dead. His grandmother was dead," she repeated slowly, waiting for that to jar something in her mind. It didn't. "So where does that lead us?"

"There's only one logical conclusion. To the cemetery." Since they hadn't seen one upon entering, that meant it was probably on the other side of the town. Shawn dropped her hands and began to lead the way back to the Jeep.

"Oh." The prospect left her cold. She didn't like cemeteries. "Couldn't you come up with another logical conclusion?"

He stopped at the Jeep. Why was she dragging her feet? "Like?"

"I don't know." Mikki shrugged helplessly. "Something a little less ghoulish."

She *was* afraid of things that went bump in the night. He found that endearing. "Right now, nothing else comes to mind."

He was right. She didn't like it, but it made sense. "Okay, let's visit the cemetery." She looked up at the sky. There wasn't a cloud in it. "At least it's not raining." She saw Shawn looking at her, confused. "It's always raining in those scary movies."

Hadn't she spent any time playing outside with neighborhood kids? Had watching old movies been the only pastime she had had? "This isn't a movie, Mikki."

"You mean it might not have a happy ending?" she asked, her eyes opened wide, her tone slightly sarcastic.

"Just get in the Jeep." He got in himself.

"When do I get to drive, Shawn?" she asked as he started the car.

He hoped he'd never get the chance to find out if she drove the same way she sped through life. "When I up my life insurance policy." The Jeep roared into life.

"Chicken."

"Wanna see my feathers?"

"No, but seeing you lay an egg might be interesting," she mused.

"Behave or I'll leave you at the cemetery." He turned the Jeep toward the other end of town.

"Yes, sir."

"Better."

"Don't get used to it," she murmured, staring at the road and bracing herself for the ordeal ahead.


They drove to the outskirts of Borachon. The cemetery was located on a hill that overlooked the town. It was small and bore the look of decades of neglect. Markers were scattered around without any apparent thought to order.

The more Mikki thought about it, the more it seemed to her that Klaus had come here after the town had already died. It would have made what he had to do easier. No one would have been around to watch him or disturb his work. That made Shawn's theory about burying the diamonds in the graveyard the likeliest one.

To confirm her suspicions, she pulled the diary out of her purse as Shawn stopped the Jeep and skimmed the last pages, skipping the foreign words and looking for something that would prove the theory.

Taking the shovel he had packed with him, Shawn began to head toward the squared-off plot of land. Mikki stayed where she was. "Aren't you going to get out and help me look?"

She raised her eyes from the diary. "You search, I'll be the lookout."

"Lookout for what?" He gestured around them. "This is a ghost town, Mikki. There isn't anyone around for miles."

She gave him a serene smile. She had absolutely no intentions of budging from the Jeep. "You can never tell, Gallagher."

"Right."

Shouldering the shovel, Shawn moved around the grave sites, taking his time and carefully reading each marker. Some were made of wood and bore just a name. Others were headstones of cheap marble, badly cracked and decayed. Some of the graves had no markers at all, just a mound of dirt that had been disturbed and then replaced. He had trouble reading the faded names. He picked his way through them slowly, as if he were stepping through a mine field.

Finally, shovel still shouldered, he returned to the Jeep and Mikki.

"Well?" She had watched his progress and didn't take it as a hopeful sign that he had come back rather than calling out to her.

Tossing the shovel into the back seat, Shawn climbed into the Jeep. "I found a lot of Johnsons and Smiths and O'Rileys."

"But no Jeremiahs?" She knew the answer before he said it.

"None."

She closed the diary, marking her place with her index finger. "How about as a first name?"

It was only a pipe dream. That's what he had thought when they had started out. There was nothing to change his opinion. "Not first, last or middle."

Mikki leaned back against the seat. "So it's not out here."

She didn't sound as upset as he thought she'd been. "Apparently not."

"I'm glad."

Now he was really confused. "What?" Then why had he gone through all this trouble?

"I don't like to think about digging up someone's last remains. It makes me feel like a grave robber."

Now he understood. "I wasn't exactly keen on that myself."

She caught her lower lip between her teeth, thinking. "Maybe it's in town?"

He wouldn't know where to start. "Mikki, we haven't a clue. He saw her indicate the diary with her eyes. "At least, not one we can make sense of."

Her body turned toward his as every fiber of it supplicated. "Shawn, please?"

He didn't stand a chance. Maybe he would have once, but not anymore. "I can't resist when you use my first name." He resigned himself. "C'mon, since we're here we might as well look around."

He drove them back to the center of town. It looked no better than before. Absolutely nothing came to mind. He turned to look at Mikki. "Any suggestions?"

None that were really viable. She pressed her lips together. "We could search the buildings." It was more of a
question than a statement.

It was a possibility, but not one he wanted to seriously
entertain. "That could take days, Mikki. Weeks. We
haven't got enough supplies to last us."

She didn't want to give up. Klaus had come all the way
here to leave the diamonds so that they could be put to good
use. She had read all about how heartsick he had been over
his son's becoming part of Hitler's army. This was his way
of getting revenge. Leaving the diamonds here would have
meant that he had gone all through that for nothing. She
couldn't do it.

They had stopped being just diamonds and had become
a symbol to her. She owed it to Klaus. She had shared his
mind, and now she wanted to achieve his goal for him.
Since Alfred was gone, maybe she could donate some of the
diamonds to a charity in his name. But first she had to find
them.

She looked at Shawn, an expression of hope on her face.
"We could go back and get more supplies."

The trusting optimism in her eyes got to him. How could
he refuse her? But there came a time when reality had to
intervene. "I suppose we could, but I do have a job to get
back to."

She had gotten so caught up in this adventure that she
had forgotten. He had a job, a life that didn't involve her.
All right, if need be, she could go on by herself. She hadn't
planned on him when she had started out.

She hadn't planned on falling in love, either, she thought.

"Okay—" she kept her voice deceptively distant "—we'll
look around now and see if we get any ideas."

The disinterested inflection caught his attention. What
was she up to? "Fine with me. I never took a date to a ghost
town before."

"Another first."

Reaching for her, he caressed the back of her neck lightly. "There seem to be a lot of firsts with you."

She wished he'd mean that the way she wanted him to, but that was just wishful thinking on her part. If she let herself get caught up in the treasure hunt, then maybe, just maybe the pain of losing him at the end wouldn't be so bad. Closing her eyes to pull herself together, she tried to ignore the bittersweet sensations that nipped at her. "Let's go over this again."

Shawn got out of the Jeep and leaned against the side. "There's not that much to go over."

Mikki held up a finger. "One, there's no one in the cemetery whose name is, or was, Jeremiah."

He nodded. "Not unless it's an unmarked grave."

"Two, Klaus specifically spoke of this town. The map points to it. And he mentions it in the letter. So it has to be here."

"Okay," he conceded. "But where?"

Pulling out the letter again, she scanned it. She hardly needed to. It was burned into her brain. "'The same malady as our beloved relative.'" she read aloud. A thought hit her. "Okay," she said, tucking the letter back into her purse. "What's another word for *dead?*"

Several came to mind. *"Extinct. Terminated. Deceased. Defunct. Departed."* Nothing seemed to click for her. What was she after? "I'm out of synonyms."

Popping a mint into her mouth, she chewed as she thought. "How about 'not alive'?"

A red-tailed hawk flew by. Probably looking for lunch, Shawn thought, his own stomach reminding him that his was overdue. "That's a definition." He was about to suggest a break, but the intent look on Mikki's face stopped him.

"If it's not alive, maybe it never was." Her voice rose excitedly at the end of the sentence.

For a moment, food was forgotten. He was mystified at how she linked thoughts up in her mind. "What are you getting at?"

Mikki grabbed his arm, shaking it excitely. "A statue, Gallagher, a carving, some inanimate object." It made sense to her.

The skeptical look on Shawn's face did have a slight dampening effect, though. "Named Jeremiah?"

She shrugged, letting go of his arm. "Statues have names."

"I didn't see any in the town square. For that matter, I didn't even see a town square when we came in," he pointed out.

She sighed and sagged against the Jeep, looking up and down the long, lonely streets. He was right. There weren't any statues in the town. No marble testimonies to bygone heroes stood anywhere as far as she could see. And they had pretty much covered the area in the Jeep. There was nothing but an old wooden Indian standing on the decaying wooden step in front of the general store.

Mikki straightened up.

"Shawn." She drew out his name as if it were made up of four syllables.

He stopped watching the hawk's progress and looked at Mikki. "What?"

She was already walking toward the general store as if she were in some sort of trance.

He looked, but saw nothing that should affect her this way. The general store she was walking toward was a run-down building with rotting wood. Its sign, which once proudly proclaimed the store's ownership, hung by one hinge, drunkenly swaying in the breeze. He couldn't even make out the lettering at this distance, not that it really mattered.

"Mikki, wait up." He caught up to her in three long strides. The look on her face told him she was onto something. "What do you see?"

"The Indian."

He looked. The wooden Indian standing in front of the general store was not unlike many he had seen scattered throughout the West. Once there had been many; now the ones that remained were relics, collector's items, conversation pieces. This one was in rather poor condition, with part of its face missing. That had probably saved it from being carted off by some collector. Did she want it to take home as a souvenir of her adventure?

Home. Her home. No, she wasn't going to cart that thing off anywhere except maybe to his apartment in Houston. The lady was staying put in his life. He'd just have to find a way to convince her once they got this minor detail of a treasure hunt out of the way.

"What about the Indian?"

He didn't see, she thought. But it was so obvious. "Look at it," she cried.

The carving, standing nearly five and a half feet, had weathered badly. The elements had had their effect on it. The long headdress that ran down the Indian's back must have once sported gleaming white feathers. Now the paint was chipped and flaked. What remained was a dirty hue. The chief's arms were crossed before him in defiance. Or perhaps in prayer to a Great Spirit that had turned his back on his people.

Shawn saw nothing out of the ordinary, but to a Californian, he mused, it might hold some sort of fascination.

She didn't look fascinated, he realized. She looked excited.

"You don't see it, do you?" she asked.

He wasn't about to concede that point yet. After all, he was supposed to be a trained observer. "What am I looking for?"

"His arms are crossed."

"And?"

She felt like shaking him. Where was his imagination? "What if he was hollow?"

Shawn leaned against the post. Holding the diamonds to his bosom, that was the way Klaus had put it. "You're reaching."

The post swayed, throwing Shawn off balance. He fell against the rickety sign at his back. Steadying himself on it, his eyes focused on the faded writing.

It bore one word: *Jeremiah's*.

## Chapter Sixteen

"Maybe it's not so farfetched after all." Shawn let go of the general store sign and stepped back. "Let me take another look at the chief."

Mikki was already way ahead of him. Using her handkerchief, she wiped away some of the dust that the old Indian statue had accumulated over the years.

As she cleaned away the dirt at the junction formed by the statue's wrists, Mikki discovered that the wood had been carefully split there. The cut was too neat and clear to have been a result of time and nature. It had been deliberately put there.

Mikki looked at Shawn over her shoulder. "Are you thinking what I'm thinking?"

"I'm not sure." He ran his finger along the slit. Dust accumulated on his finger. "With you it's hard to tell."

"Gallagher." She was in no mood to be teased. Tension coursed through her veins.

He watched the flush of excitement that rose in her cheeks. Maybe he had been wrong. Maybe she did put riches ahead of everything. The man and the reporter stepped back to observe her, if not dispassionately, at least with a semblance of calm. Time would tell. For the moment, he applied himself to the problem at hand.

He leaned back, deliberately holding back even though he wanted to help. This was her show. He'd let her run it.

"Ouch!"

Mikki pulled back her hand and popped the wounded area into her mouth, then examined it. There was a jagged red scratch on it.

"Hurt yourself?" Shawn asked.

She shook her head. "No." Closer examination proved her right. "It didn't break the skin.

She looked closer at the wooden Indian. Right above where she had been cleaning was a nail. It looked as if it were hammered straight through the Indian's heart. The opening she had uncovered was small, just barely large enough to accommodate her hand.

Experimentally, she touched the nail. It looked terribly slender. "Where would he get a hammer and a nail?" She looked questioningly at Shawn. "That's not exactly something he'd be carrying with him."

His hands on her shoulders, Shawn moved Mikki aside and looked closer. "That's not a nail, Mikki." He laughed. "That shows me how domestic you are."

"What are you talking about?" Mikki took a closer look.

"That's a large tapestry needle," Shawn told her. "The eye of the needle is stuck in the wood. It's a clue."

Her eyes widened with excitement. "Klaus was a tailor," she cried.

"Tools of his trade," Shawn agreed.

"This was to let his brother know that the diamonds were here." Her heart began to hammer hard. Warming to her task, she refolded her handkerchief to find a clean spot and rubbed again in earnest, using her nails beneath the cloth to help. A clump of dirt fell off, revealing what was beneath. "This is more than a clue, Gallagher. There's thread attached to this." She tested it gingerly and felt a weight pulling it down. "And there's something at the other end!"

Shawn started to help, then stopped himself again. This was her treasure, her moment. He curbed his impatience. It was Mikki's hard-earned right to be the first to get to the diamonds. If by some chance there weren't any diamonds, they'd deal with that later.

With her tongue caught between her teeth, Mikki eased her hand through the small opening. It was a tight fit, but she managed it. If her hand had been any larger, it wouldn't have made it through.

Cautiously, Mikki stretched her fingers, feeling around, not knowing what she might come in contact with first. The statue was rotting in several places. A little farther and—

Her fingers hit something.

"Shawn!"

He came alert. "You must have found it. You don't use my first name unless we're making love or you're feeling good—or both." Though he thought of himself as a disinterested observer of this unfolding drama, he couldn't deny that he felt the thrilling twinge of anticipation as he watched her.

She didn't hear him. Her heart was pounding too hard. Her fingers had closed around something that felt like a small pouch deep inside the opening. Holding her breath, she angled her hand, working it back up. It wouldn't fit through the opening.

"Damn." Exasperation etched every feature of her face.

Shawn was at her elbow then. "What's the matter, Mikki?"

She blew out a frustrated breath, pushing her hair angrily out of her eyes with her free hand. "I can't get my hand out."

Shawn was ready to add his strength to the tug-of-war. "It's stuck?"

She tried again. Nothing. "If I hold onto the pouch, yes."

"Then you did find the diamonds?" He couldn't believe he was actually saying that. He had come along on this adventure to write a story about a modern-day treasure hunt—and because she had fascinated him. He never expected to really find the diamonds. But then, he had never expected to have his soul returned to him, either. "You found a pouch?"

"I just said that, didn't I?" she said impatiently. She flashed him an apologetic look. "I didn't mean that the way it sounded. God, I feel like a kid with her hand stuck in the cookie jar." She tugged. Her wrist was beginning to feel raw where it was rubbing against the opening. "I can't get my hand out unless I let go."

Pulling would do no good. It might even make her hand swell. "Can you still feel the string around it?"

She fed the pouch slowly through her fingers until she could feel the top. "Yes, just barely."

"Okay, let the pouch go."

"But—" Now that she finally had it in her hand, she didn't want to let it go.

"Once you get your hand out of the way, we'll pull the pouch out by the string."

Mikki held on stubbornly. "But what if the thread breaks?"

The answer was simple. Time consuming, but simple. "Then the chief is going to become next winter's firewood very quickly."

He peered through the emporium's broken panes, trying to make out what lay beyond. There were things strewn around the inside of the store.

"I'm sure there's an ax or something handy to work with in the general store. They must have left some of their inventory behind."

She nodded and licked her lips. But she hated to think of the statue reduced to kindling. It would seem a shame to destroy something so old. With a great deal of time and professional restoration, it would be almost as good as new.

But she had touched the pouch and was certain the diamonds were in there. She could feel them. The soft leather allowed her to make out shapes. Either she was holding a pouch full of diamonds, or pebbles. She didn't think Klaus would have gone to all this trouble just to play a practical joke. The man she had met in the pages of the diary had had little sense of humor, only a strong sense of honor and morality.

Very slowly, she pulled her hand away from the pouch, taking care to disturb the slender connecting thread as little as possible. Mikki held her breath throughout the ordeal.

Her shoulder ached from tension when she finally pulled it free. Although her hand was red, and some of the skin had been rubbed off, she scarcely felt it.

Shawn wrapped his hand around hers. "You okay?"

Mikki wiggled her fingers. "I won't be able to do any hand commercials for a while," she quipped, "but my concert career doesn't seem to be affected."

He knew her by now. The quips came fast and furious when she was especially nervous. He gave her a reassuring smile. Taking a tenuous hold of the thread, Shawn eased the pouch up an inch at a time. Finally, after what seemed like an eternity, the top of the pouch poked through the opening in the statue.

"Want to do the honors?" He offered the thread to Mikki.

She was surprised and touched that he would be so sensitive to her.

"I'd love to."

She seemed unaware that her voice came out in a hoarse whisper, or that she had been holding her breath as he had worked the pouch up. But he wasn't.

Mikki pulled it up the last few inches until it was entirely free. For a moment, she just held it in her hand.

Shawn put his arm around her. It was a gesture of support. "Afraid?"

It was finally out. She stared at it. She was holding the pouch of diamonds in her hand. She was actually holding it in her hand. Her breath caught in her throat. This was a link to the past, to a man she had never met but had grown to know as well as she knew herself.

"Nervous."

"We could stuff it back." His hand hovered over the pouch, fingers ready to pluck it back.

Mikki jerked the pouch out of reach. "No!" Then she realized that he was kidding. Her hand dropped down again. "Sorry."

"Open it, Mikki," Shawn coaxed softly, keeping his own mounting excitement well under control.

"I am, I am, don't rush me. I'm just savoring this last moment, that's all." She stared at the old pouch in wonder. "I never got to open a gift before."

Was that the way she saw it? A gift? A gift from a dead man. But there had been more to what she said. "Didn't you ever get anything?"

"No." There was no bitterness. It was just a simple fact.

The pouch felt soft in her hand, the material worn down by time. She wondered if it had been Klaus's or if he had found it at the general store. His, she decided. He had probably brought it over with him on the ship to America. Whatever was in it, she'd keep the pouch to remind her of all this.

No one had ever given her a gift. The words rang in Shawn's head. He wanted to shower her with gifts, with boxes of all sizes and shapes to make up for all the years she had lost. When this was behind them, he'd give her Christmas and birthdays and Valentine's Day and all the other days in between that would mean special things to them alone. Gifts to pay her back for the new kind of excitement she had brought into his life. He knew he'd rather die than lose what she had given him.

Mikki sat down on the wooden step. Suddenly, her legs felt wobbly. She looked up at Shawn, and he dropped down beside her.

"Ready?" he asked.

"Ready."

Taking a deep breath, Mikki pulled the pouch open and shook the contents out. A brilliant shower of sparkling lights tumbled into her waiting palm. Rainbows winked and glimmered as she stared in fascination.

"Oh, God." She looked at Shawn, wanting to laugh, wanting to cry. "We really found them."

"Thank you," said a strange voice behind Mikki.

Mikki's hand closed around the diamonds as she jumped up and swung around to look behind her. She caught her breath to stifle a scream of surprise.

Alicia Traherne, the librarian from Mission Ridge, wearing trousers that dwarfed her and a baggy shirt, stood in the doorway of the general store. A burly man Mikki didn't recognize was at the woman's side. In his hand was a small gun pointed directly at them.

Shawn sprang to his feet.

"I wouldn't do that if I were you, Shawn," the librarian warned coolly. "My cousin isn't used to firearms, and if he gets nervous, it just might go off. At this range, I doubt he'd miss. Raise your hands, please."

Swallowing a curse, Shawn did as he was told.

Alicia Traherne turned her cold, amber eyes on Mikki and stretched her long, thin hand out expectantly. "I'll take those now."

Mikki put her hand behind her back.

"Give them to me." Alicia's mouth curved in a nasty mirthless smile. "I'm not in the mood for games. At least—" her gaze slid back to Shawn "—not with you."

"Give them to her, Mikki," Shawn instructed, his voice low and cold.

Frustrated anger burned deep within her. But, with a gun pointed at her chest, Mikki had no choice. Carefully, she poured the diamonds back into the pouch. Curbing the desire to throw the pouch at the older woman, Mikki held it out. Alicia snatched it from her.

Mikki took a step toward Alicia, but the woman's cousin cut the journey short with a wave of his gun. Mikki stepped back, her eyes spitting fire.

"How did you—?"

"Find you?" Alicia completed the sentence for Mikki. "In my line of work, research is second nature. A few inquiries, a few phone calls, an overheard conversation. My cousin, Brian, here just happens to be the bartender at the Do Drop Inn. In Mission Ridge, the bartender knows all." Still caressing the pouch, she lifted her eyes to Shawn. The hunger there was barely veiled. It was a very basic hunger that did not include the diamonds. "You really should have an unlisted number, Mr. Gallagher. We've been following you for quite some time."

"But why—?" Mikki didn't understand. She had been so careful. How did *these* people find out? For that matter, she had never figured out how the other two had stumbled on to her secret, either.

"Why did I seek you out?" Alicia smirked, obviously very proud of herself. "Aside from the obvious—" her eyes skimmed over Shawn "—there was the little matter of a diamond. The one you gave to Malcolm."

"Who?" Shawn began to let his arms drop. One small gesture from the burly bartender had Shawn lifting them high again.

"Our very talkative town drunk," Alicia explained, feeling magnanimous. "He came into Brian's tavern with a wild story about buried treasure."

Now she remembered. The man who had stumbled against her and taken the other diamond out of her pocket. Fury rose in Mikki's eyes, coloring her cheeks.

Shawn thought she looked magnificent. But now wasn't quite the time to tell her, he reflected. His mind raced in several directions, trying to find a way out of their predicament. If this scene were in one of Mikki's Westerns, the cavalry would be coming right about now. Unfortunately for them, he thought, this was real life.

"We never gave him anything," Mikki cried. "He stole it."

"I surmised as much." As she spoke, Alicia jiggled the pouch. "But he did have his use. He pointed you two out for his drinking companions. And for Brian." She glanced at her cousin.

Mikki turned toward Shawn. "They must have been the two men who stole the map. *That's* how they found out about the diamonds."

"Oh, did they steal your map?" Alicia looked mildly interested. "Well, you seemed to have found your way here despite that. I do admire people who rise to a challenge."

"We caught up to them and had them arrested." Mikki's tone of voice indicated that they didn't take setbacks easily and were not to be lightly dismissed. She meant it as a threat.

Shawn saw the way Alicia's cousin was looking at Mikki. Although not quite as blatant, it matched the hunger in Alicia's eyes when she looked at him. Maybe he could parlay that into something and distract the man long enough to get the gun. At the moment, there seemed to be no other avenue open to him.

Alicia slowly circled Shawn, her eyes measuring him from every angle. "Very thoughtful of you." She didn't spare Mikki a glance. "Then they won't be getting in our way."

Mikki didn't like the way the woman was looking at Shawn. "What are you going to do with us?"

"I have some ideas." Alicia ran her hand along Shawn's arm.

Mikki stared belligerently at Brian's gun. She hated feeling so helpless. Casting a sidelong glance in Shawn's direction, she muttered, "Does everyone in the state have a gun except you?"

His arms were beginning to ache, and he didn't like this any better than she did. "Looks that way."

"You don't need a gun, Shawn." Alicia's high-pitched voice sounded ludicrously melodic to Mikki. "Just a little common sense."

"I don't follow you." The problem was, he did. Women like Alicia were dangerous, especially when they had guns on their side.

"That's exactly what I had in mind, being followed. All the way home." She drew her words out. This was the first time in her life that she had the upper hand in something important, and she intended to savor it. "If you promise to be nice, you won't have to go to jail."

"Jail?" Mikki echoed. "You can't have us put in jail. We haven't done anything wrong."

Her back to Mikki, Alicia directed her words to Shawn. "I'm sure you've already noticed that this fine town has a jail."

This was getting to sound worse and worse. "You'd leave us here?" Mikki demanded.

"Not plural, singular." Alicia was beginning to get impatient now. "How about it, Shawn? You can dump her and come with us. I might even give you a share of the diamonds."

"Alicia," Brian complained.

An angry, ugly expression distorted her colorless face as Alicia looked at her cousin. "Shut up and hold the gun steady, Brian. Can't you do anything right?"

Brian opened his mouth to protest, then closed it again. He looked as if he was having trouble holding onto his temper. Mikki thought that the librarian was obviously pushing her luck. With one swipe of his hand, Brian could have sent her hurtling through the window of the general store if he wanted to.

Mikki's mind zeroed in on the thought: if he wanted to. Maybe she could provoke him. Something had to be done, and Shawn wasn't doing anything. To be fair, there wasn't very much he *could* do, she thought.

"You didn't say anything about locking her up. I don't want to hurt anyone," Brian growled at his cousin.

"We won't be hurting anyone." Alicia's tone indicated just the opposite. "We'll just leave her there. Someone's bound to be passing through again. These two did, didn't they?"

Brian needed a moment to chew that one over.

Mikki was getting a very uneasy feeling about all this. She looked at Shawn. He seemed to be thinking, as well. Was he actually considering the woman's offer? Well, why not? After all, she was offering him not only survival, but a share of the diamonds. And what was she to him? Mikki thought with a twinge of despair. A pleasant interlude. Mikki knew enough about people to know that survival came first, before love, before commitment. And there was the small matter of the gun to add leverage to Alicia's argument.

"Well, Shawn, do we have a deal?"

For two cents, Mikki would have bashed Alicia's head in.

He knew he could go along with what Alicia proposed, play along until he got a chance to free them both. But at what cost? Mikki would never believe him again, even if things did go their way. And there was always a chance that they might not. Luck was a very fickle lady, and Shawn doubted that his chances against the hulk with the gun were favorable.

Better to use wits than brawn, he decided.

"Sure," he answered. He saw the look of stunned hurt on Mikki's face, even as her eyes told him that she had expected as much. "When hell freezes over."

Mikki's mouth dropped open, then curved into a huge grin.

It contrasted sharply with the look on Alicia's face. "You've made your grave."

Her words made Brian blanch. "But you said—" he protested.

"Never mind what I said. Get them over to the jail!" she snapped, pointing down the street to a building that still retained a hitching post.

Brian didn't budge. "But—"

"Don't 'but' me, Brian!" Alicia shouted. She took a firm grip of the arm that held the gun and shook it. Shawn moved out of the way.

"No, let me!" Mikki exclaimed.

Before Shawn could say or do anything, she had shot by him, her head lowered. She dived straight into Alicia who went flying backward, sprawling out on the wooden step. Sliding along it, splinters ripped into her tender flesh. Alicia screamed in rage and pain.

Having been given the diversion he'd needed, Shawn didn't hesitate. Though he knew that his was not as easy a target as Mikki's had been, he had only one chance, and the element of surprise was it. He swung at Brian's lantern jaw with everything he had in him. It wasn't enough. Shawn's fist connected and stung. The big man staggered only slightly, but the gun went flying from his hand.

Mikki saw it land a few feet away from her and dived for it, falling short. Alicia's hand was tangled in her hair. Tears formed instantly as pain flashed through her scalp and down her neck. Swearing roundly, Mikki turned, pulled back her arm and swung her fist hard, connecting directly with Alicia's face. There was a slight cracking noise as Mikki's fist made contact with Alicia's nose.

The older woman crumbled in midscream. Mikki scrambled for possession of the gun. After having retrieved it, she yanked the pouch free from Alicia's unconscious grasp.

Breathing hard, keeping her back to the store and watching Alicia's inert form, Mikki turned to see how Shawn was doing. Not well.

Both men were staggering, although Shawn seemed to be getting the worst of it. His beefy opponent had at least seventy pounds on him.

"Break it up," Mikki yelled.

"Do something before he breaks me up," Shawn shouted back.

Mikki fired a shot into the air, wincing at the sound. Brian came to a jolting halt, his arm swung back, his other hand grasping the front of Shawn's shirt.

"Drop him," Mikki ordered.

Shawn was dropped, hitting the ground with a thud that rattled his tailbone. He shook his head as he got to his feet.

"You could have found a better way to word that." Stepping around Alicia, Shawn took the gun from Mikki and trained it on Brian.

"It worked, didn't it?" Mikki tucked the pouch down the front of her shirt.

He grinned at her as he backed up, keeping both Trahernes in his sight. "Did I ever tell you I'm glad you're on my side?"

## Chapter Seventeen

"What are we going to do with them?"

Mikki looked from Alicia, who was just coming around, to Brian. Alicia made her think of a vulture, and her cousin reminded Mikki of a sad water buffalo. Shawn had them both sitting on the floor, leaning against the wall of the general store next to the Indian statue.

"We could give them a taste of their own medicine," Shawn mused.

One arm slung over the Emporium Indian chief, the other deceptively at rest, the gun held ready in his hand, he regarded the pair. He'd seen their type more than once. People leading lives of quiet frustration until something made them break, made them take the big dare. In this case, it hadn't worked.

Luckily, he thought, for Mikki and him.

"You mean lock them up in the jail?" Mikki shaded her eyes and looked down toward the building Alicia had pointed out only minutes before.

The idea of leaving them there was too cruel for her to contemplate. Alicia might have had that in mind for Shawn and her, but Mikki had never believed in an eye for an eye. Besides, because Brian had not agreed with Alicia's suggestion, he had unwittingly initiated the diversion she and Shawn had needed to turn the tables on their two captors. She couldn't agree to installing them in the jail.

Shawn nodded, even though he saw what Mikki thought of the idea. "It would be just deserts." He was toying with them to pay them back.

"You wouldn't dare," Alicia half challenged, half begged.

Shawn moved away from the wooden Indian. "Not so appealing when the lock's on the other side, is it, Ms. Traherne?" Shawn leaned forward, studying her. She was a pathetic human being and would suffer enough by her own doing. There was no point in adding to it. Revenge wasn't his style.

But he didn't have to make things easy for them, either.

Scarlet-nailed fingers wrapped themselves around Shawn's arm as Alicia rose up to her knees. "Please," Alicia entreated.

Holding the gun aloft in his other hand, Shawn shook his arm free.

"No, I won't leave you there. Only because your cousin here didn't like the idea himself." Shawn lowered the gun, but his stance indicated that he was ready for anything. "What do you think about taking a page out of Rick and Neil's book?" he asked Mikki.

She looked at him blankly. "Tying them up?"

Carefully, he backed up until he joined Mikki in front of the wooden step. "No, I was thinking more along the lines of leaving them stranded with the tires on their car slashed."

Alicia's small close-set eyes widened. "But how'll we get back?" she cried. "You'll leave us out here to die." Hysteria began to build in her voice.

"Only if you have something against walking," Shawn answered mildly. As far as he was concerned, Alicia deserved no sympathy. If anyone did, it was her cousin. Shawn had no doubts that he'd be the target of plenty of verbal abuse before the two made it back to town. "There's a gas station not more than, oh, say ten or fifteen miles, give or take a few."

"Ten or fifteen miles," Alicia echoed horrified.

"Give or take a few," Shawn repeated. "Yeah, that plan gets my vote." He turned to Mikki. "How about you, partner?"

"It might teach them a lesson," she agreed. "And by the time they reach the gas station, we should be long gone."

Shawn handed Mikki the gun. "Slashed tires it is." A hunting knife was part of his camping gear, and he had brought it along just in case. It would do the trick. "Where's the car, Alicia?"

"Look for it," she spat out.

"The town's not that large. It shouldn't be difficult." If he guessed right, they had probably hidden the vehicle behind the blacksmith's shop. It was the only building that stood off to the side of the main thoroughfare.

Mikki didn't trust the woman at all. She kept her eyes on Alicia the entire time she waited for Shawn to return. A nagging feeling warned her that Alicia would try something. Mikki could feel all her nerve endings tense.

It turned out to be only verbal. Alicia rose slowly to her feet, nursing her sore nose. "You know, there's nothing stopping him from running out on you, too." The look on the woman's face was nothing short of vicious.

"Oh, I don't think so." Mikki knew what the woman was trying to do, but the strategy of divide and conquer wasn't about to work here.

"Oh?" The pointy chin raised high. "You think you're that indispensable?"

"No, but I have the diamonds." Mikki patted her purse. She hoped it wasn't the only reason that Shawn wouldn't abandon her, but it was the only one that someone like Alicia would understand.

Still, when she heard the sound of the Jeep starting up on the far end of the street, an uneasy sensation passed through Mikki. No, Shawn wouldn't run out on her, but he'd be leaving her soon, and she him. It had been a long time since she had vowed not to compromise her pride by asking someone to let her stay. Any moves in that direction would have to be his. Pride was all she had left.

That, and diamonds, she thought. Oddly enough, the sense of exhilaration she expected was missing.

Shawn pulled up in front of the general store. "All set," he announced.

Mikki still kept her eyes on Alicia. "Did you take care of the tires?"

"Hardly a whisper of air in the four of them." He looked at the sullen pair on the steps. "Just in case you have any ideas about following us." The clarification was addressed to Alicia. Brian looked utterly humbled by the gun. Of the two, Shawn had considered him the less formidable opponent.

It was the woman of the species one had to watch out for, Shawn mused, glancing at Mikki. As far as he was concerned, he was looking forward to that.

Still keeping the gun raised, Mikki slowly slid into the seat next to Shawn. Alicia began to move forward, but Mikki cocked the gun, aborting any other moves on the librarian's part. Mikki knew that if it came down to it she couldn't pull the trigger. But Alicia didn't know that. And that was all that really mattered.

"You'll never get away with this!" Alicia insisted self-righteously.

"That's the good guys' line, Ms. Traherne. And you two definitely aren't the good guys." As an afterthought, he dug something out of his pocket. "Here." He tossed it to Brian. A large paw whipped out quickly, catching the flying item.

Alicia crowded her cousin, trying to see. "What's that?"

"A compass," Shawn told her. "The gas station's due northeast. If you start now, you'll be there by nightfall." A rumble of thunder was heard. Yesterday's storm sounded as if it was returning. "I'd get a move on if I were you."

With that, he put the Jeep in gear and drove away. A torrent of creative, high-pitched curses followed in his wake.

Shawn made two phone calls from his house. One was to his neighbor, Hank, to arrange for transportation to the nearest airport. He wanted to leave his Jeep at the ranch house. The other call was to a friend who owned a Cessna. A little coercion and five minutes later, he and Mikki were set to fly that evening into Houston's William P. Hobby Airport.

Mikki listened quietly until he hung up, then shook her head. Given his lead, the man was a wheeler-dealer. "You certainly do have your uses."

"Nice of you to notice." He wasn't sure if she meant it as a compliment or as a flippant comment. Right now, he wasn't sure of many things. "C'mon, get your things together. Hank drives like a maniac and should be here in a couple of minutes."

"Reassuring." She started for the bedroom to get her suitcase. "Life with you is never dull, is it?"

He flashed her a grin. "God, I hope not."

Hank's driving lived up to Shawn's description. The man drove the back roads to the airport as if he was practicing for the Indy 500. He got them there in record time. *His* record, Mikki found out.

Barely catching her breath. Mikki found herself being hurried aboard a single-engine plane owned by someone named Chester. During the trip to Houston, she did manage to ask Shawn why they were going there in the first place. Secretly, she had been looking forward to spending one last night at the ranch house. One last night in his arms before the final tally was taken on this adventure. Shawn answered with something evasive about turning in his story to his editor.

Since it sounded plausible enough, she didn't pursue it. In truth, Mikki didn't want to ask too many questions because if she did, inevitably the question of how much longer they would stay together would come up and she already knew the answer to that one. Not long. She didn't want to hear it just yet.

A cab from the airport brought them to his apartment. It was wide and spacious, with a minimum of furniture.

"You know," Shawn said as he closed the door behind him, "even after taxes, you're going to be one rich lady. For a rich lady, you don't look too happy." She had been unusually quiet during the flight, and it made him uneasy. Was she trying to find a way to say goodbye?

She didn't trust herself to look at him just yet. Instead, she was drawn toward the panoramic view of the city that the huge, juxtaposed windows offered her. Twilight was setting in. The view was breathtaking.

Mikki leaned her palms against the cool windowsill, staring down on the city. A myriad of lights danced below her, each representing a life in progress. A home, a family. People at a party. It was all so removed from her.

"Only half-rich," she corrected softly.

Shawn came up behind her. The light touch of his fingertips on her shoulders made her ache inside. How long would she remember this? Not long. Just until the day she died.

"Half?" she heard him ask.

She turned then, her body brushing against his, humming with excitement. "Half is yours."

Shawn threaded his fingers through her hair. His eyes kept her prisoner. "That wasn't the agreement."

"Not in the beginning. And then only because I was afraid you wanted it all." Her eyes began to drift shut as her body absorbed the comforting warmth of his nearness.

"And you don't think that now?"

She heard the question and the strange note in his voice. "No."

"Well, I do."

Mikki's eyes flew open in surprise. Had it all been a ruse? Had he been pretending all along to keep her off her guard until the diamonds had been recovered? Oh God, had she been so wrong? So stupid? After all the promises she had made to herself to stay aloof, untouchable, it was all happening to her again.

She ran her tongue over her lips. They felt dry. Everything felt like dust.

"Where are the diamonds?"

"In my purse." She pointed to the sofa, her heart breaking.

Silently, he crossed to the sofa and picked up her purse. Mikki watched numbly as Shawn rummaged through it. The diamonds didn't matter anymore. Nothing ever would again. She had thought that she knew him, understood him, that they might not have anything lasting, but at least she would have memories of the time they had spent together. If he did this to her, the memories weren't worth anything.

Tears gathered, shining in her eyes. She blinked hard, praying they wouldn't spill out. She wouldn't cry. Not in front of him. Not ever.

Shawn was still looking. "For such an organized person, you certainly keep a messy purse. Oh." He drew out the revolver they had taken from Brian. "I forgot you still had this. Good thing we flew with Chester instead of a national airline. I'd probably be busy making bail for you right now."

Or running off with the diamonds, she thought bitterly.

Checking to see if the safety was on, Shawn tossed the gun onto the sofa, then emptied out the contents of her purse on the coffee table. Mikki refused to say anything.

"Ah, here it is." Finding the pouch, he threw her purse onto the sofa, as well. It landed on top of the gun. Moving the rest of her paraphernalia aside, he carefully spilled the diamonds onto the coffee table. Almost involuntarily, Mikki looked down at them. Funny how they had changed their hue. They had held rainbows for her only this morning. Now they were only transparent rocks.

"This one." Shawn selected the largest diamond and held it up for her inspection. The light from the fixture overhead shattered it into a million brilliant fragments. The spectacle left her cold. "Like it?"

"It's very nice." Her tone was flat.

He studied the diamond carefully. Obviously, it didn't appeal to her. "Well, if it doesn't suit you, we can always pick another one out for the ring."

"Ring?" she asked numbly.

"Engagement ring."

She couldn't be hearing him right. "What engagement ring?"

By now, she recognized that innocent look he assumed. "Yours, of course." He considered the stone again. "I don't like rings myself, although I suppose you'll probably want me to wear one. I could conceivably be talked into a simple gold band. Maybe florentined."

She grabbed hold of his shoulders. He was talking even faster than she usually did, and she couldn't keep up. Was afraid to keep up. It almost sounded as if he was saying— No, he couldn't be.

"Shawn, what are you talking about?"

He cocked an eyebrow. "And I thought you were clever."

Her mouth dropped open. "Are you—?"

"I am." He grinned, taking pleasure in her reaction. "What did you think when I said I wanted it all?"

She looked down at the diamonds. "I thought you meant them."

He laughed and hugged her close. "I meant you. You're all the treasure I'll ever want or need. I love you, Mikki Donovan. Any objections?"

She threw her arms around his neck, weak with relief. She *had* been right about him after all. "Probably, but for the life of me, I can't think of one right now."

He kissed her, letting the kiss deepen by degrees until it had them both wanting more.

"Very touching."

Mikki's eyes flew open again as she stared at Shawn. She jumped back. "I can't believe this. It's like being stuck in a bad rerun."

They turned in unison. This time, the intruder pointing a gun at them was Harold, the desk clerk from the hotel in Mission Ridge. Mikki let loose with an oath. Then she *had* seen him in the hotel lobby, talking to the desk clerk. Harold had been following them all along. How many more were out there?

"What do you want?" Mikki all but cried. She was getting very, very tired of this.

"Guess." Harold moved over to the coffee table. His owl eyes widened. "Since you two are so chummy, you won't miss these a bit." He clumsily waved his gun at them. "Raise them up!"

Shawn left his hands were they were. He sized Harold up and decided that the man wasn't going to take any unnecessary chances. "Where did you come from?"

Harold pointed with his gun, then quickly turned it back on Mikki and Shawn. "The bedroom."

Shawn let out an impatient sigh. "I've really got to get an unlisted life. I meant," he enunciated slowly, "what are you doing here?"

"I've been waiting here for you for two days, just after I lost your trail. Figured you had to come back sometime.

Sure took your time about it. I've almost cleared out your 'frigerator.''

The nerve of the man. "We ran into a few problems," Mikki said sarcastically.

"Got 'em here, though, I see." Harold's eyes were large with wonder as he took stock of the diamonds.

"Mind if I sit down?" Shawn asked casually. "It's been a hell of a day."

Harold shrugged. "Just as long as you stay clear of me, I don't care if you stand on your head."

Shawn sat down, taking hold of Mikki's arm and pulling her down with him. She looked at him, confused, then realized that he had deliberately sat down right in front of her purse. And the gun that was under it.

"Now what are you planning to do?" Mikki asked Harold as Shawn allowed one hand to slowly move behind him.

"Rob you," Harold answered.

Mikki kept her eyes on Shawn's profile. The way it relaxed slowly told her that he had the gun in his hand. "And then?" Her voice encouraged Harold to go on talking.

The foolish grin on Harold's face was lopsided. "Live happily ever after—away from Mission Ridge and my wife's lousy disposition."

"What do you plan to do with us?" she wanted to know.

Keeping one eye on them, Harold tried to sweep the diamonds back into the pouch. It couldn't be done with only one hand. He used the heel of his gun hand to complete the motion. "Nothing if you don't give me any trouble. I'm a peaceful man."

"Greedy, but peaceful. Sounds like a good epitaph," Shawn commented, waiting for Harold to look up again. Shawn held the gun in front of him, braced with both hands.

Harold glanced around to make certain that he had all the diamonds in the pouch. He did. "I don't plan to be dead for a long time."

When he raised his eyes, Harold was looking down the barrel of Shawn's gun.

"Plan again," Shawn advised.

The corners of Harold's mouth turned way down. "Oh, shoot."

"Only if I have to." Shawn held out his hand for Harold's gun. "Do I have to?"

Harold huffed dejectedly and surrendered his handgun. "No."

Shawn took the gun and gave it to Mikki. "Good. Now get out of here. If you ever so much as show your face in Houston again, I'll have you put in jail so fast and for so long, you'll be too old to remember why you were there in the first place."

Taking him by the back of his collar, Shawn separated Harold from the pouch and then unceremoniously ushered him out the door, giving him a shove for good measure. Leaning a shoulder against the door, he turned both locks, put the chain in place and then crossed to Mikki.

"Alone at last—maybe," he cracked.

Mikki ran her hands up and down her arms and glanced around nervously. "They seem to keep coming out of nowhere."

"Just means you're still not safe." Tucking the gun into his waistband just in case, Shawn put his arms around her. "If you recall, the reason I teamed up with you in the first place was to keep you safe. I also told you that I never leave a job half-finished."

Her skin warmed to his touch, as did her soul. Diamonds might be a girl's best friend, but love was always a woman's best bet. "When do you think it will be finished?"

"Oh, in thirty or forty years," he estimated, "give or take a decade." And he'd make love to her every day of that time.

Mikki sighed, disappointed. But her eyes danced. "That soon?"

"You can never tell. Might be longer." He lightly touched his lips to her forehead. The responding sigh quickened his pulse. "How does that sound to you?"

"How does what sound to me?"

He lifted her chin slightly, then kissed each eye closed. "Having me around as your bodyguard for that long?"

The words came in a sigh of contentment. "I couldn't think of anyone I'd rather have guarding my body than you, Gallagher."

"Good." His lips brushed hers. "Because nobody else is ever going to get the chance."

"Gallagher?"

"Hmm?"

"Shut up and kiss me right."

"Nothing would give me greater pleasure." He gathered her in his arms, his hands molding her body to his. "Well," he considered, "almost nothing."

"Show me."

"I have every intention of doing just that."

And he did.

\*     \*     \*     \*     \*

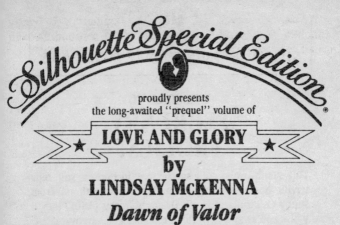

*Silhouette Special Edition*®

proudly presents
the long-awaited ''prequel'' volume of

## LOVE AND GLORY
### by
### LINDSAY McKENNA
#### *Dawn of Valor*

In the summer of '89, Silhouette Special Edition premiered three novels celebrating America's men and women in uniform: LOVE AND GLORY, by bestselling author Lindsay McKenna. Featured were the proud Trayherns, a military family as bold and patriotic as the American flag—three siblings valiantly battling the threat of dishonor, determined to triumph . . . in love and glory.

Now, discover the roots of the Trayhern brand of courage, as parents Chase and Rachel relive their earliest heartstopping experiences of survival and indomitable love, in

*Dawn of Valor*, Silhouette Special Edition #649

This month, experience the thrill of LOVE AND GLORY—from the very beginning!

Available at your favorite retail outlet, or order your copy by sending your name, address, zip or postal code, along with a check or money order (please do not send cash) for $2.95, plus 75¢ postage and handling, payable to Silhouette Reader Service to:

In the U.S.
3010 Walden Ave.
P.O. Box 1396
Buffalo, NY 14269-1396

In Canada
P.O. Box 609
Fort Erie, Ontario
L2A 5X3

Please specify book title with your order. Canadian residents add applicable federal and provincial taxes.

 *Silhouette Books*®

DV-1A

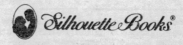

# SILHOUETTE·INTIMATE·MOMENTS®

## NORA ROBERTS
## Night Shadow

People all over the city of Urbana were asking, Who was that masked man?

Assistant district attorney Deborah O'Roarke was the first to learn his secret identity . . . and her life would never be the same.

The stories of the lives and loves of the O'Roarke sisters began in January 1991 with NIGHT SHIFT, Silhouette Intimate Moments #365. And if you want to know more about Deborah and the man behind the mask, look for NIGHT SHADOW, Silhouette Intimate Moments #373, available in March at your favorite retail outlet.

NITE-1

 *Silhouette Books*®